Philip Henry was born in 1974. I sketches while studying Performing on to short stories and a couple of scripts. During long shifts at one of the more had, he began making notes for a novel, which he then wrote on his days off. That novel, *Vampire Dawn*, was released in 2004 and proved so popular it was extended into a trilogy with *Vampire Twilight* in 2007 and *Vampire Equinox* in 2009.

Mind's Eye, a novel about the monsters of high school, was released in 2006 to great critical acclaim, as was *Freak*, the story of a boy like no other, released in 2008.

Philip continues to write novels, screenplays and short stories, all based around his home on the North Coast of Ireland.

Also by Philip Henry

Vampire Dawn
Mind's Eye
Vampire Twilight
Freak

VAMPIRE EQUINOX

PHILIP HENRY

Best Wishes
Philip Henry

CORAL MOON BOOKS
www.philiphenry.com

VAMPIRE EQUINOX
By
Philip Henry

Published By Coral Moon
www.philiphenry.com

This is a work of fiction. Names, characters, places and incidents are either products of the author's imagination or are used fictitiously. Any resemblance to actual events or locales or persons, living or dead, save those clearly in the public domain, is purely coincidental.

Vampire Equinox Copyright © 2009 Philip Henry

All rights reserved. No part of this work may be reproduced or transmitted in any form or by any electronic or mechanical means, including photocopying, recording, or by any information storage and retrieval system, without the prior written permission of the Publisher, except for short quotes used for review or promotion. For information address the Publisher.

ISBN: 978-0-9556556-4-7

Cover art by Ron McCann

10 9 8 7 6 5 4 3 2 1

eastern lies

Mito, Japan

The thief was a woman.

Even though the figure that approached the palatial house was dressed from head to toe in black, there was no mistaking her feminine curves. She crept across the immaculately manicured lawn with the speed and grace of a cat. She pressed her back to the wall. The night was still. She moved quickly around the skin of the building until she reached the kitchen door. She dropped to one knee and picked the lock. In a matter of seconds she was inside.

She ran quickly to the other side of the large kitchen and silenced the bleeping panel on the wall with the six-digit code. Takamura's cleaning lady was an honourable and honest woman, but her teenage son, who had accompanied his mother to work on several occasions, had a drug problem and was easily coerced into selling the alarm code. She opened the hall door a crack and looked around. The hallway was bathed in moonlight and quiet as a tomb. She stepped out and closed the door gently behind her. She got her bearings and made her way quickly to the east wing of the house. The marble echoed beneath her feet as she ran. The portraits of Takamura's ancestors hanging on the walls watched her progress with solemn expressions.

She reached the large oak double-doors at the end of the hallway and once again set about picking the lock. As the cylinders surrendered to her manipulations a large clunk echoed in the silence. She paused, looked over her shoulder and waited. No lights came on. No footsteps rushed towards her. Before opening the door she entered the second six-digit code on the panel beside the doors. The light on the panel changed from red to green. She turned back to the door and pushed it open enough to admit her slim form.

Lights were on in this room. Not the main lights, but smaller display lights that permanently illuminated Takamura's most prized possessions. She moved slowly along the wall. Though she could speak some Japanese, she couldn't read it, so the importance of most of the items behind glass cages was lost on her. There were quite a few antique samurai swords – one in particular appeared not to have been cleaned after battle and still bore the dried blood of the enemy it had slain. There was a quite inhuman-looking skull in a case with what appeared to be a snake pickled in brine next to it. She looked closer and the snake lurched for her. Teeth that seemed to grow from the skin of the lifeless creature clinked against its glass prison as it tried to bite her. She looked down at the illuminated plaque and saw one English word among the Japanese – Siren. She moved on.

Past several ancient parchments she found the petrified remains of some kind of winged demon. It sent shivers up her spine. There were three full shelves containing jars of blood. Then she saw it. What she had come here looking for. It sat on its own stone pedestal. A cylinder of glass surrounded it. A single red light blinked inside assuring her that it had its own independent alarm system. She crouched lower and got as close as she dared to the glass. Though the balaclava she was wearing hid it, she was smiling broadly.

Three black sedans skidded to a halt outside the Takamura mansion. A dozen oriental men and one Caucasian, all identically dressed in black suits, white shirts and black ties, got out quickly and ran up the steps to the front door. As one of them rang the bell repeatedly, the Caucasian pointed to six of his men and directed them to check the perimeter of the house. The men obediently split in half and ran off around either side of the house. A light came on in one of the windows above them, then another. The Caucasian stepped forward as his second-in-command ceased ringing the bell. The sounds of confusion inside grew louder. The door was edged open and a small man with untidy hair looked questioningly at the group on the doorstep.

The Caucasian stepped forward. 'Please apologize to Mr Takamura for the lateness of the hour. My name is Agent Fenton. I'm with The Ministry of the Shield based in Tokyo.' His second-in-command quickly translated. Takamura himself appeared at the door in his robe, looking irritated. He was a large broad-chested man who was greying at the temples and he was unaccustomed to being disturbed at home. He spoke angrily to his manservant, who related what he knew to his master, then turned to Fenton as Takamura barked in his ear.

'Takamura, san, is of course familiar with your organization, but wishes to know what cannot wait until tomorrow, Mr Fenton?'

'We've had a tip-off that you are going to be robbed tonight. A very precious and, in the wrong hands, dangerous artefact that Mr Takamura is in possession of is the target.'

The manservant related this to his master, who answered gruffly. The manservant turned back to Fenton. 'Takamura, san, is confident that all security measures have been taken to safeguard his collection.'

Fenton exhaled slowly into the night air. 'I would still feel safer if I could check for myself. We would be very quick and then if everything is secure, with your permission, I will leave some of my men here to ensure no one attempts to steal the piece.'

Takamura and his manservant talked back and forth quickly for a few moments before the master of the house relented. The manservant stepped aside and bowed, admitting Fenton and his men inside. He closed the door and he and Takamura led the seven Ministry agents down the hallway at a brisk pace.

The thief observed the glass cylinder from every angle. It rested on pressure-sensitive pads; the slightest change in weight would set off an alarm. Her prize was only inches from her grasp. The necklace sat on a black velvet neck display, just like it would in a jeweller's window. The object inside had never been in a jeweller's window, though. The stone that hung on the gold chain might not even be worth very much comparatively speaking. However, in the right hands, that stone was priceless. In *her* hands it was worth more than any piece in any museum in the world. And after spending the last few minutes studying the security measures that surrounded it, she had come to the conclusion there was only one way to get it out of there.

She lifted the cylinder up and alarms started shrieking all through the house. She turned and watched the doors through which she had entered being blocked by a heavy steel plate that descended from the ceiling. The steel hit the ground with a solid thud. She turned to the windows and noticed horizontal bars across them, cemented into the walls every six inches. She heard a loud click and turned to see what had caused it. A section of wood panelling had just opened into the wall – a secret door. Could her escape really be this easy? Her optimism was short-lived as a few seconds later the purpose of the door became apparent. From behind it stepped a samurai in full battle dress. He took a few steps toward her and stopped. The warrior removed his helmet and she noted how grey his skin was and how dead his eyes seemed. The warrior bowed to her and then smiled. She saw the pointed teeth and realised what she was facing was another item in Takamura's collection. The warrior cast his helmet aside, reached over his shoulder and drew his sword.

For one stupid second she realised she was still holding the glass cylinder. She hurled it at the warrior and ran for the other side of the room. She heard the air being cut behind her and then hundreds of pieces of glass raining down on the floor. She drove her elbow into the display case, shattering the glass, and grabbed the sword inside. She turned to face the warrior. His movements were disciplined and deliberate. He was well trained in the ancient martial arts. They circled each other, sizing up the other's strengths and weaknesses. The warrior attacked and she defended herself with all her skill and strength. Blades clashed in the air as the two warriors from different centuries did battle.

Fenton and the rest of the agents reached the doors, having ran past Takamura and his manservant when the alarms went off. Fenton pulled the door open and was faced with a steel plate. He turned to the manservant and his master who were hurrying towards them. 'What the hell is this?'

'Countermeasures. In attempted robbery, Takamura, san, has secondary security to stop thief from escaping,' the manservant answered.

Fenton had heard rumours that Takamura had a vampire "guard dog" but found it hard to believe until now. 'Disable the security systems. We need to get in there now!'

The manservant relayed this to his master. Takamura turned around and ran back towards the front entrance. He looked up and saw his wife and teenage daughter in their pyjamas looking anxious on the stairs. He shouted something at them. The girl screamed and her mother grabbed her and quickly escorted her back upstairs. Fenton watched Takamura disappear round a corner at the other end of the hall.

'Where does he have to go to disable the security?'

The manservant looked scared to answer without his master's approval but did. 'His study in the south wing.'

'How long to get there?'

The manservant shrugged.

Fenton listened as the muffled sounds of fighting on the other side of the steel grew more intense.

The warrior had her around the throat, pressed against the wall. He tightened his grip; the ice-cold fingers dug into her flesh until she was sure the skin must break. She reached out on either side of her looking for something, anything, she could defend herself with. She considered herself fairly expert with a sword, but the ease with which the warrior had disarmed her displayed a talent like she had never seen. Her fingers found a glass case on her left. She had no idea what might be in it but punched it anyway. The case shattered and she groped inside, blindly trying to find a weapon. Her fingers probed but found nothing. Bright spots began to pop before her eyes. She was going to pass out soon. She reached out desperately one last time and a shard of broken glass slit through her glove and cut the top of her hand. She turned her hand the other way and grabbed the shard of glass and broke it off. With all her remaining strength she brought it back and drove the point into the warrior's merciless eye. He released his grasp and she dropped to the ground.

She scrambled along the floor towards her fallen sword. The point was facing her. She reached along the blade to grab the handle but was only halfway when she was grabbed by the scruff of the neck. She grabbed the blade and thrust it backwards. The sword found a join in the samurai's armour and penetrated his upper hip. She tightened her grasp on the blade and pushed back. The blade sliced into her palm and fingers, but she had hurt the warrior too. She got wearily to her feet as the warrior tried to remove the sword from his lower torso. Then he saw her move. Momentarily putting his own pain aside, he stepped forward and punched her square in the chest. She flew backwards and smashed into several display cases. She got up, taking deep breaths, and shook the dizziness from her body. The warrior had almost removed the sword from his body. Dark liquid dribbled from his punctured eye. She turned around and looked for something to give her the advantage. The snake-thing floating in liquid lunged at her again. She lifted the tank that contained it and walked towards the warrior.

 The samurai pulled the last few inches of steel from his body and stood up just as she brought the tank crashing down on his head. The snake-thing wrapped itself around the vampire's throat and squeezed. The warrior tried to remove it but the snake-thing bit at his fingers. It looked like it was trying to get down his throat. She ran to the other end of the room and searched among the debris for the necklace. She glanced over her shoulder and saw the samurai struggling with the snake-thing. She crawled around the floor among the various pieces of gold and precious jewels. The warrior grabbed the snake-thing and a collar of spikes shot into his hand, but still he held on. He pulled it close to his mouth and bit it. Dark yellow liquid sprayed from the snake-thing. The vampire continued to gnaw at it until it was torn into several pieces and had stopped twitching. The samurai turned and saw her on the floor. He walked towards her and drew his sword once more from behind his back.

 She looked down and there it was, right below her palm. She grabbed the gold chain and stood up. She held the necklace out before her and closed her eyes, hoping the legends about this necklace were true. She opened her eyes and saw the vampire was almost upon her. Sunlight exploded from the stone on the necklace in all directions. She had to close her eyes it was so bright. She heard the warrior scream – something she would not have thought possible. Then the light dimmed and faded. She looked down and saw a suit of armour with a burned skeleton inside smoking at her feet.

The steel door began to rise into the ceiling again. She turned, exhausted, and saw six oriental men pointing guns at her. Fenton stepped forward and smiled. He nodded at the necklace. She didn't realise she was still holding it out in front of her. She looked at it and then set it back on its pedestal, which hadn't been toppled in the fracas. She took a few steps forward, as did Fenton. They stopped, facing each other. Fenton reached forward and grabbed the top of her balaclava and pulled it off. She brushed the hair out her face and clipped it to the side. She looked at him defiantly.

Fenton smiled smugly. 'Agent Nicholl. Oh how the mighty have fallen.'

Ministry of the Shield Field Office
Tokyo, Japan
Nicholl sat in an interrogation room. Her cuffed hands rested on the table before her. The chair opposite was empty for now, but Fenton's second-in-command stood by the door eyeing her suspiciously. The only sound was the unrelenting tick of the clock on the wall. There were no windows – the type of individual this room had been designed to accommodate didn't care much for the light. The door bleeped and Fenton stepped in carrying a folder. His second-in-command stepped out. Fenton stood at the door as it swung shut and bleeped behind him. He spent another few seconds tucking his pass-card into his pocket while looking at Nicholl hungrily. Finally, he walked over to the opposite side of the table, dropped his folder and sat down. He adjusted his chair backwards and forwards a few times before settling and looking Nicholl in the eyes.

'HQ is sending someone for you on the next flight,' he said. Nicholl remained stony. 'They said I was free to question you until then.'

'What a treat.'

'Nicholl, I suggest you drop the attitude and talk because what you tell me could mean the difference between you ending up in Section Zero or not.'

'You don't have the authority to send anyone to Section Zero, Fenton.'

'We'll see. We'll see.' He opened the folder in front of him. 'Now, let's see. That little trinket you were trying to steal; The Fist of Merlin, it's called. Discovered by Chloe Knight back in two-thousand and one outside the town of Portstewart in Northern Ireland – your old stomping ground, isn't it?' Nicholl's face remained blank. Fenton carried on. 'The Northern Ireland Home Office declared the find Treasure Trove in two-thousand and two, making the piece legally the property of the aforementioned Ms Knight, who then went on to sell it at auction for the sum of seven point nine million pounds to Mister Toshiki Takamura. The piece was reappraised four months ago by Takamura's insurers who estimated its value now lay at twelve point one million pounds. That's almost two billion yen.' Fenton laid the folder down and looked at Nicholl. 'And yet, somehow I doubt you were in this for the money. Am I right?'

'You wouldn't understand, Fenton, so there's no point in me trying to explain it to you.'

Fenton smiled. 'I'll bet I can guess. I'll bet it all has to do with some obscure prophecy you think you've found in The Book of Days to Come.'

Nicholl forced a smile back at him. 'That's right.'

Fenton laid back in his chair. 'I never took you for gullible, Nicholl.'

The door bleeped and opened. Fenton's second-in-command walked in carrying two cardboard cups of coffee. He set one down in front of Fenton and the other in front of Nicholl, then returned to stand by the door. Fenton leaned forward and sipped his coffee. He smiled and nodded to Nicholl's cup. Nicholl lifted the cup and slowly emptied it onto the floor. She looked inside the empty cup and saw the remains of a powdery substance. She looked at Fenton. 'Sodium Pentothal in the coffee? You really thought I'd fall for that?' She dropped the cup to the ground.

'A few years ago I would have said no way, but ever since Bradley died you've been going steadily downhill. Led a lot of people to assume that Bradley was the brains of your little partnership and without her you're struggling. That and your

– what are we calling it – relationship? with Rek Hughes has made you a serious security threat, Nicholl. No one knows what the hell you're going to do next. There have been a lot of wild rumours about you over the last few years and I didn't want to believe them at first. It couldn't be possible. Not Nicholl. Not the ministry's golden girl. But this latest stunt just goes to prove that maybe the rumours aren't wrong. The ease with which I caught you tonight only proves you're getting older. Older and slower. Maybe you *are* losing it.'

'You don't want to listen to rumours, Fenton,' Nicholl said calmly. 'I mean, I heard a rumour that you were sent over here to babysit Takamura's collection because Kyle said you were a "grossly incompetent field agent".'

Fenton winced, choking back the rage. Nicholl smiled. Fenton shot his second-in-command a look, which the man deliberately avoided. Fenton looked back to Nicholl. 'Fine. You go on believing your little fairytale prophecy. You believe everything Rek Hughes tells you when your face is buried in a pillow. Do you think Bradley would be proud of you? Betraying the Ministry just because some guy gave you an orgasm!'

Nicholl leapt across the table and pressed the chain of the handcuffs against Fenton's windpipe. The chair fell backwards and they both landed on the ground. Nicholl pushed down on his neck with the handcuff chain. Fenton fought to release himself but couldn't. A second later Nicholl was grabbed by the hair and yanked backwards. Fenton's second-in-command pulled her to her feet and then threw her to the other side of the room. Nicholl hit the corner and slid to the ground.

Fenton got to his feet slowly. He undid his tie and massaged his bruised windpipe. He lifted the toppled chair and slammed it down on its legs again. He glared over at Nicholl. 'Get up!'

Nicholl slid back up the wall but remained in the corner. Fenton walked over to her and stood face to face, their noses almost touching. He locked eyes with her. Nicholl never saw the punch coming. She dropped to the floor again, clutching her mid-section.

Fenton leaned down and whispered, 'I'm going to make sure you end up in Section Zero for this. You mark my fucking words, Nicholl.'

There was a bleep behind them and the door opened. A junior agent appeared. He was about to speak when he saw Nicholl buckled-over on the floor. 'Well, what is it?' Fenton yelled impatiently.

The young agent told his second-in-command, who relayed the message to Fenton. 'An urgent phone call for you, sir, from Takamura's manservant.'

'You still using a translator, Fenton? Most people pick up a language in about a year. How long have you been here now?' Fenton grabbed Nicholl by the collar and pulled her to her feet then dragged her back to the table and pushed her down into her seat.

'Look at me.' Nicholl continued looking forward as she pushed her hair out of her face and clipped it in place. Fenton grabbed her mouth and twisted her face towards him. 'I said look at me!' He moved closer to her. 'We're going to have a lot more time to talk before your escort gets here. I'll be back soon.' He let go of her face with a push. He could see how full of rage Nicholl was, but also impotent to do anything about it. He felt how stiff he was in his trousers.

Fenton walked towards the door. The young agent left first, followed by his second-in-command. Fenton looked back over his shoulder at Nicholl and smiled before pulling the door closed behind him.

He stood in the corridor until the door bleeped and gave it a pull to make sure it was secure – he was taking no chances with Nicholl. Fenton walked up the corridor and paused at the top of it. He directed the other agents to go ahead while he went into the toilets.

There was no one else in the toilets but he went to a cubicle anyway and locked the door. He unzipped his trousers and released his erection. He looked down at it, smiling. He took out his phone and got a photo of it at full strength. He looked at the screen of his phone and smiled broadly at the photo. 'That's what I'm fuckin' talking about,' he said in an excited whisper. He swayed his hips back and forth gently. It took all his willpower not to make lightsabre noises. He waited until the muscles started to relax and then zipped himself back up and left the cubicle. He threw some water on his face and dried it with a paper towel. He looked in the mirror and adjusted the remains of the bulge in his trousers. He took a deep breath and left the toilets.

He strode confidently through the office. He had a sense of seniority he had not felt since being dumped in this field office nine years before. It was all he could do to suppress a smile. As he walked through the maze of desks he could tell that the junior agent had already passed on what he had seen. They looked at him with respect now. Or it could have been fear. Or even awe. Whatever it was, Fenton would take it. They had looked at him for almost a decade like he was little more than a night watchman at an empty building. He reached his office and closed the door behind him when he entered. He watched them chatter quickly back and forth to each other, stealing glances at his office every now and then. Fenton sat down at his desk. He took a deep breath and allowed himself a smile now. He saw the flashing button on his phone and remembered his call.

He took out his mobile phone and went to the photos folder. His suspicions were correct; in the photo he had just taken his penis was definitely bigger than the other two pictures he had taken of himself aroused. There it was: scientific proof. When you compare manual arousal and chemical arousal against the aphrodisiac that is power; power wins, by at least a quarter of an inch. Though in the interests of scientific objectivity he should compare those three to an erection given to him by an actual three-dimensional, living, breathing woman in close proximity. That was the only theoretical aspect in his research at the moment. Still, with his newfound sense of power it was only a matter of time before one of the secretaries gave in to her desire and then all his photocopier-room fantasies would come true. He smiled, snapped his phone shut and dropped it in his pocket. He pressed the flashing button on his office phone.

'Fenton.'

'Ah, yes, Mister Fenton. Takamura, san, wishes to know if your man has finished?'

'What man?'

'The agent you left to do an inventory of Takamura, san's, collection. It is most late already. He has most important meeting in morning and…'

'I didn't leave anyone to do an inventory, you must be…' Fenton's smile disappeared and his heart sank into the pit of his stomach. His mouth was dry. It took three attempts to get the question out. 'Is the… the Fist… is it still there?'

'Excuse please, why would it…?'

'Is The Fist of Merlin still there?' Fenton shouted.

'I will check.'

The line went quiet. Fenton waved frantically through his office window and attracted his second-in-command's attention. He rushed into the office. 'We didn't leave anyone behind at Takamura's, did we?'

'No, sir, you said there was no need since we had caught the thief.'

Fenton held up a quieting hand as the manservant came back on the line. 'The Fist of Merlin is not here. Takamura, san, is most upset.'

'What did he look like? The man you thought we left behind, what did he look like?' Fenton barked.

'He was white man. He had the accent of the Irish.'

'Fuck!' Fenton slammed the phone down and then threw both parts of it across the room. He ran his fingers through his hair and tried to get his thoughts straight. 'Shit! I should've known. I should've fuckin' known if she was here, *he* would be here too.'

The second-in-command spoke cautiously. 'Who would be here too, sir?'

'Hughes! Rek fuckin' Hughes. Get his picture out to all the law enforcement agencies and the airports. He's on the Ministry's database. That bitch was just buying him time. She'll know where he is.'

Fenton stamped out through his office and across the main office floor, now wanting to avoid the stares of his subordinates. He strode down the corridor to the interrogation room, his blood boiling. He reached the door and felt his jacket pockets one by one, then again. Then he tried his trouser pockets. 'Where's my fuckin'…?' His sentence stopped short as he remembered Nicholl lying on top of him during the scuffle. He turned to his second-in-command. 'Open it!'

The second-in-command swiped his card through. The door bleeped and unlocked. Fenton pushed him aside and ran into the room. The room was empty apart from two chairs and a table. Resting on the table were a pair of handcuffs and a hair-clip. 'Fucking bitch!' he screamed. He upturned the table and slammed it against the wall. The crash made his second-in-command jump. Fenton took a few deep breaths. 'OK, she didn't come past us, so she must have gone out the back entrance. Get everyone out to the back car park now!'

The second-in-command rushed away at once. Fenton seethed as he stared at the handcuffs lying on the floor. He turned and ran out to join the chase.

Dawn was just breaking as Fenton stepped out into the back car park. A dozen of his men were spread out over the large car park, shining torches into cars, under cars and between cars. The roar of an engine broke the silence. Everyone looked around trying to pinpoint where the sound had originated. A pair of headlights came on, full beam, and a car bolted out of its parking spot. A few agents ran after her on foot but they had no chance. Nicholl just had time to smile at Fenton as she sped past him and out into the Tokyo night.

Fenton screamed at his second-in-command, 'Get after her. Shoot her if you have to, but she does *not* leave Japan. Understand me?' Eight agents bundled into two cars after his orders had been relayed. With a screech of tyres, they took off after Nicholl. Fenton grabbed his second-in-command and said, 'Get the helicopter prepped and ready for take-off.' His second-in-command nodded and ran off. Fenton stared at the lights of Tokyo.

Rek walked down the back ramp of the plane as a fork-lift carried another crate inside. He looked at the rapidly dwindling cargo sitting on the runway waiting to be loaded. He loosened the tie around his neck. He was still wearing the Ministry suit he had used to gain access to Takamura's house. He patted his jacket pocket again and was relieved to find The Fist of Merlin hadn't disappeared in the last three minutes. He looked towards the terminal building and saw no sign of

Nicholl. He knew this was a bad idea. It was way too risky from the beginning. He looked over at the crates. Once they were all loaded this plane would be taking off. He should have gone with her. It was madness to expect her to escape from a Ministry field office on her own.

Promise me, Rek.

They had arrived in Japan early yesterday morning. After acquiring the security codes and making their return flight arrangements, they had been back in the hotel by late afternoon. They had lunch in their room and spent the rest of the day in bed. Nicholl had become less and less worried about the Ministry finding out about her relationship with Rek. He was on the Ministry's Watch List after Takamura had reported being harassed by him by phone, mail and email. So much for trying to get the Fist legally. It had also put Rek on the outside, and any Ministry agent consorting with him would be viewed with suspicion. Nicholl had been careful in the beginning but now Rek felt that she sensed the same as he did; that bigger things were happening. The Endtime was close.

She had sat up in bed, facing away from him. He ran his fingers down her naked back. Her skin was so soft and smooth in places, but there were many scars; knife wounds, bullet wounds, scratches and bites, each tied to a place and time in her career. Her skin was a map of the path that had led her here.

'Is your mobile fully charged?' she asked.

'Yeah, it is.'

'As soon as I go over the wall you should call in the tip-off to Fenton.'

'OK.'

She kept her back to him. 'Rek, if I don't make it back in time…'

'You're going to make it back. Remember your great escape plan.'

'Yeah, I *will* get away, but I may not get away in *time*, and if that happens… you have to leave without me.'

'Let's not talk about this.'

'Rek, you have to get the Fist back home. This is bigger than either of us. Bigger than both of us. Everything depends on it. Promise me, Rek.'

Promise me, Rek.

The fork-lift climbed the ramp. There were less than a dozen crates left now. Rek stared over at the terminal building. No one emerged from the doors. He whispered, 'Come on. What the hell's keeping you?'

The back window of Nicholl's car exploded amid a hail of gunfire. She pulled the car hard right and ducked down an alleyway. The streets of Tokyo were empty at this time of the morning so she was keeping her foot down as much as possible. The black sedans were still behind her. Another burst of machine gun fire erupted and Nicholl heard metal being punched and the tail-lights shattering. She threw the car into a hard left, then a right. She put her foot down and the car lurched forwards. Behind her was clear. She raced down the neon-lined street ignoring the early-morning traffic lights.

Her freedom was short-lived. One of the black sedans appeared in her mirror again. They were still quite a distance behind; she might be able to outrun them. Explosions of steam ripped from the car's bonnet as bullets ploughed into the engine. Nicholl looked up and saw a black helicopter shooting down at her. She started swerving wildly back and forth across the street. The black sedan in her mirror was gaining ground.

The other black sedan appeared on the street ahead, coming straight at her. There was nowhere to go. No side streets. No alleys. Nicholl put her foot down and set a collision course with the oncoming car. Just yards from impact she pushed open her door and threw herself out. The sedan tried to swerve at the last moment but the car Nicholl had been driving slammed into it at full speed. The force of the impact slammed both cars into a nearby shop-front.

Nicholl had fallen hard on the street, but her training had taught her to roll so she had got off fairly lightly. She turned around and saw the second sedan was almost upon her. She got to her feet, a little unsteadily, and ran to the pavement and started trying doors. The agents were out of the second sedan and running towards her. She found an open door and ran inside. She closed and dead-bolted the door behind her then ran for the stairs. She heard the agents pounding as she raced upwards. She was in a small apartment complex. It was three storeys high. She reached the roof access and slammed the door open.

She turned, closed and dead-bolted the roof access door. She ran to the far side of the roof. The next building was at least fifteen feet away and a little higher – there was no way she could jump. She ran back across but was stopped halfway by a gust of wind. She looked up and saw the helicopter. Long black ropes dropped from either side and two men started to slide down. Nicholl was landing punches on the first one before he'd let go of the rope. Though he was trained in martial arts, he was small and of slight build. Nicholl punched his face and torso repeatedly and finished off by kicking him in the groin. The agent grabbed his testicles and dropped to his knees.

Nicholl turned around and was punched square in the face. She didn't fall over but stepped back far enough to administer a front-kick to the face of her opponent. His nose exploded and within seconds blood was pouring over his lips and chin. The agent staggered forwards, blinded by his own tears. He was about to walk into the other agent, still on his knees, when Nicholl grabbed him by the tie and jerked him down, hard. The bleeding agent's skull cracked loudly off his kneeling colleague's and they both fell to the ground. Nicholl could hear the agents from the sedan now throwing themselves against the roof access door.

She grabbed one of the ropes hanging from the helicopter and tied it to the railing around the roof. The pilot saw what she was doing and manoeuvred the helicopter backwards and over the street but he was too late. The rope was tied and the helicopter was tethered to the roof. Bullets started to rip through the roof access door around the dead-bolt. Nicholl took a few steps backwards and then ran at the side of the building. She jumped off the side and caught the other rope dangling from the helicopter. She immediately started to shin down towards the street.

She was fifteen feet from the ground when the pilot saw what she was up to. He lurched the helicopter forwards. Nicholl was propelled towards a brick wall in front of her. She let go and dropped to the ground. She heard a screech of brakes and the crash of metal. She got up and tried to rub feeling back into the shoulder she had fallen on. She looked up at the helicopter bouncing around on its leash. The agents were on the roof now and desperately trying to untie or cut the rope. She turned around and saw a bike messenger had fallen off his motorcycle while trying to avoid hitting her.

Nicholl limped over to him quickly. She asked if he was all right in Japanese. She couldn't see his eyes through his visor, but his helmet nodded. She lifted his motorcycle and brought it to life. 'Sorry about this, but I really need to be somewhere.' She painfully threw her leg over the motorcycle, kicked it into gear and was gone in a gust of exhaust fumes.

By the time the helicopter caught up with her, Nicholl was racing towards the entrance to Narita International Airport. Fenton took out his handgun and fired a few shots at her from the air as they closed in. Nicholl increased her speed towards the barrier gate. The guard had just waved a car through. The barrier was lowering again. The guard put his palm up to halt the motorcycle screaming towards him. The barrier was almost down. Nicholl leaned into the corner and just managed to get under it. The guard fired two shots into the ground and then got on his radio.

'Why have we stopped?' Fenton screamed at his second-in-command. The pilot spoke slowly and clearly.

'He says airport is restricted airspace. He cannot fly in there.'

'I don't give a fuck! You tell him to follow her.'

The second-in-command relayed this to the pilot and came back with: 'He says he's not losing his licence over this. He'll put us down outside the gate.'

The helicopter started to lower and Fenton punched his seat.

Rek watched as the back of the plane closed. He looked out the window. The loud roar of the engines meant he could pretend not to hear the co-pilot the first time he spoke. The co-pilot took Rek by the shoulder, turned him around and repeated himself. 'We must go now. We cannot wait any more. We have only small window to take off. We must go!'

Rek took one last look through the window at the terminal then gave the co-pilot a small nod. He rushed up to the cockpit. Rek dropped into his seat.

Three airport security cars were now chasing Nicholl through the grounds of the airport. Luckily they had scouted the airport the day before, so she knew where she was going and she knew she was close, but there were ten feet wire fences all around the runways. She couldn't see a way through.

She spotted her plane. It was the one the pilot had pointed out to them yesterday. She was sure of it. It was moving. She raced towards the wire, the sirens and flashing lights of three cars following her. Then she saw her chance. Someone was driving a mobile set of stairs, the kind used for boarding passengers, around the perimeter of the wire fence. The stairs were higher then the fence. Nicholl twisted her right hand down and raced towards the trundling vehicle.

Rek had failed her. He should have went with her. He touched the Fist in his pocket again. She was right of course. This was more important. Didn't mean he had to like it. He looked out the window and saw a motorcycle fly over the fence. It must have shot twenty feet into the air before landing on the runway and chasing after the plane. The pursuing cars screeched to a stop on the other side of the fence.

Rek ran to the back window and looked out at the motorcycle. Nicholl waved at him casually. He laughed out loud. The co-pilot appeared beside him. 'What do we do? We stop?' Rek looked out the back window and saw that airport security had found a way onto the runway and were now chasing Nicholl again.

'No. Tell the pilot to keep going but don't take off.' The co-pilot ran towards the cockpit. Rek pulled the lever on his left hand side. Alarms started to sound and wind rushed in. The loading ramp of the plane started to lower.

Nicholl looked over her shoulder and noticed there were now five cars chasing her and they were closing. From her left, a refuelling truck crashed through the wire fence and raced towards her. Fenton was driving. He pulled out a machine gun and opened fire. Sparks jumped off the ground around Nicholl. Fenton fired again and sparks jumped of the back of the plane. Two of the pursuing cars now broke off and were moving to intercept Fenton. They screeched to a halt in front of him and he had to hit the brakes to avoid crashing. Airport security pulled Fenton out of the truck and cuffed his hands roughly behind his back as he tried to explain his importance to them in a language none of them understood. He watched over the roof of the security car as Nicholl's motorcycle flew up the back ramp of the plane. He watched the back of the plane close again as it gathered speed and left the pursuing cars behind. Eventually the security cars just stopped and watched the plane take off. Fenton dropped his head onto the roof of the car.

Rek ran forward to the heap of smoking metal. Nicholl had come in at such speed it took her a few seconds to slow down and she had shot right past him and crashed into a heap of tarpaulin. The motorcycle's engine ticked as it cooled. Rek lifted the bike off her and set it aside. He looked down at Nicholl lying in the tarpaulin, still trying to get her breath. She smiled at him. 'Please tell me after all that, you got it.'

Rek took out The Fist of Merlin and dropped it in her lap. She looked at it and smiled at him.

The co-pilot stepped out of the cockpit. 'Narita is ordering us to return to airport immediately.'

Rek took out a wad of rolled notes and held them out to the co-pilot. 'Are you still experiencing communication problems?'

The co-pilot looked at the cash, then took it from Rek. 'Yes. Unfortunately our radio is still down.' The co-pilot bowed to them both and went back to the cockpit.

Rek sat down next to Nicholl. 'So that was your fool-proof plan, eh?'

'It worked, didn't it?' She grinned.

Rek took her in his arms. 'I guess it did.'

They kissed, The Fist of Merlin temporarily forgotten. It would take seventeen hours to reach Belfast International Airport.

the third moon

Sarah sat in the car, waiting. Hal had been so excited. She hoped that the surprise he had gone upstairs to prepare didn't involve a velvet covered ring box. He wouldn't. Surely he wouldn't. They had only been going out for three months. Still, why else would he bring her to this strange address in Portstewart? She looked at herself; why had she got dressed up? Showing a lot of leg and cleavage was not sending out the right signals. She looked in the back seat and found Hal's denim jacket and pulled it on. It smelled like him and she remembered the good times they had spent together. Some of the best times in that very back seat.

Things were different now. She was different.

Hal came running out the front of the building. Sarah pasted a smile on her face. She had never done this before but if TV and movies were anything to go by there was no good way to do it. No way that wouldn't hurt him. Hal opened her door with a grandiose bowing gesture.

'If m'lady would care to step this way.'

Sarah got out and took his proffered hand. Hal slammed the door closed and linked her arm. He led her inside.

They got out of the lift on the fourth floor. Hal led her quickly down the hallway and stopped at the door marked 4D.

Sarah was starting to get a bad feeling. 'Hal, what's going on? Who lives here?'

Hal smiled and took out a key. He unlocked the door. He turned back to Sarah and took both her hands in his. 'I'm hoping that... we do.'

'What?'

Hal put his hand on the small of her back and gently pushed her inside. He closed the door behind them. The main living area was empty except for a few cushions that had been scattered in a circle on the floor. Candles were placed all around the room, bathing it in a soft orange glow. A radio sat on the fireplace. Sarah recognized the deep voice of the DJ; it was Beatmaster Burden from the Late Lounge, playing three hours of non-stop love songs. In the centre of the cushions was a bottle of wine and one glass. Hal looked at her expectantly. Sarah couldn't find the words.

'Wait, you have haven't seen the best bit yet.' Hal took Sarah by the arm and dragged her across to the window. He unlocked the glass doors and took Sarah out onto the balcony. 'Just look at that view,' Hal said, putting his arm around Sarah and taking a deep breath.

Sarah looked out over the lights of Portstewart and heard the unceasing sound of the ocean close by. 'Hal...'

'Hey, look at the third moon.'

Sarah looked up. The moon was full and red. 'They call that a blood moon.'

'Is it good luck? Since, you know, a red moon only happens every once in a blue moon.' He smiled.

She laughed. He could always make her laugh. 'In the old days they used to regard a blood moon with dread. It was supposed to signify great change or disaster.'

'Shit!' Hal said, then laughed. 'Do you believe that?'

Sarah turned to him. 'No. It's just the earth's atmosphere refracting and bending the light from the sun.'

'Another fun fact from Sarah. I don't know where you pick all this stuff up. Though I know something about that full moon too.'

'What's that?'

'That's the third full moon this year.' Hal looked proud, so Sarah pretended to be impressed. There was a full moon every twenty-nine and a half days and this is March; it didn't take a lot of working out.

'The March full moon is also known as the Storm Moon, did you know that?'

Hal held up his hands. 'OK, I give up. You win. Let's go back inside.'

They stepped back into the living room and Hal rushed over to the cushioned area and sat down. He began uncorking the wine. 'Come on, sit down.'

Hesitantly, Sarah walked over and sat opposite him. She watched him fumbling with the wine bottle. Trying so hard to be suave and debonair and failing miserably. She remembered why she had been attracted to him in the first place. He tried so hard to be everything he thought she would want him to be.

He finally uncorked the wine and poured a glass and handed it to her. She took the glass and set it on the ground before her.

'What, you not drinking?'

Sarah shrugged, lifted the glass and took a sip.

'You know you drink less now that you're legal than you did before you turned eighteen. What's up with that?' Hal reached behind his cushion and brought out a bottle of beer.

'Yeah. A lot of things have changed since I turned eighteen.'

He twisted the cap off and took a long drink. 'So what do you think of the place?'

'It's lovely, but how can you afford this? I don't know too many hospital porters that live in penthouse apartments.'

'Well, if you promise to keep it a secret…' Hal leaned in. Sarah leaned in closer to him. 'I have a secret benefactor and he says he has great expectations for me.' Hal laughed. Sarah sat back and smiled. She took another sip of her wine.

'So, are you going to put me out of my misery?'

'What?'

'I'm asking you to move in with me. That's what the wine and the cushions and the fire hazard are all about. So what do you say?'

The words jammed halfway up Sarah's throat. Hal sensed her hesitation.

'I know what you're going to say. You're going to say that we've only been going out together for three months. We haven't even gone all the way yet, but…' Hal got onto his knees and took a couple of steps towards her. He looked her in the eyes. 'Sarah, I have loved you my whole life. Since we were kids. Since before I even knew what love was, I knew that you and I were meant to be together. You know what I mean. You've felt it too.' The two second gap after that sentence was there for Sarah to agree emphatically with Hal, but instead, those two seconds were silent. Hal hung his head. He climbed back over to the other side of the circle of cushions and took another long pull on his beer. 'Well, I hope that little speech gave you a laugh if nothing else.'

'No, I'm not laughing. That was beautiful. I just… I don't feel the same way. I'm sorry.'

Hal finished his current beer and opened a fresh one before speaking again. 'What changed between us, Sarah? When we first got together we were great. Things were great. We were in love. Then sometime... it was your birthday. Ever since your birthday you've been different. What happened to you on your birthday?'

Sarah took another sip of wine. 'A lot of things happened on my birthday.'

'Go on.'

Sarah took a deep breath. 'Remember Tom from when we were kids?'

'Tom? Tom Ford? Yeah. His house burned down and he moved away.'

'You don't remember what happened when we went to investigate the remains of his burnt-out house?'

'Yeah. There were a couple of psychos there who tried to kidnap us but this policewoman in a wedding dress showed up and arrested them.'

'They weren't psychos, they were vampires.'

'They were *not* vampires, Sarah.'

'You saw them fly just like I did, Hal.'

'That was just my imagination. My mum told me I was just remembering it wrong.'

She could hear the anger rising in his voice but she pushed on. 'Why would a policewoman be wearing a wedding dress?'

'I don't know! Maybe she was getting married when the call came in.'

'What, they didn't give her the day off for her wedding?'

'Maybe she was undercover, then.'

'Yeah, that could be it. You can't get any more inconspicuous than a wedding dress.'

'All right then, your explanation is better. Fucking vampires! Jesus Christ, Sarah. Most of us stopped believing in those stories in primary school.'

'Why do you think there are so many stories about vampires in this area?'

'Because they're real?' he said sarcastically.

'That's right. They are.' Sarah took a bigger drink from her glass. 'A few weeks ago I got a message through my Facebook account... from Tom.'

Hal got to his feet. 'I fuckin' knew it. I knew you were cheating on me!'

'I haven't been cheating on you. We haven't even met face to face yet. We've just been talking online.'

Hal was breathing hard. He threw his beer bottle across the room and it smashed against the far wall. 'Son of a bitch!'

'Maybe I should go.' Sarah started to get up, but Hal put a hand on her shoulder.

He took a deep breath and exhaled slowly. 'No. Wait. Please.' Sarah sat down again. Hal walked back to his side of the circle and dropped down onto the cushions. He grabbed himself another beer and drank half of it in one gulp. 'I always knew you had a crush on him when we were kids. I was relieved as hell when he moved away.'

She was about to say that it wasn't anything to do with attraction; it was purely business, but she knew that was a lie. She had been thrilled when Tom contacted her. He was able to explain a lot of things to her. He was able to warn her what was going to happen after she turned eighteen. 'We haven't even discussed anything like that. I don't know even know if he thinks about me that way. I have no idea what he looks like these days or what sort of person he is. He might be gay.'

Hal gave a mirthless laugh. 'Like I could be that lucky.' Hal finished the bottle in his hand and opened another. 'Where's he been all these years?'

'He didn't say. We talked mostly about… vampire stuff. He's part of it.'

'Part of what?'

'Something… it's hard to explain. Something's going to happen soon. There's this prophecy and he's a part of it and he thinks I'm a part of it too.'

'And how do you know he's not yanking your chain? Didn't Tom's dad write books or something? Maybe he's following in his old man's footsteps and this is all some story he working on.'

'It's true. I've seen a vampire.' She took a gulp of wine. 'I've killed one.'

Hal sat forward and whispered, 'You killed somebody?'

'Not somebody, some*thing*.' She took another sip of wine and a deep breath. 'Tom told me some things his mum had told him, about my father.'

'I thought your dad was killed in Iraq?'

'That's what my mum told me. And I believed her until a few months ago. Until Tom told me the truth. Looking back I should have realised. For months before my eighteenth birthday my mum and my Uncle Derek were always arguing about something. I only ever caught bits of what they were saying, but after Tom's email…'

'What *did* happen on your birthday? We were supposed to go out that night but you called me and said you were sick.'

'I had a vision. Weirdest damn thing that ever happened to me.' She took another couple of sips of wine. 'I saw these two girls being killed on a beach by a vampire. I got in my mum's car and took off towards Castlerock to save them.'

'How did you know what beach it was?'

'The vision, it was… it's hard to explain. It's not like watching a TV show. There's more. It's almost like joining the person you're seeing. Being inside their mind. I knew everything these girls knew. From boys they fancied to their favourite song, to their shoe size. Even though the vision only lasted a few seconds, I had all this information, including where they were.'

'Did you take a weapon with you?'

'No. When I got there I saw the girls in the distance on the beach and I could feel something close. I could sense danger. My heart was beating so fast. And then I was running. Almost like I wasn't in control – a passenger in my own body. I intercepted the vampire before he got to the girls. We fought. I was so strong and I knew how to fight.' She laughed. 'I knocked seven types of shit out of him!' She gulped the rest of her wine and Hal refilled her glass. 'I finished him off with a piece of driftwood I found on the beach. Rammed it straight through his chest and out the other side. He shrivelled into a skeleton in seconds.'

Hal finished his beer and cracked open another. 'What did you do with the body?'

'Someone had left the embers of a fire burning on the beach. I found some more wood and stoked it up again. Then I burned him.' She took a sip of her wine. 'Do you believe me, Hal?' He remained silent. 'I need you to believe me. This is really important. When Tom comes back we're going to need all the...'

'When's he coming back?'

'Tomorrow. The dates of this prophecy aren't that accurate since they were written thousands of years ago, but he says all this stuff is supposed to happen after the third moon and before the fourth.' Sarah's brow furrowed.

'What's the matter?'

'That's what you called it; the third moon. Why did you put it that way?'

Hal glared at her but didn't answer. 'What exactly did Tom tell you about your father?'

Sarah felt dizzy. She had been drinking the wine too quickly. 'He told me... he told me that my father was a vampire. With a vampire father and a human mother, I would be a natural warrior against the undead. I'm a...' Hal nodded slowly, urging her to continue. Sarah suddenly felt scared. Something wasn't right here. She got to her feet and swayed as dizziness hit her like waves.

'Are you all right?' Hal asked flatly.

'I must have got up too quickly. I just...' The room was spinning. Sarah put out her hand and tried to steady herself on the wall, but found the wall was an illusion. 'I'm a... I'm a dhampir.'

Hal looked at her without emotion. 'I know you are.'

She fell forwards and knocked over the wine bottle. The red liquid rushed from the bottle. She was on her hands and knees. She took long blinks, trying to right the churning world before her eyes. She looked over at Hal. He hadn't moved. Why wasn't he trying to help her? Had he said he knew what she was? With all her remaining strength she pushed herself to her feet again and staggered towards the door. She only made three steps before she dropped onto the ground and blackness enveloped her.

Hal walked over and kneeled before her. She was lying face-down. He rolled her over onto her back. He ran a finger down her face and pushed a lock of chestnut hair behind her ear. He ran the finger down her neck, across her breasts, down her stomach and on to her knee. He ran his finger back up her leg under her skirt and up the inside of her thigh. He looked at her. This is where she usually grabbed his hand and relocated it to her waist. She wasn't saying anything tonight, though. He cupped the soft skin of her upper leg in his hand. He looked at her face again. Her eyes closed, her face still looked pained, even in unconsciousness. He pulled his hand out from under her skirt. He sat looking at her for a long time, but as soon as he heard the first weak groan from her, he got the syringe from the fridge and injected the contents into her veins. She was silent again. He watched the gentle rise and fall of her chest.

Hal had crept into Sarah's room on occasion. She and her mum lived in a bungalow so it was fairly easy. The house was dark as he let the car roll silently down the last hundred yards of the lane. It wasn't much of a hill but it was enough to carry the car along. He knew this from past experience. Sarah's mum was pretty cool and didn't wait up to interrogate her about what she had done while she was out. Her bedroom was at the other end of the house too, so as long as he didn't set off any fireworks, he should be able to get Sarah inside undetected.

He laid her down on her bed and took her shoes off. The devil sitting on his right shoulder told him he should take all her clothes off. Let's face it, after tonight it was something he'd probably never get to see. He lifted the duvet and covered her up. He kneeled down at her bedside and leaned in close to her.

'I really do love you, Sarah.' He kissed her forehead and left.

From the outside everyone would assume the house was empty. The windows were boarded up, the garden overgrown and the paintwork in dire need of redoing. In fact the only thing that was pristine were the locks. The house might look like a strong gust of wind would knock it over, but it was in fact a fortress. Hal walked up the driveway and brought out a key. He looked around the deserted streets before letting himself in.

He still hadn't got used to that smell. He stood in the hall waiting for his eyes to adjust to the darkness.

'Welcome back, Harold.' The low voice made him jump. He saw something move in the darkness. Then the voice was to his right. 'I can feel your anger and sorrow. Why don't you tell me what happened this evening. Though I must first ask, does the dhampir sleep?'

'Yeah. I gave her the stuff. She'll be out until morning.' Hal debated whether or not to share his humiliation and decided that it could only ingratiate him further. 'You were right about her.'

'So she was deceiving you? I'm so sorry. With Tom Ford?'

'Yes. He's coming back to town tomorrow.'

'Excellent news. We'll make them both pay for their betrayal, Harold.'

utv

Blackness.
Fade in.
Morning. The shot consists of the dilapidated house in background right, with the female presenter, Imogen Collins, in foreground left.
'Three. Two. Good evening, and welcome to tonight's show. I'm standing here on Millenium Terrace where... what? Oh, shit. Go again.
'Three. Two. Good evening, and welcome to tonight's show. I'm standing here on Millenium Close where residents have...' A car horn beeped loudly followed by raucous shouts.
'Fuckin' wankers! Go again, Terry.
'Three. Two. Good evening and welcome to a very special edition of *Ghosts of Ulster*. We're not in a castle this week, or a graveyard. I'm standing on Millenium Close. It's a quiet suburb of Portrush that has been here just over twenty years, but the building we're interested in, the one behind me, number twenty-nine, has been here less than ten years. In that short time, it has become known as one of the most haunted buildings in the UK.' She smiles into the camera.
'Cut.'
Blackness.
Morning. The shot is showing the boarded up windows of the house. The tips of the overgrown grass are just creeping into the shot at the bottom. A head and shoulders shot of Imogen Collins stands to the right, a middle-aged man in a smart suit stands opposite looking nervous.
'You getting my tits in Terry?'
The camera zooms back slightly. The shot now shows Imogen Collins and her interview subject from the waist up.
'OK, Imogen. Got the tits.'
'I paid enough for them, may as well let the public see them.' She smiles and slaps the man opposite, who nervously smiles back at her.
'We ready for a take, Terry?'
'When you are.'

'Three. Two. I'm here with Martin McCaw, a local estate agent. What can you tell us about the history of this house?'

'Thehousewasbuilttenyearsagothefirstcouplewholived...'

'Whoa, whoa. Slow down there, Martin.' Martin takes a deep breath. 'Ready?' Martin nods. 'Still rolling? Three. Two. Martin, your firm has been letting this house since it was completed. What can you tell us about its gruesome history?'

'It was... it just... the, the house, the house was...'

Imogen flaps her hand at the camera.

Martin says, 'Shit, I nearly had it that time.'

Imogen pushes the camera down but it is still rolling. The shot is of the grass. 'What do you need, Martin? I've got some Valium in the car, or if you want a wee nip of something I have a bottle in my bag.'

The camera angle creeps up surreptitiously and shows Martin lean in to Imogen, clear his throat and say, 'What we were talking about earlier.'

'What, now?'

Martin nods with a nervous smile. 'Guaranteed.'

Imogen looks at the camera. 'Cut, Terry.'

Blackness.

Morning. The shot is of Martin coming out the front door of the house. He is smiling broadly and is relaxed and swaggering confidently. He checks his zipper is up. Imogen comes out the door behind him wiping the dirt from her knees. She looks at the camera. 'Oh, wait, Terry. Cut. I need to brush my teeth first.'

Blackness.

Morning. The shot is the same as before. Imogen and Martin from the waist up. Boarded windows behind, overgrown garden below.

'Three. Two. Martin McCaw is the estate agent who has been representing this house since it was completed. Martin, what can you tell us about this house's sordid past?'

'Well, Imogen, as you said the house is barely ten years old. I had the dubious duty of leasing the house to the first occupiers. They were a young couple that had only been married a few months. On the few occasions I met them prior to signing the lease I got the impression of two young people, very much in love.'

'But after they moved into number twenty-nine, that all changed.'

'Indeed it did. When I called to collect the first month's rent I hardly recognized them. They looked gaunt, almost ghostlike. I expressed my concern and they said they were both suffering from near-constant headaches, which in turn was depriving them of a good night's sleep. Well, I've been in this game long enough to know the symptoms of a gas leak when I see them. I called in the gas board immediately and had the whole house checked.'

'But they found nothing?'

'No. The gas main in the house was perfectly safe. But it was only three days after that that the tragedy occurred.'

Imogen turns to face the camera. 'That tragedy was the murder and suicide of these two newlyweds. From what police can piece together, it appears Georgina Maitland bludgeoned her husband, Gerald, to death in the kitchen with a sledgehammer, then went down into the basement and had some kind of psychotic fit. She scraped at the walls of the basement until she had broken all her fingernails off. Then, in perhaps a moment of sanity, she hung herself from the basement stairs.' Imogen turns back to Martin. 'How many tenants have you had since then?'

'Three. The first were a ghoulish couple that seemed fascinated by the deaths. You know the type; dress all in black, black eyeliner, black lipstick, listen to rock music. They lasted four days before running, screaming from the place in the middle of the night.

'Then there was a family on benefits. We couldn't get professionals so we decided to open the property up to DHSS tenants. There was a mother and three children; two girls and a boy. The eldest girl was only eight, but she was still strong enough to hold the other two down and cut off their fingers with a hammer and chisel.'

Imogen is noticeably shaken. 'Where did that happen?'

'In the basement.'

'And the third? The last tenants?'

'A group of parapsychologists. They gave me one month's rent in advance. They'd heard all the stories and wanted to investigate the claims of ghostly activity. They had all sorts of electronic monitoring equipment. There were four of them. They planned to take it in pairs, twelve hours on, then the other pair would relieve them for twelve hours.'

'And what happened to them?'

'The first night, when the second pair came to relieve them, they found one of their colleagues, a woman, mumbling incoherently. She had blood all over her. They never found her partner. To this day. Though tests determined the blood on her clothing was his. I don't think she ever remembered what exactly happened that night. She was convicted of his murder but found Not Of Sound Mind. To the best of my knowledge she's still in Sycamore Acres.'

'The local asylum,' Imogen Collins says dryly. She turns to the camera. The colour has gone from her cheeks. She holds up her flattened hand and cuts it across her throat.

Blackness.

'That's it?' the producer cried.

His young assistant puffed out his chest as best he could. After all, it wasn't his fault. 'Yes, sir. It was the first day's shooting. The tape was messengered to us that evening so we could start editing it.'

'That was four fuckin' days ago! What have they been doing since then?'

'I don't know, sir.'

'You don't know!' It seemed like all the furniture in the small office was shaking. 'I'll tell you what I know. That show's supposed to air in two days and we only have enough footage for three minutes. Call her.'

'I've tried calling her, sir. There's no answer. I've also tried calling the cameraman and the soundman. Neither of them are picking up either and both their wives have called in worried about them because they haven't phoned home.' He took a deep breath. 'Sir, you don't think...'

'What don't I think?'

'Well. It's just. The estate agent. The story he told sounded pretty convincing to me. I even checked what he said online. Those stories *were* reported in local papers and that woman *is* still in Sycamore Acres. I'm just wondering if maybe...'

The producer roared with laughter. When he got himself under control he wiped the tears from his eyes. 'You think we've actually found a real haunted house? Son, how long have you been working on this show?'

'Almost four months, sir.'

'Well, I've been on this show since the beginning. Six years. And I've seen every piece of footage from every castle, farmhouse, graveyard, pub, stately home and abandoned hospital. I've never seen a ghost. What I have seen is those places' takings go up by seventy percent after we've done a show on them.'

'A graveyard's takings went up? An abandoned hospital?'

'Now don't get lippy, son.' The producer reclined in his chair. 'We have to throw a couple of non-commercial premises in each series. I don't want to get too obvious.'

'You get kickbacks?'

'Perks! Perks of the job. If people want to show their appreciation, who am I to argue? And I don't want this gravy-train to end, so you're going to get your arse down to Portrush tonight and find out what the hell is going on and bring me back something I can edit.'

'But, sir, it's a two hour drive and I was supposed to see my girlfriend tonight.'

'Oh, really? Were you going to take her somewhere nice?'

'Yes, actually. It's sort of an anniversary for us. I was going to take her to her favourite restaurant and then to this little bed and breakfast we know where we…'

'Yeah, yeah, yeah. Would you be able to afford any of that shit without a job?'

The assistant exhaled and lowered his head. 'No.'

'Then we understand each other. Call me when you get there. I want to speak to Imogen. She better have a damn good explanation.' The producer opened a file on his desk, then looked over the top of it. 'Well, what are you still doing here?'

The assistant left.

The Sisterhood of the Kissed met on the roof of their founder, Danielle Rhodes's building at this time every year. Every other week of the year they would take turns gathering at one of their houses. Danielle had heard some people call her a cult leader, but maybe she was just mis-hearing; she did spend almost all her time in the company of women. There was actually nothing sexual about her group. What they were was a collection of women who had been touched by immortals and lived to tell the tale. Bitten but not killed. Kissed.

They had seven members now. As each new member joined they would tell their story to the rest of the group, who then in turn would tell the story of their brush with death. Danielle's was far and away the most dramatic story and always got left to the end. She told them of her fall into prostitution, then depression, and how, on the brink of suicide, a vampire had saved her from plummeting to her death. From that moment on she had changed her life for the better. She had been given a second chance. The two circular scars on her neck were a badge of honour and since then she had been campaigning for equal rights for vampires. They picketed the long-closed Ministry field office in Portstewart with placards saying STOP UTV! (Unequal Treatment of Vampires). For some reason, the local television station, Ulster Television, did not cover any of these protests so they largely went unnoticed. Danielle believed a vampire had saved her life, and if that were true, then vampires weren't all bad, they were just misunderstood. And they had as much right to live on this planet as anyone else. In fact if longevity was a factor, they had probably more right.

The meetings of the sisterhood were a light-hearted affair most of the time, the women would drink cocktails and swap stories they had heard about local vampire activity, then they would mix more cocktails and watch a movie. That was how their weekly meeting usually went, but everyone noticed Danielle get very serious around this time of the year. She had found fragments of a book called the Vampyre Corpora on the Internet and one passage in particular obsessed her.

As the third moon rises, the dark is released. And they looked to the west and lo, the heartsblood guided the seven and they knew their path.

Danielle stared at the setting sun. She closed her eyes and the negative of the picture appeared on her eyelids. She felt a hand on her shoulder. She turned and saw Esme. She was eighty-one years old and had been 'kissed' over fifty years ago.

'Come on now, you're going to melt your brain if you stare at it any longer.'

'What am I looking for, Esme?'

Esme looked sternly at her. The school-teacher she had been for forty-four years surfaced and spoke with cold authority. 'Your destiny. All our destinies. The heartsblood.'

'What does that even mean?'

Esme smiled. 'When it is time you will know.'

'I really thought this year would be the year. I had this feeling. Like… I don't know.'

'Never mind.' Esme put her arm around her friend. 'Maybe next year, eh?'

Danielle forced a smile. 'Yeah. Maybe next year.'

'The good news is, Patty's made up two jugs of *Sex on the Beach* and we've got *Ghost* and *Dirty Dancing* ready to play. Come on, we're all freezing our tits off up here.'

Danielle couldn't help but laugh. Esme led her towards the roof access door. Danielle gave the sunset one last glance over her shoulder. She stopped, jerking Esme to a stop as well. Danielle broke free of her embrace and ran to the edge of the building. The other women followed her over, each of them staring at the sky in awe.

'Do you? Do the rest of you…?' Danielle tried to ask.

'Yes,' Esme answered, 'we see it, too.'

The seven women stood there for a few seconds more watching the unmistakable shape of a heart the clouds had made, and the column of smoke rising from a house not far away that made it look like the heart was bleeding. The smoke and clouds were all the same perfect shade of red in the glow of the setting sun.

Danielle could have watched it forever. This spectacle that she had imagined for years was finally happening. There were tears in her eyes. They had to hurry. When the sun set they wouldn't be able to distinguish one column of smoke from another. She turned to the other women. 'Sisters, this is what we've waited for. Let's go.'

The assistant pulled up outside the house. He would need more petrol to make the return trip. He better get reimbursed for this. This wasn't part of his job description. He was going to have a word with his union rep about this, make no mistake. Every mile of the two-hour drive had just made him more irritable. Bad enough that his boss had sent him on this wild goose chase, but now his girlfriend who had phoned him several times on the journey and who he had intended to propose to tonight, now appeared to have dumped him. All this because Imogen Collins had gone on yet another bender. He understood now why no one wanted to work with her. She was a lush and a has-been and a raging alcoholic and just a thoroughly unpleasant woman in every respect. What was more annoying was how she always came up smelling of roses.

At the music awards last year she had gone onstage to present a lifetime achievement award to Kylie Minogue and ended up vomiting all over her. To any other presenter that would be a career killer, but not Imogen Collins. She got a crew to follow her through six weeks of rehab and packaged the whole thing as a reality show. She then sold it to a network for a ridiculous sum. And if that wasn't sickening enough, the twist of the knife was, it had been a hit!

The assistant had a full head of steam when he finally pulled up outside the house. He was going to tell Imogen Collins a few home truths. To hell with the job. If they fired him, they fired him. It would be worth it just to let her have it. And it might cut some ice with his girlfriend when he inevitably went crawling back to her. Yeah, if he showed her he had thrown caution to the wind because his weekend away with her had been spoiled, it might go some way to patching things up between them. But that wasn't the main reason. The main reason was to bring that hateful bitch down a peg.

This wasn't why he spent all those years at university getting his Masters degree in Media and Entertainment. This wasn't why he'd worked two jobs and then came home and did his coursework. This wasn't why he'd spent years getting three hours sleep a night. He didn't kill himself for all those years just to play nursemaid to a washed-up old tart like Imogen Collins. There were better jobs out there, there had to be.

The van was still outside the house and there was smoke coming from the chimney so they were probably still inside. He got out and slammed the door of his car, then marched towards the house. The front door was ajar. This halted him for a second. He knocked loudly, giving control back to his anger. 'Imogen!' He kicked the door open and the smell hit him immediately. It was like nothing he had ever smelled before. Like rotten eggs and sick and shit all mixed together. She'd been using this house as Party HQ. She probably had gangs of local students round every night. It wouldn't be the first time; stupid cow still thought she was eighteen.

He walked on into the house, covering his mouth and nose with his hand. It was dark inside, even though the sun hadn't fully gone down. All the windows were boarded up. He moved to the left and into what would have been the living room. There was no furniture but a fire was blazing in the hearth. The smell was worse in here. He looked around and stepped closer to the fire. He was reminded of the drunken barbecues at university where the meat was always burned on the outside and raw in the middle. What the hell were they burning? He could see blackened metal and melted plastic. Was that the camera? He ventured his toe forward and pushed the contents of the fire. Bones. There were bones in the fire. Human bones! He stepped back and turned to the door.

Imogen stood there in the flickering light of the fire. He yelled and stepped back. She was emaciated, like she had just stepped out of Auschwitz. Dried blood stained her face. Her eyes looked straight ahead and didn't follow him as he moved. She looked like she was in a trance. He cautiously walked towards her. She didn't react. When he was close enough he waved his hand in front of her eyes.

'Imogen? Can you hear me? What the hell happened here? Imogen!' She didn't move. He took her by the arm and led her towards the door. 'Come on, I'm going to get you to a hospital.' She staggered limply behind him until they reached the threshold of the front door. Imogen screamed and grabbed the sides of her head. She dropped to her knees. He bent down and tried to calm her. The screaming stopped after a minute or two. She released her grip on her temples and sat up. She grabbed his lapels and pulled him close.

'Downstairs,' she whispered. Her eyes were wild, pleading desperately.

'What's down there?'

She rubbed at her left temple vigorously for a few seconds then said, 'You have to see.' She clutched his arm.

'Imogen, I need to get you to a hospital.'

She grabbed her head. 'After,' she said through gritted teeth. 'After you've seen. Then we can go.'

He looked back at the open door, then ahead at the darkness.

'It has to be this way,' she whispered. Imogen got to her feet and, still clutching his arm, led him to the door under the stairs.

There was light below. Imogen descended the stairs as if she were being pushed every step. She pulled him with her. They reached the concrete floor and she led him to the far side of the basement.

He saw all the equipment first. A generator, a jackhammer, pick-axes, drills, sledgehammers. He passed a shelf and saw a mobile phone sitting on top of a credit card. He stopped and picked them up. The phone needed charging. The credit card was Imogen's company expense card. He set it down again.

'Imogen, you didn't buy all this stuff on the company's account did you?'

She was several feet ahead with her back to him. It was the first time he had noticed the seat of her trousers; it looked like she had messed herself repeatedly. Enough was enough. He was getting out of here. He stepped forward and took Imogen's arm, then stopped. She was standing on the edge of a large hole, maybe six feet long and six feet deep.

He turned to her and pulled her face around to face his own. 'Did you do this? What the hell for? Imogen? Speak to me! Why the hell did you do this?'

She raised her hand weakly and pointed to the far end of the hole.

He looked and saw nothing. He turned back to her. 'What?'

She continued to point and stare blankly. He turned and grabbed one of the battery powered lanterns off the wall and took a few steps forward. He held the light down into the hole. What was she trying to show him? He got down on his knees and held the lantern down as far as he could. There was something different at this end. A hole. She had drilled a hole at this end about ten inches from the wall of concrete. He squinted to see if he could look inside. 'Imogen, what am I supposed to be…?'

She stepped up behind him, pulled his head back and ran a knife across his throat. Blood poured from the wound instantly. He dropped the lantern into the pit and raised his hands, trying to staunch the flow. He turned and saw Imogen standing above him with the bloody knife still in her hand. She stared blankly at him and then put a foot on his back and pushed him forward into the pit.

He was choking on his own blood now. He coughed, trying to clear his windpipe, but it was no use. The lantern lay before him. He could see the red everywhere. The blood was rushing out of him too fast. He had to get out of here. He needed help. The blood was pooling under him and circling down the hole like bathwater. He had to get up. His brain told his legs to move but they didn't. He had to climb out. The lantern was beginning to dim before him. The batteries must be done, he thought. The batteries in all the lanterns in the basement must be dying. All at the same time. They were all dimming together. He'd never heard of such a thing. He wondered who he could tell such a bizarre anecdote to. The old man at his local hardware store. Yeah. He would get a kick out of that. He looked up and almost smiled as all the lanterns went out at once and darkness was quickly followed by nothingness.

Imogen stood over the body. The blood kept flowing after he had stopped moving. She hoped it would be enough. She was so tired. So hungry.

A layer of dust jumped off the floor of the pit. Imogen smiled. The dust jumped again and this time took some crumbs of rubble with it. The third time the base of the pit cracked. Imogen started to laugh and stumble backwards. Another loud crack sent a huge chunk of concrete into the air. Imogen had reached the wall of the basement. She stood frozen against it as rock and dust erupted from the pit. Imogen started to laugh maniacally. She slid down the wall to the floor just as the figure rose from the dust of the pit, ripping a body-bag off himself. She stopped laughing.

The dust began to settle and she made out the silhouette of a man standing before her with his back to her. His clothes were tattered and rotten and seemed several sizes too big for him. He turned to her and she saw skin tightly stretched over a skeleton frame. His eyes sunken deep into his skull. His cheeks almost transparent. His lips pulled back over his pointed teeth.

He took a few steps towards her and stopped, the rattle of footsteps on the stairs taking his attention. He turned back to her. He sent another thought into her puny brain – *One more duty, and then you are free.*

Imogen clutched her head for a second and then nodded. She got up and moved quickly around the dark end of the basement.

'Brother vampire. We are here as prophesied. We are the seven,' Danielle said as she stepped forward. 'We mean you no harm. We are a group who campaign to stop the Unequal Treatment of Vampires. We are your friends. Pray, how may we help you?'

The vampire turned and stepped out of the darkness. The women gasped. Some of them crossed themselves. The decayed corpse that walked towards them exuded malice from every fibre of his being. Danielle was suddenly afraid. She turned and looked behind her. She saw Imogen step through the basement door and lock it behind her. Danielle turned back to the vampire, who was getting closer. The women behind her started to shuffle backwards.

'We mean you no harm, sir,' Danielle restated. Some of the other women behind her had made it to the basement door and were banging on it, trying to force it open. 'What... what can we do for you, sir?' Danielle's heart was thumping loudly.

'You don't have to call me sir,' the vampire said in a hoarse dry voice. 'You can call me Kaaliz.' A smile cracked the taut skin around his mouth.

Imogen Collins ran out of the house and into the assistant's car. She brought it to life and raced away, just as The Sisterhood of the Kissed began to scream.

the morning after

Sarah woke slowly. Her head felt heavy, her body slow to react. It must have been at least half an hour before she realised she was in her own bed... and there was something wrong with that. Her confused mind tried to find the root of this feeling but memories were unreliable. Dreams and nightmares had intruded on reality and now nothing was certain. She threw back the bedclothes and saw she was still dressed. Wrong. Just wrong. Some primal instinct within her was warning her to prepare herself for attack. She swung her legs over the side of the bed and tried to stand. Her legs were weak. She managed to stand, holding onto the bedpost, and staggered over to her mirror. Her reflection was blurry. She moved closer to the glass. Her eyes were wrong. The pupils small, the iris bleary. She stood there for a long time, just how long she couldn't tell, but bit by bit the world started to come back into focus. Soon she could stand unaided. She walked to the window and opened it. The morning breeze had a sobering chill that she welcomed. She sat on the window-sill and let the cold air wake her.

The last thing she remembered was... the apartment. Yes. Hal had driven her to the apartment. His apartment. He wanted it to be their apartment. She drank some wine. Oh shit, she told him! She told him about the vampires. Why would she do that? Had she been drunk? This didn't feel like a hangover. She remembered being dizzy. She remembered Hal watching her. Not helping her. Standing over her as the darkness closed in. A shiver that had nothing to do with the cold wind wriggled up her spine. Had he done something to her while she was unconscious? Had he finally got what he had been asking for all these months?

Sarah jumped off the window-sill and closed the window. She pulled the curtains a second later and began pulling her clothes off. The denim jacket was Hal's. She threw it across the room. She saw the bruise on her left arm. From the crook of her arm to the wrist the skin was coloured shades of purple and black. She touched it. The muscles were taut and tender. A tiny circle at the top of the bruise was more red than purple. She looked closer. There was no doubt in her mind. She had been injected with something. And by someone who didn't know what they were doing.

She pulled off the rest of her clothes and opened the door to her wardrobe. She examined herself in the full-length mirror. She could see no other bruises or signs that she had been... she didn't want to say the word. She didn't want to even think it. Hal, her childhood friend. Her boyfriend for the last three months. How could he do this to her?

She ran into the en-suite bathroom and switched on the shower. She washed herself from head to toe and then stood under the shower while she turned the water up as hot as she could bear. She stood there until the last of the heaviness cleared from her head.

She sat on the end of her bed for a long time. The tails of her damp hair hung around her shoulders. She hugged herself, wrapped in her fluffy bathrobe. She looked into the mirror, but wasn't seeing the reflection. She was seeing the past. The boy Hal was. How could he grow up to be...? She stood up and walked to her wardrobe. She took the shoebox down from on top of it and sat back down on her bed. She riffled through the photos and keepsakes of her childhood until she found the photo she was looking for. She must have only been ten or eleven. Hal stood on her right with his arm around her, Tom stood on her left with his arm around her. They were all laughing. How did we get from there to here? she wondered.

She suddenly felt very alone. She left her bedroom and walked down the hall. Her mum wasn't in the living room or kitchen. Sarah looked at the clock; it wasn't even nine yet. Maybe her mum was still in bed. As she passed the front door she saw the mail lying on the mat. She knocked lightly on her mum's bedroom door. No reply. She opened the door a crack, then fully. Her mum's bed was made. She had either got up early this morning, or she hadn't come home last night. Sarah went to the bedside table and lifted the phone. She dialled her mum's mobile and got the answering service. She hung up without leaving a message. It was strange, but she wasn't worried. She looked out the window and saw her mum's car was gone. Wherever she had gone, she had gone of her own choosing.

Sarah went back to her room, dressed and dried her hair quickly. She left her house without breakfast and walked to the gate. She had been planning to take the bus into Coleraine, but now another thought struck her. Uncle Derek's motorbike was just sitting in the shed. Her mum hated that Derek had taught her how to ride a motorcycle and worried incessantly when she went out on it. But her mother wasn't here now, and neither was Uncle Derek; he was off with his girlfriend somewhere.

Sarah pulled the helmet on and kicked the bike to life. She revved it loudly, scaring the birds from the trees, then dropped it into gear and sped off down the lane towards the main road amid a cloud of dust.

Sarah stormed in through the doors of the hospital and stopped the first porter she saw. 'Hi, do you know what shift Hal's on today?'

'Hal's covering the theatres today,' the porter replied brightly. Sarah had met him before but couldn't remember his name at the moment. She smiled and thanked him and made her way down the corridor. The theatres are at the very end of the first floor. She took the stairs instead of the lift and ran up them, hoping to burn off some of the excess energy that was coursing through her. It didn't help though. The closer she came to him, the angrier she got. She turned off the main corridor at the end and walked quickly past the ICU. The theatre porter usually sat in a little alcove on the left just before reception. And there he was, sitting behind a tabloid newspaper, oblivious to her approach.

Sarah slapped the paper out of his hands and grabbed him by his collar. She lifted him off the ground and pushed him up the wall, surprising herself with her strength as much as him.

'What the hell did you do to me last night?'

'I didn't do anything.' He was trying to sound bewildered.

'Bullshit.'

'I swear. You just got drunk and passed out. I took you home.'

'Really?' She dropped him and he fell awkwardly on his chair. She pulled up the sleeve of her sweater and showed him the bruise. 'And how did this happen then?'

He looked at the bruise and struggled for words.

Sarah grabbed him around the throat again. 'You fuckin' drugged me! Why? What did you do to me when I was unconscious?'

Hal got angry now and got to his feet, pushing her hand away from his throat. 'I didn't do anything to you. What the hell do you think I am?'

'I don't know who you are. That's the truth.'

Hal turned and saw the theatre receptionist was looking worried and had the phone lifted, poised to dial. He raised a reassuring hand and shook his head. He turned his back to her and faced Sarah. He took a deep breath. 'Look, we can talk about this later. I'll pick you up tonight after work.'

'Forget it,' Sarah snapped. 'I never want to lay eyes on you ever again.' She turned and started to walk up the corridor.

Hal ran after her and grabbed her. He spun her around to face him. 'Do you mean that?'

'Yes, I fuckin' mean it!'

Still holding onto her arm, Hal hung his head for a few seconds, then looked her in the eyes. 'I love you, Sarah.' She shook her head. 'Whatever I did,' he continued, 'I did for you. To keep you safe. I know you don't understand that and I can't explain it to you right now, but please, believe me, it was for your own good.'

Sarah punched him in the face and he dropped backwards to the floor. He put his hands on his erupting nose. By the time the tears had cleared from his eyes, she was gone and the receptionist was fussing around him trying to staunch the flow of blood.

Hal decided then and there.

Sarah marched back up the corridor feeling only slightly better than before. She really needed some advice. Should she go see her doctor? Would he be able to tell if she had been raped? She probably shouldn't have taken a shower. She didn't know why, but after speaking to Hal, she thought maybe he was telling the truth about that one thing. Or maybe she was just deluding herself. She took out her phone and dialled her mum again. This time she answered.

'Sarah?'

'Yeah, it's me. Where are you?'

Her mum paused before answering. 'There was a bit of an emergency last night with your Aunt Chloe.'

'Is she all right? I'm at the hospital now if…'

'No, no, she's fine. We're on our way back to her house now. Why are you at the hospital?'

'I had to see Hal about something. Ah, when do you think you'll be home?'

'I'm not sure, why?'

Sarah didn't know what to say. If there was something wrong with Chloe, who wasn't really an aunt, just a friend of her mum's, then she had enough to deal with at the moment.

'Sarah, is something wrong?'

'No. It's nothing, mum. It can wait. I'll see you when I see you.'

'OK.'

'Bye.'

Anna slid her phone closed. Chloe looked over at her from the passenger's seat. 'Everything OK with Sarah?'

Anna dropped the phone back in her pocket. 'She says so.'

'You don't believe her?'

'I'm not sure.'

'Probably just boy trouble,' Chloe said with a grin.

'She said she had just been speaking to Hal. You're probably right. Are you warm enough?'

'I'm fine.'

'The doctors said you have to keep warm. Your body's had a terrible shock.'

'I'll be fine, Anna. I can't wait to get into my own bed. You can just drop me off and then go and see what's happening with Sarah.'

Anna didn't answer and Chloe was suspicious of the silence, but said nothing. She pulled down the car's sun-visor and looked at herself in the mirror. She looked like a zombie. Pale, too thin, she didn't even think she looked like a woman anymore. She was androgynous; it was impossible to guess her sex just by looking at her face. That haircut had been a mistake. Very few women can pull off short hair; Audrey Hepburn, Winona Ryder – that's about it. The latest in a long line of mistakes made by Chloe Knight.

She leaned her head against the window and watched the countryside pass by. In truth she dreaded reaching her home. A huge mansion she had bought for herself when she sold The Fist of Merlin. She thought it was her dream house until she had to live in it by herself. Eighteen rooms for one zombie with a bad haircut. It was a joke. In the early days of course she had the Daves for company, but now even they had moved on, both married and working if you can believe it. The whole world was moving on and she was standing still.

Anna was the only close friend she had left in the area. But she had met someone now, too. Tall, good-looking, good-natured. She would be the next to move on. Another bridesmaid's dress. With every wedding she attended Chloe grew more and more sure that she was going to spend the rest of her life alone. Something inside her told her so. No matter what she tried, she never met anyone who measured up.

The money had only complicated things. She had millions in the bank. She was slim (maybe too slim) and back in her dating (and pre-bad-haircut) days she had been pretty. You would assume there would be no end of male suitors for such a catch. And there were, in the beginning. They fell into two categories; 1) old money, who looked down on Chloe for being new money and not knowing five-hundred years of in-bred etiquette, and 2) himbos (the male equivalent of bimbos), who looked very attractive when hung over your arm and would gladly accept all manner of presents, but were sorely lacking in any real personality. Her last real boyfriend was called Pedro. A Latin beauty with a vacuum between his ears. Other women used to drool over him, but they didn't have to live with him. He really was the most boring person she had ever met. He had left her, and taken quite a lot of valuables with him, while she was out shopping one day. That was two years ago. Two years she'd spent rattling around those eighteen rooms alone. She compared herself to Miss Havisham from *Great Expectations*, except she had no wedding dress to wear.

Maybe she would get some cats, just to seal her spinster status. She could fill the eighteen rooms with cats. She could be known locally as the Crazy Cat Lady. When she died she would leave the house to the cats, just to piss off any relatives that might surface. And on her gravestone would be written

Chloe Knight, spinster of this parish, Crazy Cat Lady, a life of no consequence.

'Are you crying, Chloe?'

Chloe wiped her face. 'No. I'm fine.' She looked out and saw they were on the driveway up to her house. Home sweet home. Chloe's boat was sitting on a trailer, moored in her front garden. Round the back of the house was a helicopter. And in the garage two sports cars, a four-wheel-drive SUV and three motorcycles (two vintage and one brand new). The toys of the rich. Failed distractions to her loneliness.

Anna pulled the car close to the door and stopped. Chloe reached to her trouser pocket then quickly turned to Anna. 'My keys. Did the ambulance men lift…?'

She stopped mid-sentence as the door to her house opened and Lynda stepped out. Chloe looked at Anna.

'I called her last night. I hope you don't mind.'

There were tears in Chloe's eyes, but they were tears of gratitude. She smiled at Anna and nodded. Chloe opened the door and ran to Lynda. They hugged on the doorstep as Anna unloaded the few belongings Chloe had in hospital. She followed the two women inside.

Lynda had made breakfast and they all ate. Chloe did her best but couldn't finish what was on the plate. Afterwards they all went to the living room with mugs of coffee and talked.

Lynda was showing them the latest photos of her children.

'They've got so big since the last time I visited,' Chloe said.

'Well, that was nearly a year ago.'

'Was it?'

Lynda sat forward. 'Yes. Why didn't you come at Christmas like you said you were going to?'

'I didn't like to. I know you invited me and all, but, well, it's a time for family isn't it?'

'Hey, I wouldn't have invited you if I didn't want you to come. I had planned to set you up with this doctor friend of Frank's.'

Chloe forced a smile.

Anna joined in. 'A doctor, eh? What's he like?'

'If I weren't a happily married woman, I wouldn't say no!' Lynda and Anna laughed.

Chloe smiled a little more naturally. 'I don't know if I can stand striking out in the north *and* south of Ireland.'

'Now what sort of attitude's that?' Anna asked.

Lynda was staring at her solemnly now. Chloe's jokes masked a deep sadness inside her. They were all friends so the best thing was to ask her straight. 'Chloe,' she started. 'This accidental overdose…'

Chloe lowered her head, avoiding both women's eyes. 'Yeah?'

'It was accidental, wasn't it?'

It took her a long time to come back with, 'I think so.' She took a sip of coffee and continued. 'I don't remember too much from before. But I remember… I think I almost died.'

'You did,' Anna said. 'The ambulance men said they barely made it in time.'

'I felt it coming; death, and you know what was going through my mind as I died? What have you done? You leave no children behind, you haven't made the slightest difference to the world, even with all the charities I support; they try, but nothing ever changes. I'm leaving the world the same as I found it. I might as well not have lived at all for all the impact I made. And then I thought, now I'm going to die on my bathroom floor. Not even a heroic death. Not even dying so someone more worthy can live. When I thought of how many people have died fighting vampires over the years, people with families, people who would be missed, and I thought, why not me?'

Lynda sat forward and took her hand. 'Chloe…'

Chloe stood up and said, 'Let me show you something.' She quickly left the room.

Lynda and Anna exchanged worried looks. 'How long are you staying?'

'I told Frank it would be a few days at least. He has some time off so he can take care of the wee'uns.'

Anna leaned in. 'I think one of us should stay with her at all times.' Lynda nodded.

Chloe came walking back in carrying a scrap-book. She sat between Anna and Lynda and they both leaned in close. Chloe opened the scrap-book to page one. Stuck there was a yellowed news article with the headline JEDI? KNIGHT. The picture showed Chloe flipping in mid-air clutching a baby as two cars crashed below her. 'This is the first vampire I ever killed,' she said. 'The first and the last,' she added. 'His name was George. He wasn't much of a vampire really, but he gave me a good run for my money. As he was trying to escape he pushed this baby out into traffic. I grabbed the baby out of its pram and launched myself into the air just as two cars crushed the pram below me. Some tourist took this photo of it happening and I was big news for a few weeks. And then…' She flipped over the rest of the pages of the scrap-book. They were all empty.

'Is that what you want?' Lynda asked. 'To be on the front page of The Coleraine Times?'

Chloe shook her head. 'It's not the fame I want. It's… knowing, that I made a difference. That in some small way, the world is better because of me. That's all I want before I die.'

'You've still got a lot of years left before then. Plenty of time to make your mark,' Anna offered. Chloe hung her head and didn't answer.

'You have helped, anyway,' Lynda said. 'You've helped the Ministry more times than enough. OK, you may not be on the front lines anymore, but you're doing your part.'

'Yeah, maybe,' Chloe mumbled.

The doorbell rang. Chloe looked confused.

Anna got up. 'I'll get it.'

Lynda looked at Chloe, trying to catch her eye. Chloe made a point of avoiding her gaze. After a few moments Anna walked nervously into the living room again.

'Who was it?' Chloe asked. 'Jehovah's Witnesses or door-to-door salesman?'

'No,' Anna said. 'It's my brother.'

Rek Hughes and Agent Nicholl walked into the living room. Chloe got to her feet, her eyes dancing with anticipation.

Agent Nicholl stepped forward. 'Chloe, we need your help.'

Chloe smiled widely, her eyes full of tears.

returning

Kaaliz lay naked among the bodies of The Sisterhood of the Kissed. His form was so wasted after all those years of not feeding that it had taken all their blood to regenerate his body. Afterwards he had felt quite dizzy and had passed out while his body repaired. He had no doubt the skeletal hand wrapped around his heart quickened his recovery. When he woke he could sense it was still daylight. That was OK. If all that time not being able to move had taught him anything, it was patience. He wandered around the basement and found an old radio that still worked. The DJ mentioned the date. Kaaliz couldn't believe it. Ten years he had been buried in that concrete. How had the world changed? Were there more of his kind now, or less? And most importantly, where was Sin?

Alone in the cold darkness as the immeasurable time passed, days just as dark as nights, he had waited for her. As insects crawled over his face and he couldn't raise his arm to move them, he waited for her. As he lost his mind a thousand times and then regained it, he waited for her. She was looking for him. That much he was sure of. Unless she were dead. And if she were, whoever killed her would pay.

In his underground prison he had focussed his rage. If he couldn't use his limbs, he would use his mind. He could sense when there were people close. His mental abilities had been limited to controlling the actions of flies and mice previously. He had never successfully kept a human under his control. Now all he had was time to learn. And learn he did. Strong wills could not be broken, but a weakened mind, like a child's or an adult who was tired, or someone who watched a lot of reality shows was easily manipulated. Sometimes the connection was so strong, he saw flashes of what was happening through their eyes. He saw them hurt and kill. Their bodies carrying out his desires.

Unfortunately, he could not hold the subject under his power over distance; as soon as they left the area immediately above him, he lost the connection. But his hold on those close to him was getting stronger all the time; culminating in the moment that hapless woman had walked through the door. She had been so easy to control. Maybe she had low intelligence or was weak of will, or maybe in the years since the last visitors his powers had increased. Either way, she had set him free.

Kaaliz walked around the basement and found an old mirror. He rubbed the dust from it and wished he could see his reflection; his body restored to perfection. The clothes he had been wearing were rotted and he had ripped them off during his attack on the women. For some of them, the sight of a naked man scared them more than his pointed teeth. And this had aroused him. He had taken ten years of sexual frustration out on the best looking one of the bunch; the mouthy one that had wanted to be his friend. He was sure Sin would understand.

The temperature of the air in the basement changed minutely, but it was a change all vampires were subconsciously attuned to. The sun had gone down. Kaaliz was heading up the basement stairs when he realised he was still naked. He looked at the dead women below him. Most of their clothes were saturated in blood. He pulled a pair of dark trousers off one. They were too big for him so he secured them with a belt from another. None of their footwear fitted him. In the end he ripped the laces out of a pair of trainers and squeezed them onto his feet. The only top that didn't have a noticeable amount of blood on it was an old woman's cardigan. It was beige. He put it on and buttoned it up. He ran up the stairs again and pulled the locked door off its hinges. He walked up the hall and out the open door into the night air. He breathed in its sweet fragrance; fresh air for the first time in ten years.

He was in the middle of a housing estate. He started walking. He could have flown, but walking was a simple pleasure he had been dreaming about for years while his legs had been unable to move.

He hadn't been walking long when he came to a clearing; a large patch of grass in the middle of the housing estate. There was a pond in the middle where a species of amphibious shopping trolleys seemed to be thriving. Two youths sat on a bench by the pond smoking cigarettes and no doubt feeling very grown-up about it. They saw him approach and started laughing.

'What is you wearing, man?' one asked.

His friend turned and said, 'Transvestites just don't put in the effort they used to.' They both laughed. They jumped down off the bench, discarded their cigarettes and blocked Kaaliz's path.

'What is you doing here, homes? You don't belong in this 'hood.'

'Fo' Sho'. That's the true, baby,' his friend agreed.

Kaaliz wondered why these two boys with complexions nearly as white as his own were doing their best to be black. 'My attire *is* quite laughable,' Kaaliz said.

'His attire!' they both said and then laughed.

'Dawg, those threads is nasty. You is charity shop chic gone every kind of wrong.'

'You're right.' Kaaliz eyed the clothes they were wearing.

'Who is you, man?'

'Yeah, login, fool. Let's see your I.D.'

Kaaliz reached into their minds. They weren't tired, but there was something suppressing their higher brain functions. He guessed they were probably high on something. 'You don't need to see my identification.'

They turned to each other and repeated. 'We don't need to see his identification.'

'These aren't the droids you're looking for.'

'These aren't the droids we're looking for.'

'I can go about my business.'

'You can go about your business.'

'And I should take your clothes with me.'

The two boys started undressing. Kaaliz took the cleanest pair of underwear and socks, a pair of black jeans, a pair of trainers that actually fitted, a black T-shirt, a black hoodie and a long black coat. He told the two naked boys to throw the rest of their clothes -- and his transvestite gear -- into the pond, which they obligingly ran off and did. When he was a few hundred yards away Kaaliz heard the boys' shouts of confusion and laughed. He opened his arms and lifted off into the night sky.

He still remembered the code. The outline of the heart was even more weathered now, but the four letters were still distinguishable. He pressed A, P, M, T. Behind him a square of the ground lifted and ripped the weeds that had overgrown it up by the roots. The lift raised to full height and the doors opened. Kaaliz stepped inside and pressed the down button. The lift car began to sink into the earth again.

    The doors opened and he stepped back into Project Redbook. It was dark, cold and quiet. But something was alive down here. He could sense it. He flipped the main switch at the lift and the lights flickered on all over the huge space.

    She isn't here.

    He knew it right away. Sin had a distinct odour. She hadn't been here in a long time. Kaaliz walked forward and entered the room with the holding cells. The screams and roars made him wince. They were all still here. Fifty vampire/Che'al hybrids pulled at the bars of their cages, all with the single intent of ripping to pieces this living thing that had entered the room.

    Why had they never been released? he wondered.

    Something had gone very wrong with the plan.

He was the youngest one on the bus by at least forty years. He had gone with a small local firm in the hope he could slip over the border and into Portstewart unnoticed. The bus was a sixteen-seater and was filled to capacity. His hope of having a double seat to himself had been thwarted immediately when he got on the bus in Dublin. Molly had approached him before his backside had touched the seat.

    'Are you travelling alone?'

    Tom nodded reluctantly.

    'Do you mind if I sit next to you?'

    'No, that's fine.' Actually the trip hadn't proved to be as bad as he thought. Molly was full of stories and got the whole bus talking by the third hour on the road. Tom now knew everything about everyone on the bus; who they were, what they did, why they were going to the North Coast and who had a granddaughter around his age. The only one who had managed to remain a mystery was Molly herself.

    'What do you think I look like?' she asked Tom as she forced another toffee into his hand.

    Tom smiled and shook his head. 'A school teacher?'

'Oh, come on, you can do better than that. All old ladies look like school teachers but very few are.'

'You got to give me a clue, Molly.'

The wrinkled face grinned. 'OK. Let's see. It's a job you never really retire from.'

'Something you never retire from? So you must be self-employed.'

'Why?'

'Well, if you worked for someone else they'd make you retire. You must be an artist or a writer.'

'Nope.'

Tom kept trying, periodically, when another possibility occurred to him, but by the fifth hour on the bus he still hadn't guessed. They were getting close to Portrush now, so he didn't have much time left.

This road had been the same one he had left by all those years ago. He remembered the rockface on one side of the road and the sheer drop to the sea on the other. When he had walked out of this town with his mother the sea was blue, now, as he returned, it was black, except for the reflection of the full moon.

'I suppose you're going to Portstewart to meet some pretty girl,' she asked with a playful tickle of his ribs.

'Yes,' Tom answered without thinking. 'I mean no. I mean, yes, but that's not why I'm going.'

'Tell me all about her.'

'There's not much to tell,' Tom answered. Molly's eyes widened and she gave him a single nod. He knew right then that she wasn't going to be dissuaded. 'I'm going back to Portstewart...'

'Back?'

'Yeah, I was born there and lived there for the first ten years of my life.'

'So she's a childhood sweetheart?'

Tom couldn't help but smile. 'I suppose she is, yeah.' He had actually been dying to talk to someone about her but his male friends wouldn't have understood and his mum, well, his mum definitely wouldn't have understood. His thoughts drifted back to her now. She would know he was gone by now. Would she have the Garda looking for him or would she do as his note had instructed and wait for him to come back? His mum wasn't really the waiting type. And even though he hadn't told her where he was going, he felt that she was probably hot on his trail.

'They say those are the ones that last,' Molly said, snapping him back to reality.

'What?'

'Childhood romances. They say they have a better chance than most of staying together. I'm inclined to agree. I met my husband when I was fourteen. We married when I was nineteen and had fifty-one wonderful years together.'

'My mum and dad were together… a long time too.' A hundred and sixteen years to be exact, but Tom didn't want to explain that to Molly.

He had trouble remembering his father now. He stared at photographs but never really remembered what sort of a man he was. His mother told him stories of their decades of adventures as vampires, but they were told from her point of view; a woman totally in love with her husband.

The only family he had really known was the distant relations (ancestors actually) of his mother's that they had been living with for the last ten years in Dublin. As they continued along the coast road he began to get a strange feeling in his chest. He was going back to where his father had died. He didn't know how he had died. Tom just hoped he hadn't travelled all this way for history to repeat itself.

Seeing the sadness in his eyes, Molly changed the subject. 'You play hockey?'

'Hockey?'

'I saw you put the long bag up in the overhead storage. It's a hockey stick, right?'

'Hurling, actually,' Tom said. 'You don't miss much. I don't suppose this elusive occupation of yours is Private Investigator?'

Molly laughed and shook her head. 'Nope.'

Everyone lurched forward in their seats as the bus braked suddenly. Tom checked Molly was OK then looked to the front of the bus. The driver got out and hurried into the beam of the headlights, where Tom lost sight of him.

'My husband went like that near the end. It's the prostate.'

'I don't think he's going out there to pee, Molly. I think something's wrong. Can you...?' Tom gestured. Molly turned her knees out into the aisle and he squeezed past her and made his way to the front of the bus. The driver was kneeling on the road about twenty yards ahead. Tom walked down the steps and outside.

'Hey. You all right?' The driver didn't turn. All Tom could see was his more than ample backside and the soles of his shoes. Tom started to walk towards him. He noticed the driver was twitching. Then he began to rise, but he wasn't standing up of his own accord, he was being lifted. Someone, crouched in front of him, was standing up. The driver was now illuminated in the bus's headlights and Tom saw his throat had been ripped out. His limp body flew through the air and over the edge of the cliff. Tom imagined him plummeting towards the dark water beneath.

Where the driver had knelt a skinny, pale faced woman now stood. She was short; barely five feet tall. Her brown hair was in pigtails. Her eyes were completely white apart from a small circle of black in the centre. She was clothed in a patchwork coat made of children's clothes; brightly coloured bunnies, teddy bears, rainbows and the like were at odds with the thick black stitching holding it all together. Tom knew at once that she had taken a piece of clothing from every child she had killed and made her jacket from the scraps.

'Me knows who you are,' she said as she started circling him. 'You're the little boy that everyone's scared of. But you're just a baby. Tommy baby want to play with Jacqui? Jacqui wants to play with you.'

The vampire flew at him as fast as she could. Tom met her face with his fist and stopped her momentum immediately. The vampire picked herself off the ground quickly, pushing her jaw back into place. Tom braced himself for attack. The vampire clicked her jaw and smiled. 'Me told him I could take you myself... but he insisted I bring others.' Tom spun round as three male vampires dropped to the ground behind him.

Jacqui took a baby rattle from her pocket and shook it by her ear. 'Master said we couldn't have any fun with you.' She put the rattle away again. 'Just kill you,' she almost sang the words. 'Kill the baby.' She turned her back.

The three male vampires flew at him at once. Tom grabbed the closest and turned him into the attack of the next one. He pushed the two of them away as the third reached him. The vampire opened its mouth and lurched at Tom's neck. Tom grabbed him by the top of the head and under the chin and twisted his head until he heard it crack. The vampire dropped to the ground and tried to twist his head back into place. The other two were on him in an instant. Tom threw punches and drove his elbow into any opening he could see. Thirty seconds of frantic fighting ended with Tom tossing the two vampires to either side of him.

Tom was breathing heavily. This was the first time he had ever fought vampires. His mother had trained him well and told him what to expect, but now that he was here he realised the practical reality of fighting them was a lot harder than he imagined.

Jacqui turned back to them, gently singing a lullaby to herself. She looked at the three vampires, one at a time, and then skipped towards Tom. 'Baby Tom is strong… but is he wise?' Jacqui and one of the vampires attacked Tom again while the other two ran off towards the bus. Tom tried to see what they were doing but was too busy landing and blocking lightning-fast punches.

The two male vampires grabbed the bus; one by the front bumper and one by the back, and lifted it off the ground. They started to walk it back towards the cliff edge. The passengers started screaming. Tom threw the male vampire against the rockface as hard as he could and put Jacqui in a headlock and squeezed. He looked around for the other two and saw them carrying the bus towards the cliff edge.

'No,' he screamed. The male vampire was just getting his senses back at the rockface when Tom threw Jacqui at him. He didn't wait to see if he had managed to hurt her but ran for the bus.

Inside, on the steps of the bus, he saw Molly standing, looking out the open door.

'No,' he shouted. 'Stay inside, Molly!'

Molly jumped from the bus and fell awkwardly. Tom noticed she was clutching his hurley bag in her arms. The vampire at the back of the bus dropped his end and ran at

Molly. The old woman shakily got to her feet and unzipped Tom's bag. The vampire was almost upon her. She drew the sword from Tom's bag and lopped his head off when he was close enough. The vampire grabbed for its missing head for a few seconds before dropping to the ground. Molly spat on the decapitated body and said, 'Take that you godless motherfucker.'

The vampire holding the front of the bus gave it a push and dropped his end. The back of the bus started to slide over the cliff edge. Tom bolted towards it and slid like a baseball player towards home base under the bus. He grabbed it by the axle. He held on and scrambled frantically, trying to get his trainers to grip on the damp grass verge. Molly walked around to the front of the bus and held out the sword towards the three remaining vampires, who were approaching slowly.

'Grandma was supposed to be eaten by the big bad wolf,' Jacqui said shaking her head. 'Me doesn't like this story.' The vampires advanced on Molly.

A motorcycle roared around the corner and skidded to a stop. The vampires and Molly all looked towards the motorcyclist. It was obvious she was female even before she took her helmet off. Sarah set the helmet down on the bike's seat and strode towards the vampires.

Jacqui closed her eyes and exhaled. 'No one else is allowed to play,' she said through gritted teeth.

One of the male vampires charged at Sarah. She pulled a stake from the waistband of her trousers at the last second and drove it into his chest. The vampire's body shrivelled and collapsed. Sarah continued towards the other two. The bus gave a sudden lurch forward and its front wheels once again safely gripped the road. Tom scuttled out from under it, and ran towards Molly. The vampires turned and saw Sarah was dangerously close now. Tom's blade silently sliced the night air and the last male vampire found himself without a head.

Jacqui walked backwards away from Tom and Sarah. She was smiling. 'Master was right. This little boy is strong.' She took a stuffed animal from her pocket and held it up to her ear. She nodded at the toy's advice then put it back in her pocket. 'Me has to go tell him what you did. You is going to be in big trouble. Both of you.' She giggled and rose into the night sky.

Tom and Sarah watched after her as she disappeared into the night, her laughter still echoing off the rockface.

Tom turned to Sarah. She smiled at him. She was beautiful. She stepped towards him and threw her arms around his neck. Tom dropped his sword and wrapped his arms around her waist. They clung onto each other tightly, each feeling the other's gunning heartbeat. They released their embrace slightly and looked into each other's eyes. Tom wanted to kiss her right there and then, but thought it might be too soon, even though he was sure she would kiss him back. Finally they released each other. Tom looked at her from head to toe; the woman he had known as a girl. More beautiful than his dreams could imagine.

'A'hem!'

Tom turned and saw Molly standing by the bus. Inside, the passenger's faces were all stuck to the windows like novelty toys. Tom and Sarah laughed at their own self-absorption. Tom walked over to Molly.

'You weren't a Ministry agent back in the day, were you, Molly?'

'About time you guessed it. I gave you enough clues.'

'So they never let you retire?'

Molly took out a hip flask and took a swig. 'When you get too old for the fist and swords work, they ask you to use your eyes and ears. Just keep a lookout in your area for signs of vampire activity. Sometimes they give us low-risk assignments.'

Tom winced. 'And who thought my coming back to the North Coast was a low-risk assignment?'

'Tom, this assignment was not sanctioned.' She took a deep breath and hung her head for a moment. 'The official Ministry line on prophecies is to ignore them until they bite you on the arse… or neck, as the case may be. But there are some of us who believe you are the one spoken about in The Book of Days to Come. You and young Sarah, here. We believe. And we know what's at stake. What you do in the next few days will affect the whole world. You must destroy them for the time is near when they will come out of hiding and become the dominant species on Earth.'

After a moment to let the gravity of the situation sink in Tom said, 'We won't let you down, Molly,' with more confidence than he felt.

'I know you won't,' she said with a dentured smile.

'Think you can drive this bus?'

'No problem. I once drove an Alvis FV107 Scimitar tank into a nest of vampires. I think I can handle this buggy. You're not coming?'

He turned to Sarah. 'I think I'll catch a ride, if that's OK?'

Sarah nodded. Molly smiled. Tom retrieved his backpack from the bus and re-sheathed his sword in its bag. They watched the bus trundle off towards Portrush, then turned to each other. Tom couldn't help it; he just couldn't stop looking at her.

'That's a pretty cool sword you've got,' she said, eventually.

'It's my mum's. She'll probably blow a gasket when she realises I've taken it. You're just using stakes? You should get yourself a sword.'

'They're not actually that easy to come by. I mean, I've tried Argos but...' They both laughed. Tom stepped forward and took her hands in his.

'Sarah, I've...'

'Isn't this a picture?' Sarah and Tom turned and saw Hal walking towards them. 'That's my girlfriend you've got your fuckin' paws on, Ford.'

Tom let go of her hands and stepped back. He looked closer at the approaching figure. 'Hal?'

'*Ex*-girlfriend, Hal,' Sarah shouted. 'I thought I made that clear to you earlier on today.'

'You'll be mine again. I love you and we're meant to be together.'

'Oh, give it a fuckin' rest. Are you following me around now? You think the stalker approach is going to endear you to me?'

'Just wanted to see the boy-wonder.' Hal was just a few feet away now and stopped. 'I never liked you, Ford. You were always a weirdo.'

Sarah took Tom's arm and pulled him gently towards the motorcycle. 'Come on, Tom. Let's go.'

'You think you can take me, weirdo? You wanna try right now?'

'Grow up, Hal!' Sarah tugged again on Tom's arm and this time he let himself be led. Tom put on his backpack and put the hurley bag through his arm and over his head.

'Running away again, Ford?' Sarah put her helmet on and got on the bike. It started on the first kick. Tom climbed on behind her and put his arms around her waist. Hal ran over to the motorcycle and stood in its path. He stared into Sarah's eyes then took a few steps back. 'I'll see you again,' he said, nodding. Hal floated several feet into the air. Sarah jumped back in her seat. Tom grabbed for his hurley bag. Hal pointed down at them. 'I'll see you *both* again, real soon.' With that he flew off into the night.

sleepers

Sarah spread out the spare duvet on the sofa and threw all the cushions to one end. They had picked up some Chinese food on the way home and she was giving it a quick blast in the microwave while Tom gave himself a wash. He stepped into the living room wearing just a T-shirt and jeans. He rubbed at his damp hair with a towel. He sat down on the sofa and stretched his feet out towards the roaring fire.

'Your house is just the same as I remember it.'

'Really?'

'Yeah. You have a few less Barbies now, but apart from that...'

Sarah laughed. 'Hey, remember the time my mum told you off because your Action Man had stripped my Barbie naked to give her a physical.'

Tom nodded, smiling. 'I tried to explain to her that it was standard military procedure but she wasn't having any of it.'

'You were lucky you weren't here for the teenage years.'

'I don't know if lucky's the word I'd use.' Tom met her eyes and that urge to kiss her swelled within him again. She didn't look away. 'So,' Tom said, changing the subject, 'isn't your mum going to freak out if she comes home in the middle of the night and sees some stranger lying on her sofa?'

'No. It'll be dark. Just snore loudly and fart occasionally – she'll think it's Hal.'

That took the fun out of everything. The elephant in the room had been mentioned. 'I guess you guys were pretty close.'

Sarah shrugged. 'We went out a few times. Had some laughs.' She stood up and turned towards the window. Tom could hear her voice cracking when she said, 'And now he's a vampire and I might have to kill him someday.'

'Sarah...'

Beep-Beep-Beep

Sarah turned and brushed the tears from her cheeks. 'I'll get the food.'

Half-an-hour later they were sitting on the sofa by the light of the fire, their bellies filled with curry, fried rice and prawn crackers. Sarah was obviously tired. Her phone whistled for her attention. She read the message and put the phone down.

'Mum's spending the night at Aunt Chloe's.' Tom said nothing. She snuggled up close to him and rested her head on his shoulder. 'Where did you go when you left here?'

'The south. Dublin. My mum's relations.'

'Did you ever think about me?'

'Yes.'

'You never wrote. You never called.'

'My mum wouldn't let me. There were a lot of people trying to kill me. Vampires *and* humans. All because of this prophecy.'

'What was your life like?'

'Just an ordinary life. I went to school, played sports, practised sword-fighting every night with my mother – you know, the usual.'

'What are you going on for?'

'What, you mean as a career? I have no idea. If I survive this, then I'll think about it. What about you? What are you going to be when you grow up?'

'I thought about journalism maybe.'

'Not a super detective?'

Sarah's body shook as she laughed quietly into his shoulder. 'I still have my badge, you know?'

'Good. That means I can deputize you.' Tom stroked her hair. 'Hey, remember the time we all went down to the beach to investigate this big piece of driftwood?'

'It took all of us to carry it back to your house so you could run lab tests on it.'

Tom laughed. 'That's right. We got it back to my dad's shed and we all went home and came back with all different kinds of liquids.'

'Why did we do that?'

'Benny said that if all liquids rolled off it then it must belong to a ship, probably a pirate ship, and if we found the right liquid it might reveal a treasure map on the wood, like invisible ink.' Tom and Sarah laughed quietly to themselves. 'Whatever happened to Tim and Benny? I'll have to catch up with them while I'm in town.'

'Tim joined the army as soon as he was old enough.'
'And Benny?'
There was a few seconds pause before she answered, 'Benny's dead.'
'What?'
'Vampire attack. Three years ago. Newspapers recorded it as a car accident, but if you move in the right circles, you hear the truth.' Tom said nothing so Sarah looked up. She saw the tears running down his face as he stared into the fire. She sniffed back her own tears and tried to swallow the lump in her throat. She turned his face towards her own and said, 'We're going to stop this, Tom.' Tears spilled down her face as she reaffirmed, 'You and I are going to put an end to this, once and for all.'

Nicholl was sitting on the sill of the bay-window talking on her phone when Rek walked in. They were staying the night in one of Chloe's spare bedrooms. Nicholl was wearing one of Chloe's Def Leppard T-shirts that was long enough to serve her as a nightie. She said her goodbyes quickly and put her phone down.
'Who was that?'
'Just Mitzi and Emma,' Nicholl answered.
Rek sighed deeply.
'What?'
'Don't ever play poker, Mand.'
'What's that supposed to mean?'
Rek took off his shirt and twisted it in a bundle before throwing it to the ground. He walked over and sat opposite her on the window-sill. 'You always phone your sisters just before you do something really stupid.'
'Rek, I was just calling them to see…'
'You were just calling them in case you don't make it back.'
Nicholl lowered her head.
'I don't like this plan, Mand.'
'You *never* like my plans.'
'This is different and you know it. If all the big, scary things in that prophecy come to pass… I don't think we can handle it by ourselves.'

'That's why we need the plan.'

Rek hung his head. Nicholl got up and came to him. She sat on his lap with her arms around his neck. 'I know the risks are higher, Rek. But the rewards are, too. If this works we can put an end to vampires forever.'

'And if it doesn't work, vampires take over the Earth.'

'We're here to see that doesn't happen.'

He looked into her eyes. 'I have a really bad feeling that this is one battle we're not all going to be walking away from.' He pulled her close to him and held her tightly.

Sergeant Finlay's jacket had shrunk again. He inhaled and managed to slip the last silver button into its hole as he left the station. His jacket had been shrinking every week since his wife walked out on him. He didn't miss her. What was there to miss? Her bitching about eating too much fast-food? Her nagging him about stopping for a burger on the way home from work? Those endless bloody salads and low-calorie meals. She just didn't get it. Being a policeman is an active job; whatever extra calories he put on through the occasional burger he would soon work off walking the beat or chasing bad guys through the streets of Portrush. OK, so maybe his desk duty didn't actually allow him to do any of that stuff, but he kept up his fitness level just in case.

Like now, he could have got one of the officers to drive him home, but he was going to walk. It was good exercise and would more than negate the kebab he was going to pick up on the way. *'You shouldn't eat late at night!'* That was another phrase he wasn't missing. Sure he missed some of the things his wife did. The washing was piling up, for instance. And this problem with the shrinking jacket, he wondered how she had stopped that happening. He didn't want to call her and ask her because he wanted to show her he could get by just fine without her.

Maybe his mother would know how to stop his jacket shrinking. Yes, his mother *would* know – it's probably one of those things all housewives know but keep to themselves. He saw the neon lights of the kebab shop in the distance. He began to salivate at the thought of a doner kebab piled high with strips of lukewarm, highly-processed lamb drenched in garlic butter. Maybe he should get two, just to keep up appearances. He didn't want everyone to know his wife had gone. Yeah, he'd get two. And if word had reached the kebab community that his wife was surplus to requirement, well... that would be even better! Everyone would assume he had already found himself a new woman. Yeah, a younger model; better bodywork, bigger headlights and no problem with fuel consumption. Two kebabs was definitely the way to go. Two kebabs, two drinks and maybe a portion of chips (between them). Yes, the kebab community would fill in the all the blanks from that order. He increased his pace, eager to get there.

A pale man dropped from the sky and landed, facing Finlay. There was a twinge in Finlay's left-hand side. The shrunken jacket must be pinching under the arms. He would worry about his washing methods later. Even though he had never seen one personally, he had lived in the area long enough to know what was standing before him. He wished he had that kebab and garlic butter inside him already. That'll teach him to walk. 'Wha... what... do you want?'

'I want to know who the Ministry's representative is these days,' the vampire answered.

'The... the... Ministry closed down their field office here back in...'

'I know that. But don't tell me they didn't leave a lighthouse keeper. Someone to keep an eye on things just in case someone like me showed up.'

'I don't know... I don't...'

Kaaliz grabbed the lapels of his ill-fitting jacket and flew him up to the top of the Dunluce Centre's tower. The domed peak of the entertainment complex's tower seemed a lot higher than it looked from the road. Finlay's feet scrambled and skidded on the dome.

Kaaliz held him upright by his lapels. 'Now, are you going to tell me what I need to know, or shall we see if all the king's horses and all the king's men can put you back together again?'

Finlay screamed as a particularly dangerous wobble almost caused him to fall. 'Ch.. Ch.. Chloe. Chloe Knight. The big mansion on the coast road.' Kaaliz released the policeman. Finlay dropped onto his stomach and hugged the top of the dome tightly. He looked all around. The vampire was gone.

His hand crept up and inside his jacket. A silver button popped off as he fished around his inside pocket. He watched the little silver disc slide off the dome and hit the ground far below. Damn shrinking jacket. He pulled the phone from his inside pocket.

    Several numbers occurred to him. His police station. The fire brigade. Ministry HQ. The kebab shop's delivery service. They could all wait. He made his decision and dialled. 'Hi, honey. Listen, I love you. I miss you. Can we talk? Yeah, OK, great.' He listened for a few seconds. 'You're at your mother's? No, I can't come *right* away.' His face changed as he looked around again, listening. 'Why not?'

    She was never going to believe this.

Anna closed her eyes tightly, but sleep was not to be found. Chloe squirmed in the bed beside her. The restlessness of her friend wasn't the only thing keeping her awake, though. She didn't like leaving Sarah alone. She knew what she was; that was how she had met Chloe in the first place. Her daughter was a dhampir and better equipped than most people to fight the undead, but to Anna she would always be her daughter first and a dhampir second, and it was her job to worry about her. She was also worrying about Rek and Amanda. She had never known her brother so happy and she already felt that Amanda was part of the family. This plan was foolhardy, but she had to agree with Agent Nicholl; if they didn't do something, who else would?

    She had phoned her boyfriend before going to bed and left a message on his voicemail. He was away on business for the next couple of weeks, travelling through Eastern Europe. He had said that he probably wouldn't be able to get a signal on his phone. He was checking out some prospective sites for his employers to set up a new factory. The cheapest labour was often found in the poorest areas, hence no mobile phone towers.

    She had been seeing him three months now. It had lasted longer than she thought it would. The longevity of their relationship was probably helped by the fact that he travelled so much and was rarely home. But when he was home, they had fun together. The only trouble was his age. He said he was twenty-nine, though Anna suspected he was lying to make her feel better. Even if he was, by some miracle, as old as twenty-nine, that still made her sixteen years older than him. It was a lot. It was probably the reason she hadn't introduced him to her friends. Sarah had met him a couple of times and seemed to like him, but sixteen years! Not that he wasn't mature for his age, but Anna couldn't help thinking every once in a while that he would eventually find someone his own age (whatever that really was).

She decided she would enjoy it while it lasted. She liked being wooed and she felt like a teenager when she was with him so maybe a sixteen-year age difference wasn't as creepy as she thought. But it was only a matter of time before they would have to have 'the talk' and figure out where, if anywhere, their relationship was going. At least she didn't have to have the even more terrifying, 'So, are you aware that vampires really exist?' talk.

He knew that vampires existed. He said he had heard the stories for years when he was growing up and his father had fought in the 1986 street battle in Portstewart. She had dated men before and they had always bolted as soon as she mentioned vampires. Understandable, she supposed, in normal relationships, but she'd never had a normal relationship.

Telling him about Sarah was a gamble, but she felt it was also the right thing to do; you don't invite someone into a minefield without telling them to watch where they step. He had taken the news of a dhampir in the family with excited fascination more than anything else. She smiled to herself. He was what her mother would have called 'a keeper.'

Chloe twisted over again and yanked the duvet.

'For God's sake, Chloe!'

'Sorry. I'm just not tired. All the time I was in hospital I did nothing *but* sleep.' She turned over again and faced Anna. 'Besides, aren't you just buzzing? These are some proper, history-making events about to go down. The final smackdown.'

Anna turned over and faced Chloe. She didn't like the way Chloe had embraced her role in this plan without a second thought. 'This is dangerous, Chloe. Really dangerous.'

'I know.'

'You don't sound like you know. You sound like you've just been invited onto a gameshow.'

She considered her response then said, 'I just want a chance to prove myself.'

'You've done enough over the years. You've given more than anyone I know to the fight. You've made your mark.'

'Others gave more.'

The implications of what she had just said hung in the air. Anna thought it best not to pursue them. 'How about I make you a milky drink. Hot chocolate?'

'Irish hot chocolate?'

Anna smiled and got out of bed. 'OK. Back in a sec.' She stopped and looked at the window. From the corner of her eye she thought something had moved past but wasn't sure. She shrugged it off and left the bedroom.

Kaaliz moved to the next window. The two women in bed had said (or done) nothing of interest to him. The next bedroom had a man and a woman sleeping in bed together. He could sense the post-coital satisfaction in them both. He concentrated on the woman. She was in a deep sleep so her mind should be open to visitors. The fragments came slowly at first.

The streets of Japan.

A vampire samurai warrior.

Kissing. Holding. Touching. Rek.

Sisters. Holding her sisters' babies.

Prophecy. Vampires. The plan.

Chloe. Rek. Sarah. Dhampir. Tom. Tom Ford. Back in town. The chosen one. Claire. Xavier. Dead. The bridge. Carrick-a-rede. Sheridan. Sin. Vampire. Betrayed. Jumping. Stabbing. Falling. Fighting. Impaled. Sheridan. Sin. Dead. Killed. Murdered. Executed.

Kaaliz seethed. The old rage that used to rule his life rushed back to the surface. The woman stirred in bed next to her lover. This is the woman he had been looking for. Agent Amanda Nicholl of the Ministry. She had killed Sin. He would make her pay, starting with killing everyone in this house. The door clicked to his left below him and he looked down. A woman walked outside and lit a cigarette. She looked vaguely familiar to him. Kaaliz looked back inside the Ministry bitch's head.

Anna. Rek. Sister. Sister in law?

Her lover's sister. She would do for a start. Kaaliz flew at her as fast as he could. She looked up a split-second before he reached her. Terror blossomed in her face. Two decades of the most hellish nightmares imaginable were made flesh before her eyes. She opened her mouth to scream and her cigarette dropped. Kaaliz was drinking from her neck before the cigarette hit the ground. The screams inside her were never released. She struggled but was no match for him. Soon she was limp and he was feeling even more powerful. He dropped her lifeless body to the ground and approached the doorway. Inside the kitchen a kettle boiled. Two cups and a bottle of whiskey sat beside it. Kaaliz stepped forward but the threshold pushed him back. The sun would be up soon.

Nicholl sat up in bed with a start, waking Rek. She grabbed her chest and felt her pounding heart begin to slow down now that reality had been restored. She took deep breaths.

'Hey, you OK?' Rek asked.

'Just a nightmare.'

'What about?'

'I can't remember. I just feel... violated. Scared. Something...'

The window smashed as Anna's body came crashing through. Nicholl jumped back against the headboard. Rek jumped back too and put an arm around her. The vampire stood before them, hovering in mid-air, framed by the broken window.

He pointed to Nicholl. 'You. You killed her,' he said softly.

Nicholl winced and said, 'Kaaliz?'

'You *killed* her!'

'Who's he talking about?' Rek whispered.

'Sheridan,' Nicholl answered and glanced at her sword standing in the corner of the room. 'Yeah, I killed her,' she said loudly. 'Bitch deserved it.'

Kaaliz flew forward and hit the invisible barrier. He punched and scratched at it for a few seconds before levelling his gaze at Nicholl and saying, 'Your family, your friends, anyone you ever cared about. Anyone you ever fucking met! I'm going to kill them all, and their blood will be on *your* hands.' Kaaliz turned and was gone in a second.

Rek got out of bed and knelt by the body lying at the foot of their bed. He had thought it had been some random victim Kaaliz had snatched, but as he pushed the hair out of her face he saw his sister's eyes looking up at him. He crumpled to the floor and started crying. Nicholl got out of bed and saw Anna lying dead on the floor.

She walked to the window-sill and lifted her phone. She watched Rek cry as she waited for it to be answered. 'Hi, Mitzi, it's me. No, I don't know what time it is. Listen, I need you to get the whole family together and go to Aunt Heather's.' She looked over at Rek and tears ran down her face. 'Yes, everyone! I don't care, just do as I say!' Her voice was breaking as she tried to sniff back the tears. Her sister finally understood the severity of the warning and promised to get everyone up immediately. Nicholl hung up the phone and let it drop to the floor. Rek lifted his sister's body and hugged it.

Nicholl put her back against the wall and slid down to the ground. For the first time in years, she let herself cry.

the legend of fairhead

Ballycastle, 87 B.C.

Congal's horse was galloping as fast as it could through the fields. Torloch's arrow had wounded the beast and slowed its retreat. Congal could see its silhouette hobbling in the distance and whipped his horse again. The beast was trying for the safety of the trees, free of the moon's gaze. Congal drew his sword and directed his horse toward the fleeing creature. They were both going to reach the trees at the same time. Congal knew if it got in there he would lose it. This beast had eluded him too many times so far. He would not let it escape this time. Congal jumped from his horse and landed on the beast, rolling them both along the ground.

The beast lunged at Congal's throat. He punched the hilt of his sword into the creature's mouth with all his might. The beast's teeth shattered. Congal used the creature's disorientation to pounce on its back. He held the creature's face in the dirt with one hand while his other sought out a rock in the grass and brought it crashing down repeatedly on the beast's head until it was still. Taking no time to enjoy his victory, Congal began binding the hands of the creature as quickly and tightly as he knew how. Then he bound its feet. When he was certain of the knots' strength he relaxed and waited for Torloch to find them.

The creature awakened some time later. It struggled for a time before realising it could not escape its bindings. He turned to his captor. 'Why do you hunt me?'

'It was the king's will. You killed people of Ireland, so you are an enemy of Ireland,' Congal answered. 'I was charged with your capture.'

'And what bounty will the king bestow on you for capturing me?'

'That is not the concern of a low creature such as yourself.'

'I can give you treasures a king could never dream of possessing.'

Congal laughed. 'You try to coerce me into betraying Ireland? You are a simple-minded creature if you believe such a ruse is possible.'

'I can heal all your wounds. Cure all your disease. I can give you life everlasting.'

Congal got to his feet. 'The poor ramblings of a trickster. I will not fall under your spell.'

'If you doubt me, look at where you struck me.'

Cautiously, Congal stepped closer, drawing his sword, and looked at the creature's head. Where he had smashed open the creature's skull a short time before was healed. Not even a scar remained. 'A trick. A trick of the underworld!'

'If you remove the arrow from my leg, it too will heal. It is no trick, my prince.'

'How do you know my station?'

'Your father is the king you spoke of. You were charged with my capture to prove your worthiness for the throne.'

'How can you know that which has never been told?'

'It is another of the gifts I can give you.'

'You insult my father and his throne if you think I would yield to the bribery of a daemon.' Congal turned and saw the cart trundling towards him. Torloch had caught up with him at last. He took a deep breath then searched around and found two stones, the size of seed-potatoes. He walked over to the creature and forced its mouth open. He pushed the two stones into its mouth and then began to tie a gag around its mouth. 'I will not have you poison the mind of my friend as you tried with me.' The creature pleaded with its eyes and grunts. 'Quiet! Or I will leave you here for the sun gods to execute you.' The creature stopped grunting and struggling. 'That's right. You may know me, but I know of your kind too. I know the sun gods will not tolerate you to walk in their light.'

'Congal, I thought I had lost you,' Torloch cried. 'The beast gave you good chase.' The huge, bearded man jumped down from the cart.

'Aye, and he has spent the time since trying to bribe me into betraying Ireland. Tis why I have bound his mouth, lest he try to bewitch you, or to bite you.'

'I would take his life right here, if your father did not wish that pleasure for himself. Come, let us put him in the barrel so we no longer have to look upon him.'

Congal and Torloch forced the creature into the barrel and nailed the lid on. 'He will be safe from the wrath of the sun gods in there.'

'Tis more mercy than he deserves,' Torloch said.

They set off slowly towards home.

They had been riding a long time in silence when Congal cleared his throat and said, 'Torloch, maybe we should rest before continuing our journey.'

Torloch tried to suppress a smile. 'Oh, yes? Where do you suggest, sire?'

'Well, where are we, the North Coast?'

Torloch boomed with laughter. 'You and I know fine well where we are and I know where you wish to be.' The big man laughed again.

'It seems my secret is nothing of the kind.' Congal laughed. 'You may go on without me if you wish. I will find you after I see her.'

'No, no. I will wait. You are never such good company on the road as you are after you have seen her.'

Congal smiled. 'Then I will waste no more time pretending otherwise. You will no doubt stay in the tavern you always choose and make use of the local women when you have drank your fill of mead.'

'That I will,' the big man bellowed.

'Then that is where I will seek you when I have visited my love.' Congal turned his horse and galloped off at high speed.

Torloch shouted after him, 'Godspeed to you, sire.'

Rathlin Island

Congal waited in the banquet room of the castle while the servant woke the king. The smells of the night's feast were still hanging in the air. Congal's stomach groaned. He had been so dedicated to his task he had not eaten since the moment he picked up the creature's trail.

'Congal, my boy!'

Congal lowered to one knee and bowed his head. 'Please forgive the lateness of the hour, my liege.'

The king took his hand and raised him back to his feet. 'Think nothing of it. The nights are long since the gods saw fit to take my Finola to the afterworld.' The king chased away a tear with a smile. He was not an old man, but his face seemed to have weathered more years than his body. 'To happier times, though,' he said. 'You have come to see my daughter, I imagine.'

'That I have King Donn, but it is late and I would not wake her.'

'Then perhaps my company will suffice until morning brings her to you.'

'I would be honoured, sire.'

'If you sailed from Baile na castle you must be hungry.'

'I believe the moon has risen twice since last I feasted.'

The king nodded to his servant, who had been waiting patiently by the door. The servant bowed to his master and left. 'Perhaps you will tell me of your journey.'

'Tis a tale to scare the young, sire, I warn thee.'

'Oh, wonderful.' The king smiled.

Congal told his story while he ate. The king did not join him, but seemed pleased to be able to sate the warrior's appetite. Congal sat back and drained the last of his mead from the tankard.

The king was lost in thought. 'I have never heard of such a creature.'

'Tis the first time I have seen one. My father told me stories when I was young of such beings, but I dismissed them as superstition until these days past.'

'What you describe is an animal with the tongue of a man. A savage beast that will try to barter for its life when captured,' the king said with wonder. 'You have done a great service to your land and mine this night, Congal.'

The door opened and the king's daughter walked in. Congal got to his feet immediately and brushed the crumbs of meat from his mouth. For a few seconds he could not find the words. She stood there bathed in the morning light, almost glowing to his eyes. He drank in every detail of her; the long white dress embroidered with colourful stitching, the curling tresses of her hair coloured like a cornfield, and her eyes bluer than any a summer sky. She smiled when she saw him and only restrained herself from running into his arms because of her father's presence.

The king studied the silence between the two and smiled. He got to his feet. 'Taisie, perhaps you would show our visitor the castle gardens.'

Taisie nodded to her father.

Congal and Taisie kissed in the shadow of the castle wall. She felt safe in the arms of her warrior prince. Many times the sun had risen and set since last she saw him. Many suitors had come and gone in that time. Duty compelled her to give these men an audience, though her father knew that none would be successful until Congal returned. Congal broke their embrace and looked into Taisie's eyes.

'I have good tidings. I was sent on a quest by my father to capture a creature that had killed some of our kin. He took me aside before I left and told me this would be my final test. If I brought the creature back to him, he would let me accede to his throne.'

Taisie smiled and tears of joy welled in her eyes.

Congal ran the rough skin of his finger down the soft skin of her cheek and said, 'When next I return to Rathlin's shores, it will be to claim you as my bride. My queen.'

Taisie threw her arms around his neck and hugged him tightly.

They walked around the island until the sun had half its daily journey completed. Hunger was once again calling to them as the castle came into sight. Congal stopped and once again enjoyed the closeness of his love that would not be respectful inside the walls of the castle. Reluctantly their lips parted.

'The gods have truly blessed me, Taisie.' He looked across the sea. The day was clear. 'Do you see that rockface in the distance? From here it looks flat on top and plumb almost all the way down to the sea. Like the back of a blacksmith's anvil.' He turned his attention back to Taisie. 'Some days I would pass this way and time or duty would not permit me to sail to your shores. On those days I would stand atop that cliff and stare across the water, hoping that maybe you were looking back.'

'I have looked to that cliff many times hoping to see the sail of your boat coming this way. I am sure that we must have been looking at each other on those days.' Taisie looked across the water again. 'That is where we should be married. As far as the eye can see, everyone should know of our joining.'

'Then that is where we *shall* be married. I will arrange such a celebration even the Scots will see the flames and know of our union.' Taisie and Congal kissed one last time before returning to the castle.

They were told the king was in the throne room and rushed inside to tell him the news. A tall man with red/blond hair and beard stood before the king in his full armour. Another man, slightly shorter stood to the side dressed the same.

The king stood up. 'Ah, Taisie, there you are. We have visitors. May I present Nabhogdon, King of Norway, and the general of his army, Agnar.'

The tall man turned and eyed Taisie hungrily. He walked towards her, took her hand in his and kissed it. His eyes ran slowly over Taisie's body. Congal's blood boiled.

King Donn cleared his throat and said, 'May I also introduce Congal, Prince of Ireland.' Nabhogdon turned and regarded Congal for a brief moment then turned his attention back to Taisie.

Nabhogdon spoke in a loud, booming voice more suited to the battlefield. 'Many nights have we spent in Ireland. We have travelled from the southern most point to the north. Many women have I seen in my quest for a queen. Many were beautiful. But when I talk in taverns with the menfolk of your country, Congal, one name was said more than any other when I asked of the greatest beauty they had ever seen. Taisie, Princess of Rathlin. I could not return home without investigating the accuracy of these claims. Now she stands before me, I see the rumours are true. The mantle, deserved.' He turned to the king and said, 'I will take her as my wife.'

Taisie and Congal exchanged shocked glances.

Nabhogdon continued, 'The people of Norway will never have seen such a beauty. All women will pale in her presence and all men will envy me my bride. We will set sail…'

'Pardon me, my lord,' Congal said loudly. 'But the princess just this morning has already consented to marry me.'

'You are not a king, boy! Kneel when you address your better!'

Congal reluctantly lowered himself to one knee. 'Taisie and I have long been betrothed to each other. When I return to my father's kingdom I will be made King of Ireland.'

'Until that time,' Nabhogdon bellowed, 'you are not worthy of her hand.'

Taisie knelt before Nabhogodn. 'I beg you, sire. My heart belongs to Congal. He is…'

'Silence, woman!' Taisie lowered her gaze from his. 'You will learn your place.' He turned to King Donn. 'What sort of country is it that allows your womenfolk to argue with their master?' He strode towards the throne. 'I think I will be doing you a service, Donn, by taking this troublesome waif from your walls.' He laughed alone.

King Donn stood and faced Nabhogdon. 'My daughter has chosen Congal, my friend. Many years has he waited for her.'

'I care not for Congal or his country!' Nabhogdon took a deep breath and stepped close to Donn. He lowered his voice, but it still echoed with menace. 'Would you break the laws of your gods and disgrace me? I will have what I have claimed or our armies will clash on the battlefield. And you know you cannot triumph. For every man you have, I have fifty. I will lay waste to this entire island and darken your fields with the blood of your countrymen should you go against the will of the gods. The seas will run red around Rathlin.'

Congal got to his feet, unable to contain his anger any longer, and shouted, 'Nabhogdon, King of Norway. I challenge you for the hand of Taisie of Rathlin.'

He turned slowly. 'You challenge me, boy?'

'The gods allow that any man may be challenged to a fight to the death to prove his worthiness. You are not worthy of this prize, and I will prove it when I stain my blade with your blood.'

Nabhogdon choked back his rage. 'If death is what you seek I will indeed help you find it. Tomorrow at dawn. No armour. We fight to the death.' Nabhogdon stormed out of the throne room followed by Agnar.

King Donn gave Congal his sword. It had served him well in his younger days on the battlefield. Taisie would not attend the duel. She begged Congal to leave with her during the night. She would give up the chance to be his queen if she could still be his wife. Congal refused. He would not dishonour his father and the throne of Ireland by running away. He left the weeping Taisie in the care of her lady in waiting.

Congal took off his shirt and felt the heft of the sword. Twenty paces further down the beach, Nahbagdon made an imposing silhouette in the pre-dawn light. He whispered with his second, Agnar. Donn had sent one of the servants across to the mainland and found Torloch, who now stood beside Congal. The first light of the sun broke on the horizon. Congal swung the sword and lurched with it, getting a feel for the steel. It was a fine sword, and much better balanced than his own.

Torloch's eyes were fixed on the other pair. 'I do not trust them, sire.'

'Their gods instruct them to follow the same laws as we do. They will not try to deceive us.' Congal stuck the sword in the sand and turned to his friend. He put his hands on Torloch's shoulders. 'If I should fall under his blade, I trust you will tell my father how I died.' Torloch nodded solemnly. Congal gave one last look at the castle, then turned to his opponent and pulled his sword from the sand.

Nahbagdon drew his sword from its sheath. The blade sparkled in the morning sunshine. He lowered it at Congal and, screaming, charged forward. Congal raised his blade and ran towards him.

The sun was disappearing on the opposite horizon. The servants from the castle had come down to watch. Both warriors were exhausted and bleeding from a dozen different places. They stood facing each other, their chests heaving, their arms numb from fighting. Nahbagdon lowered his sword and raised a placatory hand to Congal. He took a step towards him and Congal lowered his sword. Nahbagdon lunged forward and head-butted Congal, smashing his nose. Congal dropped his sword. His eyes filled and he could barely make out the blurry figure before him. Congal jumped forward and toppled the giant. Nahbagdon's sword fell to the sand. Congal still couldn't see, but for the first time in this epic fight he had his hands on his opponent. He felt his way quickly to Nahbagdon's face and punched with all his remaining strength. Nahbagdon didn't have time to respond as punch after punch landed on him. Congal kept landing blows until his vision had cleared. He looked around and saw his sword and scrambled towards it. Nahbagdon was on his hands and knees crawling towards his own blade.

A wave came rushing in and covered Congal's sword. He crawled into the water and probed the dark liquid for his blade. The saltwater stung his wounds. He felt the cold steel beneath his fingers. He worked his way down to the hilt and seized it in his grasp. He turned just in time to see Nahbagdon standing before him with his sword raised over his head. Congal thrust his sword from the water and plunged it into the Norwegian's chest. Nahbagdon's sword dropped to the sand behind his back. His hand grabbed the steel in his chest and tried to pull it out. Congal drove it further in and out his back. Nahbogdon dropped to his knees then fell to the side and slid off the sword's blade into the water.

Congal was only able to take a few steps before he collapsed with exhaustion. He saw Agnar gather up his fallen king and carry him off. The last thing he remembered was looking into the face of Torloch as his friend cried to one of the watching servants to bring the apothecary.

In the days that followed Congal recovered and with Taisie at his bedside they planned their joining ceremony for three days hence. A rider was sent to tell Congal's father, who arrived the night before the ceremony was to take place. He passed the crown to his son as soon as he saw him.

Ballycastle

The handfasting ceremony took place on the top of the cliff where Congal had so often looked towards Rathlin. Everyone from miles around came to celebrate and all were welcomed by the newly-crowned King of Ireland, Congal the Brave. Taisie wore a white dress with a crown of wildflowers in her hair. The sun shone for most of the day, though the couple were glad that a light shower of rain blessed them as they approached Baile na castle's town elder to perform the handfasting.

Congal and Taisie knelt facing each other. They put their hands out before them and crossed them, Taisie taking Congal's left hand in her left hand and Congal taking her right hand in his right hand. The town elder wrapped the ribbon over Congal's wrists and under Taisie's then bound the ends of the ribbon together.

The town elder spoke loudly, 'Let it be known from this day forward that Congal the Brave, King of Ireland, and Taisie, the fair of head, Princess of Rathlin, are joined together to live as man and wife. Let no man try to undo what has been witnessed here today. May their days together be long and fruitful.'

Congal and Taisie got to their feet and held up their knotted wrists to the crowd that had gathered. The crowd erupted with cheers. Congal and Taisie kissed and the cheers grew louder.

Dusk had fallen but the celebrations were only getting started. Bonfires were lit so that the revelry could continue long into the night. Local musicians and lilters provided the rhythm for the crowds to dance, and the local ale houses provided the mead at no cost.

As was tradition, the bride sang for the assembled crowd. Everyone was silent as her voice sailed lightly over them like a cool breeze on a summer day. Even Congal had never heard her sing before and was entranced by the sound. The gathered musicians were especially impressed with the soft tone of her voice. When she finished the crowd cheered for more, but she left it to the musicians to continue providing the entertainment.

'Never have I heard sounds so sweet,' Torloch said. 'Tis what I imagine faerie song must be like. Otherworldly in its beauty.'

'It seems my bounty grows with each day I know her,' Congal said.

Congal stood next to Torloch and watched Taisie dance with the girls from the town. 'I'll bet the Scots can see the fires.'

'I hope they can. I have more joy than I can share with my countrymen alone, Torloch.'

'She's indeed a grand lass, sir.' Torloch laughed and took a long drink from the jug he was holding. When he lowered the jug his face changed. He put his hand to his sword and nodded to Congal to look behind him. Congal turned and saw Agnar standing behind him. Congal steeled himself to fight. Taisie stopped dancing and looked over, the smile gone from her face. The musicians and dancers fell silent and still.

'I apologize for intruding on your celebrations. We are setting sail and I wished to make peace with you. Ireland and Norway need not be enemies after this night. You fought as the gods decreed. Nahbogdon lost, as was the will of the gods.'

Congal regarded the man, then stepped forward and grabbed his shoulder. 'I will hold no quarrel with any man on this day. Come, drink with us and seal the peace between our two great countries.'

Torloch reached Agnar a tankard and said, 'Slainte.'

'Slon-sha?' Agnar asked.

'Good health,' Congal said. The three men drank. Taisie smiled and returned to the circle of dancing girls. The music started again. 'Will you take Nahbagdon back to Norway with you?' Congal asked.

'No,' Agnar answered. 'We have already sent him on his way to Valhalla on a burning raft.'

'Valhalla?' Torloch asked.

'The Hall of the Slain. It is a majestic hall located in Asgard and ruled over by Odin; god of the hunt,' Agnar explained. He cleared his throat and turned to Congal. 'And what of your own injuries? You have healed?'

'I was tended to by a skilled apothecary. I am not fully healed, but on this day I will feel no pain.'

'That'll be the mead!' Torloch shouted. Congal and Agnar laughed. 'I just hope you're fit for your mi na meala.'
'Have no fear, my friend!'
'And what is that?' Agnar asked with a smile.
'It means Month of Honey,' Congal said.
'I still don't understand,' Agnar said.
'Mead is made from honey!' Torloch said between gulps.

'It is our custom,' Congal explained, 'that when a man and woman are joined they are left alone together for a month with a good supply of mead. After this time, it is said the gods themselves could not stop the woman from being with child.'

The three men laughed again. Agnar said, 'It's a grand tradition. I will try to see that Norway adopts this Honey-month ritual.'

One of the town girls ran over and curtsied before Congal, then turned to Agnar and said, 'Will you have a dance?' Agnar looked to Congal for permission.

'You have a long sea voyage ahead of you, my friend,' Congal said, then smiled.

Agnar set his tankard down and allowed the girl to drag him off into the dancing circle.

Agnar danced with the girl until Congal and Torloch had stopped watching, then abandoned the girl and made his way through the crowd.

He bowed his head before Taisie. 'My lady, is it permitted that I may dance with the bride before I leave these shores?' Taisie looked to Congal but he was deep in conversation with Torloch.

She smiled to Agnar and raised her hand, which he took. Taisie and Agnar danced. He spun her around and around, faster and faster. She laughed politely, though she hoped Congal would stop this dance soon. When they did stop dancing she found herself far from the other dancers and close to the edge of the cliff. Agnar seized his hand around her upper arm, hurting her.

'Congal!' he screamed. 'Congal!' The music silenced. The dancers were still. Everyone looked to the source of the shouting. Again he shouted, 'Congal!' The crowd parted leaving a line-of-sight between Congal and Agnar holding Taisie by the cliff edge. Congal cautiously started to make his way forward with his palms facing the Norwegian. Taisie was struggling in his grasp.

'Congal,' he said, now in a lower voice befitting the distance between them. 'It was my king's wish that you witness me carry out his last command.' Agnar spun Taisie roughly around and threw her off the cliff behind him. Everyone gasped. Congal heard her scream all the way down. He screamed, 'Taisie!' and ran towards the edge.

When Congal was close, Agnar said, 'Did you really believe...?' Congal drew his sword with lightning speed and lopped his head off. His body stood twitching, spurting blood, until moments later it collapsed and was still.

Congal ran to the edge and dropped to his knees. He looked over at the dark waters far below. He got to his feet and ran back through the crowd and grabbed Torloch.

'Find the apothecary and follow me down.'

'Congal,' the big man said softly. 'She is lost. There is no hope...'

'There is *always* hope!' Congal ran and jumped on his horse. He turned to Torloch, tears in his eyes. 'Find him and follow me down.'

Torloch reluctantly nodded and Congal galloped off into the night.

Torloch arrived on the beach with the apothecary and half-a-dozen men from the town that wanted to help. They saw Congal's horse standing by the water and dismounted next to it.

They listened to the unending roar of the sea. They watched the untiring lapping of waves on the beach. They saw no one. Torloch built a fire to guide Congal back. They stood by the flames, ever watching the dark horizon.

The apothecary was the first to speak. He said what they were all thinking. 'I fear we have lost them both.' He reached up and put a comforting hand on Torloch's shoulder. Torloch continued gazing into the blackness.

The apothecary hung his head and turned to walk away when Torloch cried, 'There!' They all looked to the ocean and saw the water being churned. Someone swimming. They ran closer to the sea. They saw Congal swimming to shore, dragging a limp body in a white dress behind him. Torloch and the men ran into the water. The apothecary opened his trunk and began selecting potions and powders that would heal a drowned woman.

The men carried Taisie over to the fire. Her white dress was now heavily stained with red. 'Lower her head,' the apothecary shouted. ' Keep her feet in the air.' The men did as they were told. The apothecary slapped her back several times and sea-water gushed from her mouth as she coughed. Hope blossomed in Congal's chest. 'Lay her down now.' The men laid her down and stepped back. Congal knelt next to her and watched the apothecary run his hands over her body. He gently lifted the torn dress at her chest and looked underneath. The wound was deep and blood was pouring from it. The apothecary took a deep breath before raising his head and looking Congal in the eyes.

'There is nothing I can do.'

Congal reached across her body and grabbed the apothecary. 'There must be! There is still breath in her body. My kingdom is yours if you save her life.'

'Sire, her body is broken in many places. I cannot stem the flow of blood from her wound. I regret to say, she will not see morning.'

Congal pushed him away and got to his feet. He turned and took a few steps to hide his tears from the other men.

Congal turned and ran to his friend. 'Torloch, the beast in the barrel. Did my father execute it yet?'

'No. He wanted to take it back and make a public example of it.'

'Where is it?'

'On my cart, in the stables of the ale house.'

Congal ran to his horse and jumped on. 'Give her up to me.'

The men helped Taisie onto the saddle in front of Congal. He held her close to him with one hand and held the horse's reins with the other. He galloped off towards town.

Congal prised the lid off with his sword, then toppled the barrel on its side. The creature inside tumbled out onto the mud floor. Congal pounced on it and cut the gag from its mouth. The creature spat out the stones Congal had placed there and drew breath. Congal pointed to Taisie, lying in a bed of straw in the corner.

'You claimed you could heal any wounds. Heal her and I will grant you your freedom.'

'Do you know what you ask?'

Congal grabbed the creature and dragged him across the floor to Taisie. 'Heal her now! Her time is short.'

'Unbind my hands.'

'You think me a fool? Not until you have healed her.'

'Only my blood can heal her.'

Congal's face twisted in disgust.

'She must drink from me. It will heal her. It is the *only* thing that will heal her.'

Congal dragged his fingers through his hair, then drew his sword and brought it down sharply. The creature's hands were free. It reached down to unbind its feet and Congal put the tip of his blade under its chin. 'No. Not until she is healed.' Congal knelt down and looked the creature in the eyes. 'Do not betray me daemon, or your death will be slow and filled with pain you cannot imagine.'

The creature shuffled over to Taisie. He looked back at Congal, then bit his wrist and placed it on Taisie's lips. Congal's heart raced and his hands trembled with rage that such a creature should be touching his love.

Her lips started to move. They kissed the bleeding wrist before her. Her hand raised and pulled the wrist closer to her. The creature tried to pull his wrist back and her other hand grabbed it and held it close. She started to moan and pant as she sucked harder on the wrist. Taisie screamed and the two fell apart. She lay on the straw, her body writhing somewhere between pain and ecstasy. The creature undid the binding on its feet and stood up. Congal was too captivated by the sight of Taisie, moving again, alive again, to care.

The creature stood beside Congal. 'She will be like me now.'

Congal turned to him and said, 'No. Never.'

'It is the price she must pay to cheat death.'

Taisie stopped squirming.

'It is done. I suggest you find a peasant of the town. Someone who will not be missed. She will need to feed.'

'Silence your lying tongue!' Congal stepped forward.

'The first hunger after Becoming is confounding, she will not know...'

'She is pure of heart. She would never be what you are, travesty!' Congal knelt down beside her and ran his hand down her cheek. Her skin was cold, probably from being in the sea so long. Congal reached forward and lifted back her dress. There was no trace of the wound on her chest. Congal turned his head and looked at the creature in wonder. 'If I had not witnessed...'

Taisie bit into his neck and the sweet nectar she desired was given. She did not know where this liquid was coming from. She did not know how she had found it. A new instinct had been borne in her and had taken over her actions. For a few moments she had felt on the brink of death and then sweet nourishment was making her strong and clearing her head of all confusion.

She felt as if she had drank too much mead. A man. Standing before her. Not Congal. He reaches out his hand. 'Who are you?' she asks. Even her voice sounds different.

'My name is Galen. We must go. It is not safe for our kind here.'

'I am Taisie, betrothed of Congal, King of Ireland. Please see me to his side and...'

'He is at *your* side.'

Taisie turned and saw a man lying dead next to her. She drew back, then recognizing him leapt forward. She saw the bite marks on his neck. She rubbed her chin and found blood on her fingers. She began crying, the memories coming back to her.

'What have I become?' The creature lowered his head and remained silent. Taisie looked into the face of her dead husband and said, 'What have I done?' She raised her head and screamed at the heavens, 'What have I done?'

One Year Later

The cart trundled along. The man, his wife and their ten-year-old daughter were seated at the front while all their possessions rattled around in the back. The man had given the reins to his daughter some time ago but now took them back. He wanted to get there before dark if possible. Ahead of them they saw an old man walking in the opposite direction, his back bent by the load he was carrying. The man pulled the horse to a stop.

'How are ye?' the man asked.

The old man stopped and regarded the family. 'I'm grand,' he eventually answered.

'Do you know how far we are from The North Glen?'

'The old man turned away from their eyes and said, 'No such place. Not anymore.'

'How can that be?' the man asked.

The old man turned back to them. 'Do yourself and your kin a service and turn around now. There's nothing there for you.'

'I was *born* in the North Glen. I lived there until my nineteenth year. There are dozens of settlements.'

'They are all abandoned now. That land is cursed. Heed my words and go back where you came from.' The old man was beginning to get angry.

'I mean to show my daughter and my wife the place of my birth.' The old man looked at the ground and said nothing. 'I'll find it without your help, then.' The man cracked his whip and the cart trundled forward.

The old man shouted after them, 'Tis no longer called The North Glen, tis Glentaisie now. That land belongs to her. Remember my warning.'

The man waved a dismissive hand at the old traveller and continued on his way.

The signpost said GLENTAISIE.

'The oul fella must have been right,' the man said to his wife. 'This is the place. I recognize the fields and forests where I played as a child. We will be there before the moon is much higher.'

There were trees on either side of the road. The night was eerily free of sounds. 'Many nights I walked this road. We are very close now. Are you excited, Aoife?' he asked his daughter. She nodded, smiling. 'I had two brothers and a sister, so if any of them still live around here, you could have cousins. How would that be?'

She smiled and clapped her hands together. The man and his wife laughed. The man brought the cart to a stop. A branch lay across the road. 'I'm not risking breaking a wheel on it. I'll clear it away.' He jumped off the cart and grabbed the branch and dragged it into the trees.

His wife watched the trees. He didn't come out. She looked all around. 'Sean?' she called.

'Where's daddy, mummy?'

'He's just hiding to make jest.' Her worried face showed she did not believe what she had just said. She climbed down off the cart and took a few steps towards the trees. 'Sean? Stop fooling now. You're scaring the wee'un.' She looked back at the cart and saw her daughter standing on the seat looking at her. She took a few more steps forward and saw something move in the darkness. The moon came out from behind a cloud and she saw something feasting upon her husband's flesh. The creature looked up and saw her. Blue eyes glowing in the darkness. She turned back to the cart and screamed, 'Aoife, run!'

The little girl jumped down from the cart just as her mother was pulled into the trees. Aoife started running back the way they had come. Tears were steaming down her face and she was crying loudly. She heard her mother screaming in the distance behind her and then fall silent. She kept running. Screaming. Following the road in the darkness. Crying. Yelling for help. Something flew overhead casting a moon-shadow over her and she screamed louder. The figure descended from the sky and plucked the screaming girl from the road and carried her off into the night.

dave²

It just looked like a garage. Admittedly, a large garage, but a garage nonetheless. Two ramshackle cottages sat by the road separated by a small wall, but their back gardens seemed to be shared. This garage stretched over both their properties with broken parts of engines and machines piled up on either side. The businessman checked the address on the scrap of paper he had been given. This was the right place. He looked at his £600 Italian shoes, then looked at the muddy driveway. He did consider going in barefoot for a few seconds, but it wouldn't be very professional. What the hell, if these guys could do what they claimed, he would have more money than he knew what to do with. He clicked the alarm on his Mercedes, though there didn't appear to be another soul for miles. It had taken him forty-five minutes to find the place and he had directions, the odds of anyone else stumbling upon these two cottages in the middle of nowhere were remote.

His first step sunk three inches into the mud. There, shoes ruined. He didn't have to worry anymore. His second step was less concerned with dirtying his shoes and more about not slipping and ruining his suit as well. As he passed the front garden he couldn't help but stop and stare. He paid a professional gardener a lot of money to tend to his lawn and it didn't look as good as that. The immaculate lawn seemed totally out of place in these otherwise squalid surroundings. He continued on, past the houses and towards the doors of the garage. A sign was welded above the door, made up of reclaimed letters from who knew where, it bore the legend: dAve². He was definitely in the right place. He knocked timidly on the door.

The door opened momentarily and he was greeted by a welding mask. The mask lifted and Dave asked him, 'Can I help you?'

'Yes, I have an appointment. You must be one of the Daves.'

'That I am,' Dave answered. 'Are you the guy with the submarine batteries?'

'No,' the businessman said quickly. 'I represent the conglomerate of Yoshi, Goldberg and Mitchell.'

Dave looked blankly at him.

'Head of their automotive solutions department,' he clarified.

'Oh, right. You're the car guy. That was today, huh? OK, you'd better come in.'

He scraped the majority of the mud off his shoes and followed Dave inside.

The businessman gazed in awe. Everywhere was covered in machines. Some moved while others were floating in baths of water. Lights were flashing on several, for reasons he couldn't fathom. He stopped at a hamster cage and noticed the wheel was hooked up to a transformer, which in turn was hooked up to a computer that was plotting a graph.

He turned in amazement. 'You're running a computer off a hamster wheel?'

Dave gave him a smile and said, 'Add a little caffeine to his food mix. He has too much energy and needs to run it off. A simple transformer does the rest. I'll just get Dave and we'll show you the car.'

He wandered off while the businessman watched a dog cross the room to a panel of pedals; one blue, one yellow, the other six grey.

The dog stood on the blue pedal and a small amount of kibble dropped down a tube into a bowl. The dog ate the kibble then pressed a grey pedal and the same tube deposited water into another bowl. The dog drank its fill and then pressed the yellow pedal. A robotic arm came out of the wall and began extending and contracting its fingers. The dog put its head into the hand's grasp and got his head and ears scratched, then walked away.

The businessman laughed. 'My god, that's amazing,' he said, in barely more than a whisper.

'It took us ages to get that working,' Dave said, though not the Dave he'd already met, a different Dave. 'Even though it's a fairly simple machine. It was the pedals you see, we didn't realise until a vet friend of ours told us that dogs are dichromatic; they can only see two primary colours, blue and yellow, but they have a higher perception of black and white than we do, which means they can easily distinguish between dozens of shades of grey.' He smiled at the awestruck businessman. 'Hi, I'm Dave Watt. I think you've already met my compadre, Dave Drake. You're here to see the car, right?'

He nodded and followed Dave through the garage and out the back doors. 'Isn't your… the ah, the other Dave going to join us?'

'He's a little busy. He genetically engineered this strawberry and this guy's coming round to see it, so he's trying to figure out a way to get it through the doorway without squishing it. I can show you the car.'

They stepped outside and saw the old VW Jetta sitting in a field that had obviously been used for test drives. 'OK,' Dave said. 'You're not the first person who's come to see us this week, so if you're going to make an offer, I'd suggest you do it sooner rather than later.'

'Well, I'd have to speak to my superiors before…'

'Yeah, yeah, I know. OK, you guys never believe this so I'm not even going to touch the car. I'll let you do everything. First thing first, for this prototype, we made the fuel tank out of Perspex so you could see when it was empty.' Dave motioned the businessman to check, which he did. He got down on his knees and looked under the car and found one Perspex fuel tank: empty. Nothing else that could possibly be a fuel tank was under there. He stood and nodded to Dave.

'Now you'll want to get in and try to start it.'

The businessman got in and turned the key repeatedly. The starter-motor kicked but the engine didn't start. After a couple of minutes of trying he got out and faced Dave.

'Happy that it's out of fuel?'

'Yes.'

'Did you bring what I asked?'

The businessman laid his briefcase on the bonnet of the Jetta and opened it. He took out two cartons of apple juice. 'Stopped at Tesco on the way here.'

'OK, pour it into the fuel tank.'

The businessman eagerly punctured the seal on both cartons and unscrewed the fuel cap. He gave Dave a last look then poured them in.

'OK, get in and try to start it again. Remember it will take a couple of tries to work its way through the system.'

The businessman got behind the wheel again and turned the key. On the third try the car came to life and ticked over happily. The businessman started laughing out loud. 'It works! It fucking works!' Dave nodded. 'What... what's the performance like?'

'Take it for a spin and see for yourself.'

'What? Really?'

Dave nodded. The businessman clicked his seatbelt on and raced off down the field. It had amazing acceleration. He flew towards the end of the field at sixty miles an hour. He hit the brakes and pulled a one-eighty. He raced around the perimeter of the field, waving at Dave each time he passed. The engine was so quiet. This was incredible. He hadn't been this exited about driving since he was a teenager. On his fifth circuit he noticed Dave had disappeared. He skidded to a stop at the back of the garage.

He got out and looked under the car at the fuel tank – there was still plenty in it. It was even easy on juice. Literally! He laughed out loud again. My god he was going to make a fortune on this. He pulled out his phone but couldn't get a signal. He had to speak to his boss right away. If there were other parties interested, they had to make an offer *now*.

The first Dave he had spoken to walked out to him. The businessman ran to him and hugged him. 'Where have you guys been all my life?'

'Getting stoned mostly.'

'Right. And do you still...?'

'No. Special occasions only; birthdays, anniversaries, Saturdays.'

'Well, whatever works for you. This is amazing! Do you have a land-line? I have to speak to my company right away.'

'Dave's on the phone. We had a call. You can use it when he gets off.'

'Does the car work with any fruit juice or just apple?'

'Any fruit juice will do. Orange has the best fuel consumption for some reason we haven't figured out yet. Grapefruit is like high-performance petrol.'

'How? How did you do this?'

'What? Oh, the engine.' Dave looked towards the front doors of the garage and started walking towards them as he talked. He seemed distracted. 'The converter on the engine takes the fructose from the fruit juice and converts it into dimethylfuran. The first one we made ran on ethanol but it evaporated too quickly.' They were at the doors now and walked outside to the side of the house. Dave kept looking at the door. 'And the one we made that ran on water had very limited power.'

'You made a water-powered engine as well?' The businessman was drooling. He needed to get these two signed to an exclusive contract, now!

'Yeah, it extracted the hydrogen, but like I said, it wasn't very powerful. The car could only do about 15 miles per hour. Still, we used it to power our jet-ski and that worked out great. Because it was a lot smaller and even lighter because it didn't need a fuel tank.'

'Didn't need a fuel tank?'

'No. We figured since it was floating in its own fuel supply, why bother with a tank when you can just take it directly from what's below you. Took a bit of tweaking to adjust it for freshwater and sea-water, but we got there in the end. I'll take you down to the lake later if you fancy a spin. We've got a converter here but we run the central heating off it, so you can't really get a good look at the workings.'

'Your central heating runs off water, too?' he asked. Dave nodded.

If there were such a thing as an excitement attack, the businessman was having one. They reached the front garden and stopped. Dave was staring intently at the house. The businessman bent over and tried to slow his breathing. He saw the immaculate lawn again. When he had caught his breath he stood up and asked, 'How do you get your lawn so perfect?'

Dave took two steps towards the house and pushed a button next to the drainpipe. Two spheres popped up on either side of the lawn. One shot a laser towards the other then the spheres moved simultaneously up the lawn on metal tracks, the laser slicing the grass at exactly the same height the whole way up. The laser reached the top and had cut the lawn in less than four seconds. The laser turned off, the spheres returned down the track to their starting position and disappeared again.

The businessman's eyes were wide, his mouth hanging open.

Dave walked out of the house and Dave tensed. They locked eyes and Dave solemnly nodded to his friend. Dave exhaled and lowered his head. He knew this day was coming, and now it was here. Just when things were looking up.

Dave made love to his wife that night. She knew everything about him. His brief twenty-year dalliance with marijuana, the vampires he had seen and killed, his relationship with Chloe. She didn't like it, but Trina knew this was something he had to do.

Next morning he got up and pulled the Dream Director [patent pending] sensors from his eyelids. Dave had invented the Dream Director [patent pending] for Trina. When they were first married she used to suffer terrible night terrors. Then Dave had read some research on dreams. It appeared that dreams could be directed. In the experiment dreamers who were in REM sleep had droplets of water dripped on their face. All seven subjects dreamt they were either in the rain, swimming or in a bath. This gave Dave an idea. He attached paper-thin sensors to Trina's eyelids before she went to bed. When Rapid Eye Movement occurred it triggered a tape recorder filled with sounds of the beach, and voila, she dreamt she was on a tropical island. Trina went from being scared to go to bed at night to taking naps twice daily as well. The subconscious responded to verbal commands too. Dave had made himself a tape where he just said 'Showering with Marilyn Monroe' in a soft voice on a continuous loop. It worked. Brilliantly. Fortunately Trina saw the funny side and didn't mind the extra washing.

Last night he had used the Dream Director [patent pending] to dream of him and Trina on their honeymoon, probably the happiest time of his life. He didn't wake her when he got up, but kissed her lightly on the forehead before he left the bedroom. He looked back at her, savouring every moment, then left.

Dave made love to his wife that night. She knew everything about him. His brief twenty-year dalliance with marijuana, the vampires he had seen and killed, his relationship with Chloe. She didn't like it, but Darlene knew this was something he had to do.

Next morning he got up as lightly as he could but she awoke. 'I don't suppose there's anything I can say to make you change your mind,' she asked.

Dave shook his head.

'But David, listen, if…'

'Darlene, I'm not going to argue with you. I have to do this. If you'd seen the things I've seen. If you'd lost people… The bottom line is, Chloe needs help and we can help. I'm doing this for you and me and all the little Dave juniors to come.'

There were tears in her eyes but she forced a smile. 'How many Dave juniors were you planning on having?'

'Five. Just like George Foreman called all his sons George, I'm going to call all ours Dave.'

Darlene laughed in spite of herself. She wiped her eyes. 'This is really dangerous, isn't it?'

Dave clipped the Tooth Tram [patent pending] onto his front tooth. It began polishing the tooth, front and back, then rolled onto the next. It had started the third tooth before Dave nodded slowly. 'This is as dangerous as it gets, and if we fail, vampires will take over the Earth.' The Tooth Tram [patent pending] finished the top teeth. Dave unclipped it and clipped it onto the bottom teeth.

'How long will it take?'

Dave shrugged. 'I don't really know. A few days maybe.'

'Will you call?'

'If I get the chance, but don't assume the worst if I don't.'

Her voice cracked as she said, 'You better come back to me David Watt.' Tears were freely flowing down her face now. The Tooth Tram [patent pending] had completed cleaning the bottom teeth and Dave unclipped it.

'I will.'

'I love you.'

'I love you.'

Dave had already loaded the jeep when Dave came out. 'How did Darlene take it?'

'Tears. Lots of tears. What about Trina?'

'Tears last night. I got out without waking her this morning. I had to promise her I was coming back before she'd go to sleep last night.'

'I just made the same promise.'

'You got the papers?'

Dave took out a brown envelope from his jacket. They both looked at it. 'I'll leave it in the workshop.'

'Everything's in there?'

'Your letter, my letter, our wills and instructions for the transfer of all our patents to Trina and Darlene. That guy who was here yesterday is coming back next week. I think he's trustworthy. He won't try to con them. He really wants the Fruit Machine.'

'He even liked the name. Personally, I think it's way too camp.'

Dave dropped the envelope on the bench just inside the workshop's front door. They both stared at it for a moment.

Dave turned to his friend and said, 'Let's hope they never have to read them.'

The Daves turned and left the workshop, closing the door firmly behind them.

out for a scroll

Hal sat in his room. The decrepit house he had visited so often was now his home. He had left his possessions behind, and his family. The Master was his only family now. He liked his new life. He had taken to killing easily. Like an assassin, the first one is the hardest, after that it gets easier until it just becomes routine. Here he was, not even a week-old vampire yet, and killing was already routine. Nothing mattered now but his own drives and desires. No Christian dogma to tug at his conscience. No laws of man that he had to obey. He was truly free.

He took out his wallet. When he had gone to the Master to be Made he had taken all his savings with him. This made him snigger now. He had no need for money. If he wanted something he would take it. No one would try to stop unless they wanted to die. He took a lid from a rusted tin box in the corner; some kind of biscuit barrel in years gone by. He turned the lid upside down and dropped the wad of money in it. He had saved almost £700 since he had been working as a porter. It was going to pay for a foreign holiday for him and Sarah. He took out his lighter and set fire to it. He watched the notes curl and burn in the flames. He fingered through the other sections of his wallet. Credit card and ATM card went on the fire. Gym membership card, movie library membership card and a dozen other business and taxi firm cards were eaten by the fire, too. His wallet was empty except for a photo-booth picture of him and Sarah. His arm around her, pulling silly faces. He held the photo above the fire. He could feel the paper heating up. He took the photo away from the heat and put it in his pocket. He dropped his empty wallet on the fire.

Hal went downstairs. He didn't even notice the Master's smell anymore. He imagined it was because he smelled the same. The living room was still in total darkness. Even when the Master had Made him, he hadn't got a good look at him. He liked to keep to the dark.

'Harold,' the voice said from the darkness. 'You're off to feed?'

'Yeah, you want me to bring you back someone?' Hal had never seen the Master feed, or leave the house, or have anyone brought to him.

'No, but I need you to do something for me.'

'Name it.'

The voice had moved when he spoke again. 'Someone is here. An emissary of the carpenter. He means to destroy us. He must not see the dawn.'

'The carpenter?'

'The Nazarene.'

Hal thought for a few seconds before it clicked. 'Oh, *that* carpenter. Right. Consider it done.'

'Take Jacqui with you.'

'Oh, do I have to? She weirds me out.'

'The followers of the carpenter have many defences against us. You would be wise to take her.'

'What's her deal, anyway? Why's she like that?'

The voice was closer now, louder, but still he couldn't see the Master. 'When a vampire is Made its body becomes perfect, and approximately twenty-one years of age. Jacqui was only nine years old when she was Made. Her body grew in stature, but her mind did not. It is forbidden to Make children for this reason. She is a casualty of a vampire with selfish urges.'

'By urges you mean…'

'Sexual urges, yes. His preference for children led him to the mortal Jacqui. He ravished her dozens, maybe hundreds of times. When she was on the brink of death he decided he didn't want his fun to end. He didn't know that she wouldn't remain a child when he Made her.'

'So where is this guy who Made her? Shouldn't he be taking responsibility for her?'

'His actions angered me. He and I spent three years alone in a room where he learned the price of angering me. I think, in the end, he understood.'

'Three years?' Hal said, almost to himself.

'Yes, he was weak. Others have lasted longer. Much longer.' The voice moved again, and now spoke in a coarse whisper. 'You've probably yet to fully grasp what your immortality means. Three years is nothing but a long afternoon in the grand scale of things.'

Hal gulped. He stared into the darkness for a few moments before saying, 'I'll go get Jacqui.'

Hal went back upstairs and knocked on Jacqui's door. He opened it and walked in without waiting for an answer. The door hit the child-sized coffin that she squeezed into every night. She was awake and sat in the middle of her playpen, the fabric below her filthy and stained with dried blood. She was playing with dolls. She looked up as Hal approached.

'Me is playing dinner party. Do you want to come to me's dinner party?'

'No, it looks like it's black-tie and I've nothing to wear, thanks all the same. The Master's got a job for us.'

She gasped. 'Me's guests will have to leave without dessert. Is very rude of me.' She reached inside her coat and took out a baby bottle filled with blood and suckled on the teat. When she had drank her fill she put it back inside her coat. She raised her arms up to Hal, wanting to be lifted.

'Oh, for fuck's sake,' Hal said under his breath.

Jacqui burped and immediately started giggling.

It was going to be a long night.

The funeral had been hard on Sarah. Tom had been with her almost constantly since her uncle broke the news of her mother's murder. She had cried a lot but since the funeral a new drive had consumed her. She tried to find out everything she could about Kaaliz; the vampire who had killed her mother. Unfortunately there wasn't much to find. He was a comparatively young vampire and seemed to disappear for long stretches at a time.

She had learned where he had been for the last ten years from her Uncle Derek. He had told her about burying Kaaliz in the concrete. They had gone to the building site the day after the funeral. It wasn't hard to figure out which house he had been buried under. When they arrived there was yellow police tape cordoning off the whole area. Ambulance men carried out body bags while forensics specialists examined bone fragments in the fireplace. The house stank; it had taken a long time for the bodies to be discovered. The neighbours, experts in looking the other way, could finally bear the smell no longer and called the police.

Rek spoke to the police officer in charge and he let them in. They all stared at the hole in the basement floor. Rek blamed himself for everything; Kaaliz's return, his sister's death, everyone Kaaliz had killed and would kill before he was caught again.

After a thorough search of the house provided no clues to where Kaaliz might go, they all went back to the car. Another body bag was carried out. Rek stared at the house. Sarah sat beside him. Tom sat quietly in the back.

'It's not your fault,' Sarah said.

'But it is,' Rek answered coldly. 'I could have just killed him. If I'd just killed him, none of this would be happening.'

'Why didn't you?' Sarah asked. It was the one question she had been dying to ask since he told her.

'I wanted him to suffer,' he said. 'After everything he did to your mother...'

'Everything?'

Rek put his head in his hands and rubbed his face, he pushed his hands back through his hair and took a deep breath. 'I hoped... we both did... we hoped you'd never find this out, Sarah. We hoped we'd never *need* to tell you.'

She was scared now that the awful realisation was dawning on her. 'Tell me.'

He sniffed. 'You and Tom have probably put your heads together by now and figured out what you are.'

'A dhampir.'

Rek stared at the dashboard. He said quietly, 'Yes.'

'Are you trying to tell me...?'

'He's your father, Sarah. That murdering piece of shit is your father.'

Sarah's shoulders shook and she started crying. This wasn't the romantic, doomed relationship she had imagined. She thought her mum had been in love with some vampire with smouldering good looks and a brooding personality. A vampire desperate to regain his humanity. One of those nice, dull Stephenie Meyer-type vampires; good-looking but as threatening as a wet sock. A vampire who would sacrifice his life for the sake of his love and his unborn child. Not this killer. This murderer. 'No, mum would never…'

'He raped her,' Rek shouted. Then quieter, 'That bastard raped her repeatedly and then beat her half to death. That's why I wanted him to suffer.'

Sarah opened the car door and ran. Rek reached for his door handle but Tom stopped him. 'No, I'll go after her. I'll see you back at home later.' Tom got out of the car and ran after Sarah. Rek dropped his head to the steering wheel and cried. He wished Nicholl hadn't left already.

Father Fox stepped off the train onto the platform. He looked both ways. Everyone was leaving. No-one loitering behind. No-one was watching him. No-one was still on the train. He was wearing a long coat and put the cardboard tube inside it and clamped it with his arm. He joined the crowd walking towards the exit. He looked behind himself a couple of times but didn't see anyone following.

He reached the porter at the end of the platform and gave him his ticket. The porter clipped it and handed it back. Father Fox didn't move on. 'This is the port of the rushed?' he asked in a thick Italian accent.

The porter nodded. 'Port-rush, that's right.'

Father Fox took out a scrap of paper from his pocket and showed it to the porter. 'You know this woman?'

The porter looked at the paper. 'Chloe Knight? Yeah, I know of her. The town doesn't have too many millionaires, and even less that look like her, know what I mean?' He laughed and nudged the priest. His coat fell open and the porter saw his collar. 'Oh, maybe you wouldn't. Sorry, Father.'

'This address is close?'

'Not too far. There's a taxi rank just across the street – they'll get you there.'

Father Fox nodded. 'Gracias.'

'No bother, Father.'

Father Fox stepped out of the train station and onto the pavement. He looked left and saw the taxi rank. He looked right and saw a man drop a cigarette and grind it into the ground then start quickly towards him. Father Fox turned and ran towards the nearest crowd, which had assembled outside a nightclub. He ploughed through the midst of the teenagers until he was out the other side. None of the teenagers had accosted Father Fox about his behaviour because they had seen the collar, but his pursuer didn't get the same pass. A tall teen blocked his path and stopped him with a confrontational gaze that would surely impress the girls around him. The man reached into his pocket and drew out a gun. Everyone screamed and the crowd parted like the Red Sea before Moses. Bullets ripped through the air almost silently from the end of the long barrel. The man fired several shots at Father Fox, who was now running into a large amusement complex a few hundred yards away. The man ran after him.

Father Fox ran inside the amusement complex. The bright flashing colours all around and the electronic screams disoriented him. He stumbled against the nearest wall and his coat stencilled a bloody shape on the white paint. He reached inside his coat and his fingers came back red. Sweat was pouring down his face. The cardboard tube began to slip and he reaffirmed his hold on it. He ran forwards, deeper into the amusements.

It seemed like everyone was looking at him. Faces seemed to drift close then disappear. He hid behind a penny-push machine and watched the entrance. The man entered and concealed his gun before anyone noticed it. He then began scanning the area, squinting off into the distance. Father Fox lost the strength in his knees and collapsed to the ground. He turned, ignoring the pain in his side and saw the man rushing towards him again.

Father Fox pushed himself to his feet and hobbled deeper into the amusements. He ran through the maze of fruit machines and almost got kicked in the head by a hobby-horse. The brightly coloured horses spun before him as children held tightly to their reins. He staggered sideways and noticed a crowd standing by the bumper-cars. He made his way over and tried to lose himself among them. He looked back and saw his pursuer slowly walking around the hobby-horse ride. He turned his head slowly, looking for sudden movements in the crowd. He saw none and made his way to the back doors that led to the rollercoaster. He looked back over his shoulder one last time. Father Fox crouched down behind a tall woman carrying a child. When he looked up again the man had run outside towards the rollercoaster.

'You're bleeding, Father,' the woman with the child said.

Father Fox looked down and saw a small pool of blood below him. 'I'll be fine.' He patted the woman's shoulder and ran towards the entrance. He came to a stop beside the ghost train. He stared at the doors and saw two of the unholy enter. They spotted him immediately and started towards him.

Father Fox's strength went again and he collapsed. The cardboard tube fell from his coat and rolled across the floor. He tried to crawl towards it and blood spurted faster from his wound. He saw the tube next to the barrier for a ride called The Experience. Several teenagers were screaming their enjoyment of the ride, being spun round and round and upside down at great speed.

An employee appeared from behind Father Fox and knelt down next to him. 'Oh my god, what happened to you?' she asked, genuinely concerned.

Father Fox was coughing up blood now. He couldn't get the words out. He pointed at the cardboard tube. He glanced at the approaching evil. He pointed again and tried to lurch forward towards the tube.

'It's going to be all right. My name's Anne-Marie.' She took out her phone and dialled 999. 'Just don't move. I'll have an ambulance here soon.'

The two vampires stopped before them. They looked down. Father Fox tried to scramble backwards but hadn't the strength.

'Baby's made a mess,' Jacqui said.

Anne-Marie looked up at the pair and said, 'Listen, can you just step back and give him some air.'

Jacqui hung her head and mumbled, 'Me doesn't like being scolded.'

Hal smiled and said to Anne-Marie, 'She really doesn't.'

Jacqui grabbed Anne-Marie by the head and lifted her up to her feet. She was ripping at her throat before Anne-Marie could say a word. Blood from her jugular sprayed Jacqui's face as she fed sloppily from her prey. The phone in Anne-Marie's hand dropped to the floor and the emergency operator, who had been becoming more and more worried by what he was hearing, was finally cut off.

Jacqui dropped the body, her face and clothes drenched in the mortal's blood.

Hal looked at her and said, 'Baby needs a bib.'

Jacqui smiled and her eyes danced. They both looked down at the squirming priest below them. The screams all around them were no longer from the thrill of being spun at high speed or winning a prize, they were screams of blind panic as everyone flooded towards the doors, front and back.

Hal bent down to the priest and bullets ripped into his chest. Hal fell backwards, more out of years of conditioning than any real pain. He had been shot. He lay on the ground and actually panicked for a few seconds before he realised what he was now. He was pretty sure bullets couldn't hurt him and when his fingers searched his chest for holes, he found he was right. He sat up and started laughing. The man walking slowly towards him slapped another magazine into his gun and unloaded it into Hal's chest. He continued laughing. He looked around for Jacqui but couldn't see her.

The man with the gun kept glancing to his right. Hal followed his look and saw a blood-stained cardboard tube lying by the barrier. Hal shuffled across and snatched it into his grasp. Smoke rose from his fingers and pain shot through his entire body. He dropped it again.

Hal turned to the priest, who was now barely conscious and said, 'That's sneaky. What have you done to it?' He put his hand inside his coat pocket and reached to lift the tube with his hand covered. Again came the smoke and the pain. He turned back to the priest. 'You're a tricky one, aren't you?' Hal stood and kicked the tube so it was between his legs. He turned and faced the gunman. 'You want this?' He tapped the tube with his shoe.

Hal had heard the man's gun click empty but still he held it before him like it might save him. The gunman didn't know what to say. He gestured with the gun that Hal should step back. Hal glanced behind the gunman and then put up his hands. 'OK. It's a fair cop.' Hal took two steps backwards from the tube on the floor and then turned his back to the gunman.

The gunman saw his chance and ran for the tube. He didn't make it two steps before Jacqui dropped on him from the ceiling. She clutched him around the neck like she wanted a piggy-back and bit into his throat. Hal, his back still to them, heard the sound of someone choking on their own blood, closed his eyes and smiled. He had come to love that sound.

When he opened his eyes and turned back, the gunman was lying on the floor. Jacqui stood up and took a deep breath. She took a pack of baby-wipes from her pocket and cleaned her face. Hal knelt down to the priest and said, 'Who are you guys? And what are you doing in my town?'

The old priest said a Latin prayer in barely more than a whisper, then died. Hal walked over to the gunman, bent down, and opened his coat. He reached into the inside pocket and brought out his ID. He read it with interest. 'Vatican police. You're a long way from home.' He looked to Jacqui for her reaction, but she just pulled a lollypop from her pocket and began sucking it. Hal looked at the tube lying on the floor. 'Whatever that is, I think the Master will want to see it.' He stood up and looked at Jacqui. 'Any ideas how we get it back to him when we can't touch it?'

Jacqui stared at him vacantly, sucking on her lollypop, then said, 'Put the baby in a pram.'

'Good idea. I'm sure there's a basket or a trolley around here somewhere. Wait here, I'll be right back.'

It took Hal almost ten minutes to find something suitable to carry the tube in; a student's backpack would do nicely once he emptied out the books and got rid of the student attached to it. He dropped from the sky outside the amusement complex and ran inside.

Jacqui wasn't there. Neither was the cardboard tube. The two bodies still lay where they had fallen, but there was no one else around.

The door to the ghost train opened and Sarah stepped out carrying the tube. 'You looking for this?'

Hal eyed her cautiously then said, 'No. Just here to try to win a stuffed toy on the grappler.'

'Those things are a rip-off.'

Sarah knelt down and felt for a pulse on the priest's neck while still keeping her eyes on Hal. 'You did this?'

Hal shrugged. 'You a follower of the carpenter now?'

'I've got their greatest hits album, does that count?' She covertly took a piece of blood-stained paper from the priest's grasp and put it in her pocket.

'Maybe you're just here for the candy-floss. Maybe you need to get a bag and leave, Sarah. While you still can.'

'I'm here for you, Hal. But first I want to know what you know about this.' She stood up and held the tube before her. 'And I *do know* this is what you came back for. That crazy bitch you were here with tried to pick it up a few times when we came in but she couldn't. Is that what the backpack's for?'

Hal dropped the backpack. 'Where is Jacqui?'

'Tom and her went out the back to talk things over. Kudos on your choice of girlfriend, by the way.'

'Yeah, I always seem to pick the bitch of the bunch, don't I?'

She waved the tube at him. 'You going to tell me what this is?'

'I don't know what it is.'

Sarah eyed him as he got closer. 'Do you know a vampire called Kaaliz?'

'No.'

'Bullshit.'

'I find that a very racist statement. Just because I'm a vampire you assume I know every other vampire. Next you'll be saying we all look alike.'

'He killed my mother, Hal.'

Hal hung his head. 'I am sorry about that, Sarah, but you've made your choice and I've made mine.' Hal charged at her and knocked her off her feet. The tube rolled across the floor. Hal grabbed it and screamed as he ran a few steps towards the backpack with it. When he couldn't hold it any longer he dropped it and shook the pain from his hands.

Sarah kicked him in the stomach, then quickly twice to the head before swinging a punch that sent him hurtling backwards. She grabbed the tube and ran through the doors of the ghost train. Hal got to his feet and shook the dizziness from his head, then ran through the doors after her.

Hal felt the train tracks below his feet and followed them. He could see in the dark, but there was nothing to see. Blank walls. He walked faster. A skeleton jumped from the wall followed by a loud screaming noise. Hal swung instinctively and punched it, shattering the plastic frame into pieces. He chastised himself for being so easily spooked. He walked on and a mummy pounced forward. He ignored it. Then a witch. Then a vampire in a long cloak. Hal stopped and smiled at it for a second, then continued. Some rubber bats flew in his face. Frankenstein's monster made an appearance. A werewolf with red eyes. A white-sheeted ghost. Sarah with a jug of water. She threw it in his face. He raised his hands to his face, expecting the inevitable burning that accompanied holy water. It didn't come.

He blinked his eyes and smiled at Sarah. 'Sorry, I don't think that was holy water.'

Sarah struck a match. 'I know it wasn't.' She threw the match at him and his chest and face exploded in flames. Hal screamed and beat helplessly at the fire. He ran screaming back the way he had come, bumping into the walls like a pinball. Sarah ran after him.

Sarah burst out the doors of the ghost train just in time to see a six-foot ball of flames rise into the air and head towards the sea, which was only a couple of hundred yards away.

Tom ran up behind her, out of breath. 'We need to go.'

'Did you kill the other one?'

'She flew away when things got rough. We really shouldn't leave the house without weapons. I could have had her a dozen times if I'd had a stake.' Tom bent over and took deep breaths. 'Next time, for sure.'

Sarah looked at the cardboard tube in her hands and then at the dark sky that moments ago had been lit by fire. 'Yeah. Next time.'

taken in

The two agents stank. Their car stank. Their clothes stank. Their breath certainly stank, and their mood most definitely stank. So when the two agents appeared to relieve them, the handover was short and to the point.

'That's the door you have to watch. Twenty-four-hour garage half-a-mile that way has a good shop, microwave and public toilet. Chip shop is four streets that way: they do a nice kebab. Nothing to report. See you in forty-eight.'

The two new agents parked in the same position as their colleagues had and watched the green metal door. And they watched. And they watched.

By three a.m. the younger agent was getting restless and the older agent was getting annoyed.

The young agent switched off the radio.

'What did you do that for?'

'I've fuckin' had it, listening to news.'

'It might do you some good to know what's going on in the world.'

'I know what's going on, OK? People killing other people. All news, all depressing, all the time. A list of who's died for what bullshit reason, that's all the news is. And you, you're like an old lady checking the obituaries in the newspaper when you listen to it. It's ghoulish.'

The older agent considered his young partner for a moment before answering, 'And what do you consider a bullshit reason for dying?'

'Religion for a start,' he answered quickly. 'Half the mass-murder on this planet is caused by people saying "My god's better than your god" or "My god could beat your god in a fight." It's ridiculous. It's getting to the point... I don't think we need vampires anymore. I think we're quite evil and selfish enough to kill ourselves.'

The older agent studied him, taking it all in, then said, 'How many times has that little speech got you laid?'

The younger agent tried to hold a straight face but eventually smiled. 'Yeah, OK. I admit I've used that line more than once to some hottie in HQ and it works more often than not.' His partner nodded, smiling. 'Still, it doesn't mean it isn't true.'

'You ever try it on our target?'

'Nah, Nicholl was a bit before my time. I remember seeing her about HQ a few times the first month I started, but she hasn't been around much lately.'

'Once seen, never forgotten,' the older agent added.

'Yeah, she's still a MILF.'

'She's not a mum.'

'Isn't she? OK, then she's a… OWIB.'

The older agent chuckled. 'What's an OWIB?'

'Older Woman I'd Bone.' The two agents laughed.

The older agent glanced at the green door as a cat ran past. 'This is so stupid. I know Nicholl; she isn't going to come here.'

'You *know* her?'

'No, not like that. I worked with her briefly years ago when she lost her partner.'

'Bradley, right? I've seen the pictures. Nice.'

'We didn't work together very long. I think she was already drifting away from Ministry protocols. She started to do things her own way, and more and more often by herself. She still got the job done, but HQ didn't like it. We went our separate ways soon after. She's never had a partner since.'

'You think she's finally gone over the edge?'

'No. Just because she stole something from Takamura doesn't mean she's turned to a life of theft. Whatever she took, she took for a specific reason. Try telling HQ that, though. No, they know better. So that's why they've got agents all over the country watching every possible mystical object she might steal. A complete waste of time.'

'What is it that's in there, again?'

'The Sword of Light. Very famous in Gaelic mythology. Apparently it can slice through vampires like a hot knife through butter.'

'Sounds pretty handy. Maybe she *will* show up if she believes this whole prophecy crap. She might be desperate enough.'

'Not a chance. She's smarter than that. Besides, she does quite well with an ordinary sword.' The older agent squirmed in his seat. 'These stakeouts are murder on my haemorrhoids.'

'You want me to go over and get the old Sword of Light and lop them off?' The young man laughed.

'Ha, ha, dipshit. Wait 'til you have twenty years of stakeouts behind you and see how your ass is doing.'

The younger agent stifled his laughter. He looked out at the green door. 'If this sword's such a big deal, why's it kept in a storage room in a dodgy part of town?'

'The guy who owns it used to keep it in his house, but there were a lot of attempted robberies. No one knows it's here except him. And us, of course.'

The young agent yawned. 'I'm hungry. You want anything from the shop?'

'You could see if they have any cream for... you know.'

'I am not buying you ass cream!'

'Why the hell not?'

'What if it's a good-looking bird behind the counter? I'm not going to ask her if she has anything for piles.'

'So typical of the younger generation, always thinking with their dicks and about their dicks.'

'If it's a choice between thinking about my dick and your ass, that ain't no choice at all.'

'I'm in considerable pain, here.'

The younger man considered it. 'OK, here's what I'll do; if it's a bloke at the counter I'll get your ass-cream, but if it's some tasty bit, I'll bring you back a bag of frozen peas or something. That's my best offer.'

'For God's sake, it not like the girl behind the counter is...' The older agent's attention drifted to the street outside. The younger man followed his gaze. They saw Nicholl creeping towards the green door. She was moving slowly and checking over her shoulder often. The agents' car was sitting in the shadow of the alley so she didn't spot it. The older agent spoke in a whisper, 'I don't believe it.'

They watched as Nicholl bent down and started picking the lock. A few seconds later the door was open. She pushed it up high enough for her to squeeze underneath, then disappeared inside the building.

'OK, grab your Taser and follow me,' the older agent said, already exiting the car.

The two agents ran towards the storage depot. They put their backs to the wall on either side of the door, their Tasers ready. The younger agent waited for the nod, then yanked the door upwards and ran inside. The older agent followed him and hit the lights. There was a long corridor with locked doors all the way up on both sides. One was open. The younger agent went charging down the corridor and straight into the open room without pausing. There was sounds of a scuffle and then the young agent flew backwards out of the room again and hit the metal door opposite. Still dazed, he got up and charged back inside the storage room. The older agent walked slowly towards the room. He could hear the noises of the fight that was raging inside the room. The younger agent flew backwards out of the room again and landed with a groan on the floor. He tried to lift himself up but this time couldn't manage it. He collapsed with a grunt.

Nicholl stepped out holding the sword, ready to run. She stopped when she saw the older agent.

'Hello, Nicholl.'

She was surprised. She took a breath before answering, 'How's it going, Ward?'

'Not too bad. I hope you weren't too rough on the young boy.'

Nicholl glanced at the agent at her feet. 'He'll be OK.'

'Remember when we were that young and impetuous?'

'He'll learn. Give him time. How are the haemorrhoids, Ward?'

'Still a pain in the ass.'

'I hope I didn't keep you waiting too long.' She took a deep breath and looked him in the eyes. 'You don't have to do this, Ward.'

'I'm sorry. I do.'

'If you knew what was going on…'

Ward shook his head.

'You know I can beat you.'

'Maybe ten years ago. Have you seen the latest intake of agents? They're fitter, faster, better than we ever were.'

Nicholl looked down. 'Like him?'

Ward raised the gun. 'I am sorry.' He fired and the two wires rushed at Nicholl. She brought up the sword and cut the wires in mid-air. Ward dropped the Taser and reached into his jacket. Nicholl ran at him and knocked him down. She took the gun from his jacket and stepped over him, heading for the door.

She turned and said, 'When you see Kyle, tell him...'

Two prongs hit Nicholl in the chest and in the split second before the charge hit her, she saw the bloodied young agent had picked himself up to a sitting position and had fired his Taser. The last thought Nicholl had was to bring the sword up and sever the wires. The darkness closed around her.

Nicholl woke up in the back seat of Ward's car. Her hands were cuffed behind her back. She sat up straight but said nothing. The younger agent tended to his injuries in the passenger seat as Ward drove. Ward glanced at her in the rearview mirror but said nothing either. Nicholl hung her head. She noticed enough of the signposts to know they were heading for Ministry HQ. They were still a couple of hours away. She settled back.

Ward and the younger agent made a spectacle of marching Nicholl through the front doors of HQ. She saw the looks of her one-time colleagues. Secretaries who used to look at her with awe and pride, now looked at her with disgust. Nicholl hung her head to avoid their stares. They took the elevator one floor down and again marched her through the desks of dozens of admin personnel. Nicholl saw them all jumping up from their desks so they could get a better look at her. She saw them whispering to each other with looks of distaste on their faces. She saw the younger agent who had hold of her left arm smiling and drinking in all the attention. Ward, who had her right arm, had a neutral look on his face but she sensed he was enjoying it too.

Finally they arrived at Kyle's office and Ward knocked. They were beckoned from within and Ward opened the door.

Nicholl had been in this office many times, usually to be commended. It looked bigger now, more foreboding. Kyle must be in his sixties, Nicholl thought – a good record for anyone in this business – and was even more distinguished and handsome now that the grey had finally won the fight for supremacy in his hair. On either side of Kyle behind the long desk were two other senior agents, people Nicholl had once looked up to and admired.

Ward and the younger agent marched her forward and sat her down in the chair to face her accusers. Nicholl squirmed to get comfortable, but it wasn't easy with her hands still cuffed behind her back.

'Do we really need the cuffs, Kyle?' she asked.

He considered her. 'Yes. I think we do.'

Ward and the younger agent left her at the desk and retreated back to the door to stand on either side of it.

'You've led us quite the merry dance, Nicholl. Fenton had all sorts of bad things to say about you. Were they all true?'

'Probably. Though, in my defence, I gotta say, that guy's a fuckin' dick.'

'Yes, well. Do you want to offer anything else in your defence?'

She looked into his eyes. Kyle was a reasonable man. She had to try. 'Kyle, you know me. I'm not impetuous and I'm not gullible, but there have been things happening, things prophesied in The Book of Days to Come. You must know. You must be keeping an eye on it, too.'

'Ministry Intelligence took over the prophecy department, remember? I'm sure they would tell us if the world was about to end.'

'How many jokes have you and I shared about Ministry Intelligence? They don't know about this, and if they do, they aren't doing anything about it.' She leaned closer. 'Kyle, this is happening right now! All that stuff is coming true and if we don't do something the thousand years of darkness will become a reality.' She heard the younger agent snort behind her, but ignored him. 'Even if you're not a hundred percent convinced, where's the harm in putting a few agents on it just in case?'

'Where is The Fist of Merlin?'

Nicholl sat back in her chair and exhaled. 'It's safe. I need it for a few days.'

'Your little stunt has created quite a controversy.'

'When did you turn into such a bureaucrat, Kyle? This job used to be about killing vamps and saving humans. That's all I'm trying to do!'

'Anglo-Japanese relations....'

Nicholl got to her feet. The two agents at the door tensed but didn't advance on her. 'Fuck Anglo-Japanese relations! I'm trying to save the whole goddamn world and you're worrying about politics?'

He raised his eyebrows. '*You're* going to save the world?'

'I know what that sounds like.' Kyle flipped through the folder on his desk. 'You missed your last two medical evaluations.'

'I was busy!' She took a deep breath and sat down again. 'Look, I'm not cracking up and I'm not having a breakdown.' She looked into her superior's eyes and said softly, 'Please, Kyle, if I ever needed your trust, I need it now.'

'Will you disclose the location of The Fist of Merlin?'

Nicholl shook her head and smiled at the absurdity of the question. She looked at him defiantly. 'No.'

'Then you leave me no choice.' He conferred briefly with the two agents on his left and right in whispers then said, 'It is the opinion of this board that Agent Amanda Nicholl is a security threat and as such is no longer fit for active duty. We believe her judgement to be questionable and her motives highly suspect. You will therefore be taken to Section Zero immediately, where you will spend the rest of your natural life.' Kyle stamped the front of Nicholl's file in large red letters that said SECTION ZERO.

Nicholl got up and lunged across the desk at Kyle, her hands still bound behind her back. 'You fuckin' moron! You're not going to believe this is true until it comes up and bites you on the arse!' The two agents grabbed an arm each and started dragging her back towards the door. 'Kyle, I'm right about this!' she screamed. She kept on screaming that same phrase until she was out of earshot of the board.

He looked at her file and then put it in the inactive filing cabinet. He shook his head. One of the other board members patted his shoulder and said, 'Damn shame.'

'Even the best agents can crack up and get a "Hero complex" about themselves, but I never thought it would happen to Nicholl,' Kyle said. He closed the filing cabinet drawer.

The two agents pushed her down the corridor, past the shocked and disappointed looks of her ex-colleagues. They reached the door. Ward entered a code on the keypad on the wall. The door opened and they pushed her inside.

The room was almost bare. The only things that interrupted the straight lines and glaring whiteness were a door at the opposite end from where she came in, a bench bolted to the middle of the floor with a plastic bag sitting on it, and a hatch mounted on one wall. She walked over to the hatch and could feel the heat through the metal. She walked back and sat on the bench. A few minutes later a large woman in her forties came in. Nicholl had seen her around HQ but never knew what she did. She carried a metre-long rod that Nicholl was quite sure delivered an electric shock from the end. The woman walked over and unlocked Nicholl's handcuffs. She put them in her pocket, then stepped back.

'OK, Nicholl. I hope you're not dumb enough to try anything.'

Nicholl shook her head silently.

'Good girl. Well, come on. You know the drill.'

Nicholl got up and started taking off her clothes. It wasn't so much the large woman with suspiciously short hair and tattoos on her forearms that bothered her, but the security camera hidden in the light fitting. She knew it was hidden there because she had seen people in this room before. The IT nerds hacked the security footage and passed it among their friends. Just another humiliating perk of being expelled from the Ministry.

When she stood there, naked, her clothes in the bag provided, the large woman approached her. First she took the clips from her hair (once bitten, Nicholl thought), then she took the rings from her fingers, her earrings, her watch and her necklace, and placed them in the plastic bag too. Then she seemed to take great pleasure in looking where only Customs Officers dare to look. When she was satisfied she told Nicholl to go and stand at the door at the other end of the room. The large woman opened the hatch and dropped the plastic bag of Nicholl's belongings into the incinerator.

The door before Nicholl opened and she stepped inside. She found herself in a small cubicle with another door facing her.

There was a bench with an orange boiler-suit on it and a pair of rubber slippers. The door behind her closed. Nicholl put on the boiler-suit and the slippers.

On the other side of the door before her a hatch dropped down, leaving a circular hole.

'Wrist,' a coarse voice said.

Nicholl got up and tentatively put her hand through the hole. Her arm was seized roughly and held as an injection was delivered into her wrist. The grip on her arm was released. She pulled her hand back through the hole and examined the puncture.

The room started to blur. The floor seemed to be tilting in all directions. She put out her hands to steady herself, but a second later dropped to the ground. There were noises above her. Talking maybe. She couldn't be sure.

The world melted into darkness.

offspring

Kaaliz sat in Project Redbook watching the creatures in the cages. Was one any different than another? Would a Che'al/vampire hybrid in a Garth Brooks T-shirt be more vicious than one in a Shania Twain T-shirt? Cowboy boots versus trainers? A neckerchief could be a positive sign of evil, or maybe a waistcoat. Did it really matter? They were all going topside sooner or later. He didn't think it made a difference which went first, though he could hear Sin's voice in the back of his head saying it did. She would know which to send first and she would have a damn good reason. His mind just didn't work like that.

He got up and wandered into the lab. This is where Sin had spent most of her time working and it still smelled of her. The door had an air-tight seal that had captured her scent and stored it for all these years. Kaaliz sat there, breathing her in.

She was the only one he had ever felt a true connection to. Women had always been something he had to take by force. She had given herself to him, freely. Before he was a vampire women had always been repelled by him. But he had drives, needs. And one way or another, he needed to sate those urges.

When he was a mortal he had kidnapped a psychiatrist, a pretty one with long hair and a short skirt. He had asked her why he was the way he was. She had screamed for nearly an hour, then realised the only way she had a chance of living through her abduction was to co-operate with him. She had asked him about his childhood. He had no mother and didn't know what had happened to her. His father would beat him whenever he mentioned her, so he soon learned not to ask. He lived in a ramshackle house on the edge of a forest, with no other houses for miles. He went to school briefly and remembers being ridiculed for the smell that followed him around.

His father had lots of girlfriends. None of them stayed very long. Bruises seemed to appear on their faces like welts, as if they had walked into a contaminated area when they entered the Higgins house. His father didn't talk to them, he gave them orders. If they didn't obey the orders, the bruises came.

When Kaaliz, or Edwin as he was then, was eleven, his father woke him up in the middle of the night and hurried him out to the forest, to a clearing. There was a body of a woman lying there, looking brilliantly pale in the moonlight. She had the bruises like the others. And some bruises around her throat that the others didn't have. She had no clothes on and was so white in the glow of the moon that she almost didn't look real. The boy looked at her and began to stiffen in his pyjamas. His father told him she had been in an accident and they needed to bury her.

Father and son began digging a hole. The boy stole glances at the woman's nakedness when his father wasn't looking. The hole was about four feet deep when his father decided it was deep enough. He said he would run back to the house and get her things. The boy waited with the body.

When his father was out of sight he knelt beside her. He touched her cold breast and ran his fingers over the smoothness and grabbed the nipple. He pinched the nipple while his other hand raked through the hair between her legs. The boy felt an ecstatic shudder surge through him and then noticed a wetness in his pyjamas. He scurried back quickly and tried to dry the wet patch with leaves and dirt. The last time he had wet the bed his father had beat him with the fireside poker. His father was returning. He scrambled to his feet and stood with his hands clasped before the wet patch.

His father ran into the clearing with her belongings bundled under his arm. He threw her clothes, underwear, shoes and (after he had taken the money from it) her handbag into the hole. He then instructed the boy to get her feet and they rolled her into the grave. She landed face down with a thump. The boy looked down at her, fascinated by the flip-side of what he had been staring at all night. His father unzipped his trousers and urinated into the grave, laughing as he sprayed her back, buttocks and hair with his piss. He zipped up when he was done and handed the shovel to his son. They filled in the grave.

The psychiatrist called this a pivotal moment.

She tried to explain to Edwin Higgins the psychological damage his father had done to him. She said his actions were the result of mental illness borne of that night. She said she would testify to that in court. She seemed to get more scared when he told her they were in his father's house now; that was where he had taken her. He told her not to worry – the old man was long gone. He didn't elaborate on the hows and whens.

The psychiatrist was saying all the right things and being perfectly reasonable in her pleas to help him, but there was no way he could let her go. She knew too much about him. She called it understanding him, he called it knowing his weaknesses.

He had stabbed her in the heart. There was very little blood. He cut the ropes around her hands and feet that bound her to the chair and let her fall to the floor. He just sat there and watched her for a long time. Looking at her. Becoming more and more aroused until he could stand it no more and he did what every instinct in his body had been telling him to do.

He undressed her slowly...

No one knew about that. Not even the cops who built a case against him. They knew he had kidnapped her but they had never found the body, so they didn't know what he had done. When the prosecutor was trying to shock the jury with the crimes of Edwin Higgins, he was sitting smirking. They didn't know the half of it.

He had been planning to tell Sin. He felt sure she would not judge him. He didn't think she'd wholeheartedly approve either, but she had a mind thirsty for knowledge and experience. She would know why he had done it. She would probably find it fascinating. He could imagine the hunger in her eyes as she quizzed him about his thoughts and feelings as he did it.

And now that Ministry bitch had taken all that away from him.

Kaaliz got to his feet and stormed out of the lab. He looked at the creatures all clawing at their prisons. This was Sin's legacy. These were their children. He pushed the button on the wall and the lift doors opened. He grabbed the swipecard from the desk and stood before the cages.

She had been a slim and pretty girl once. Maybe she had even modelled herself after the picture of Shania Twain on her T-shirt. Any beauty was hidden now, forever buried below the ridges and growths that had been the result of combining Che'al and vampire blood. She would look harmless from a distance (maybe that's how Sin would have thought about it). Kaaliz swiped the card through quickly and her cell door swung open. She pounced from the cage and caught him on the arm. Her nails sunk into his skin before he levitated upwards and shook her off. Kaaliz looked down from the ceiling as the hybrid growled and screamed at him. The deep gouge in his arm repaired in a few seconds. He patted his heart and smiled. Jumping as high as she could she would never reach him, but that fact didn't seem to register. Kaaliz imagined if he stayed above her forever, she would probably keep jumping forever. Any semblance of intelligence she had as a human was gone.

Kaaliz flew over to the lift. She followed him, still jumping and clawing at the air. Kaaliz asked, pleaded and commanded her to get in the lift, but his words were lost. She didn't understand him and even if she did, she wouldn't obey him. She had one thing on her mind: feeding on whatever was available.

Kaaliz looked inside the lift. If he went in there she would follow, but there wasn't enough ceiling height for him to stay out of her reach. He looked around for emergency exit signs and saw none. Wasn't there a stairwell out of this place? Someone should get onto Building Regulations about that. He stared down at the screaming hybrid and was lost for a way to get it outside.

Once again, he wished Sin were here.

Chloe armed herself with a sword before answering the door. She looked out the peephole and then dropped it into the umbrella stand. She opened the door and Sarah and Tom came in, trying to catch their breath.

'Are you two OK?'

'We just got into it with a couple of vampires,' Tom said between breaths.

Chloe looked concerned. 'Rek said you ran off, upset when you found out about... it wasn't him, was it?'

'No,' Sarah said in little more than a whisper.

'One was this girl dressed in... like a coat made out of old baby clothes. The other was...' Tom nodded to Sarah.

'Hal was the other one,' she said.

Chloe hung her head briefly and then asked, 'Did you kill them?'

'We didn't have any weapons,' Tom said. 'They killed a couple of people.'

Chloe looked at Sarah, but she didn't meet her eyes.

Tom felt the awkwardness and took the cardboard tube from Sarah. 'This is what they were after. Do you know what it is?'

Chloe finally took her eyes off Sarah. 'No, why would I?'

'The priest was on his way to give it to you,' Sarah said. She reached Chloe the bloodied piece of paper with her name and address on it. Chloe looked at the paper, then at the tube. 'You didn't look to see what it was?'

Tom glanced at Sarah, then back to Chloe. 'We didn't want to. The vampires couldn't touch it. We figured there must be some protection on it. Maybe you're the only one who can open it.'

Chloe took the tube from Tom and rolled it over in her hands. 'OK, let's go into the kitchen and let the Daves take a look at it before we try anything.' The two of them started moving. Chloe took Sarah's arm and stopped her, then turned to Tom. 'Oh, ah, you might want to go into the living room first, Tom. Second on the left.' Tom nodded and walked through the door.

Chloe lifted Sarah's chin and made her look into her eyes. 'No weapons, huh?'

'Yeah.'

'That the only reason Hal's still walking around?'

Sarah tried to look down but Chloe wouldn't let her. 'Sarah, every day you let him live is another couple of innocent people in the morgue.'

Tears welled in her eyes. 'I've known him since...'

'I know. I'm sorry. But eventually you, or some one of us, will have to put him down.'

Sarah nodded and wiped the tears from her cheeks.

Chloe put her arm around her. 'Come on. Let's go and see if we can figure out what this thing is.' The two of them walked towards the kitchen.

Tom had walked into the living room to an unexpected shock.
'Hi, mum.'
Claire got up, walked over to him and hugged him tightly. When she released him he saw she was crying. 'What the hell do you call this? Running away?'
'You knew this day was coming, mum.'
She turned her back on him and shouted, 'I know. I was training you for it. We were going to face it together.' She turned back to him and spoke softly. 'I thought I'd lost you.'
'I left you a note.'
'What note? I didn't get any note.'
'I put it in your movie jacket. You always go to the cinema on a Tuesday with Ciara and you always wear that jacket. You couldn't miss the note.'
Claire smiled. 'I bought a new jacket on Monday. I wore it instead.'
Tom let out a snort of disbelief then dropped into the nearest armchair. Claire sat on the sofa opposite him. 'How did you find me?'
'I was a vampire for over a hundred years. I read The Book of Days to Come a lot. The North Coast is where it all goes down. The final battle. The vampires and the humans. And the chosen one.'
Tom leaned forward. 'Yeah. The chosen one. Not the chosen one and his mum.'
Claire looked hurt.
'Mum, I love you, but you're human now. You can be... You should just go home.'
'We trained for this together and...'
Tom got to his feet. 'No,' he shouted. 'This is my fight.'
Claire smiled. 'You sounded just like your dad, then.' She looked away briefly, then turned back to her son. 'This is everyone's fight, Tom. A thousand years of vampires ruling the earth is everyone's problem. Even a broken down old housewife like me can help. I've still got some moves.'

Tom knelt down and kissed his mother's forehead. 'I know you have.'

'Come on, shall we go and see what Chloe's planning?' Claire stood up and put her arm around her son.

'How do you know Chloe?'

'She helped us escape when you were ten. Don't you remember?'

'I thought this house looked familiar.' Tom cleared his throat. 'Listen, mum, Sarah's in there.'

Claire smiled. 'Who's Sarah?'

'Would you believe she's Kaaliz's daughter?'

Claire stopped in her tracks, lost in thought for a few seconds. Tom didn't see his mum scared very often, but now he saw it he didn't like it. 'Who... who's her mother?'

'Her name was Anna.' Tom looked at the concentration on his mother's face. 'She worked as an undertaker's assistant. Her family...'

'Oh, shit! I know who you mean. I sort of introduced him to her. OK, there's a conversation I'm not looking forward to.'

'You won't have to. Kaaliz killed her a few nights ago.'

'Oh, no.' Claire let it sink in for a few seconds, then her eyes brightened. 'Wait, if she's his daughter that means...'

'She's a dhampir, yes.'

'Well, that's something we've got going for us. Wait a sec, this isn't Sarah who you used to play with when you were young, is it?'

Tom nodded. 'Yeah.'

Claire shook her head. 'How did I never know who her mother was?'

'I think she laid low after what he did to her. Anyway, mum, when we get in there, don't act... well, just...'

'You like her.' Claire smiled again.

Tom exhaled through his nose then said, 'Yes, I do.'

'I always thought you did. Is she pretty?'

'She's beautiful, mum.'

'Aw, that's sweet. Don't worry, I won't embarrass you.'

They walked through the door into the kitchen. The Daves, Chloe, Lynda and Sarah were all huddled around the table where a large piece of paper was spread out. The Daves were examining it closely.

Chloe looked up and saw them enter. 'You didn't kill him after all, then, Claire.'

Sarah walked over to Claire with her hand outstretched, 'Hi, Mrs Ford. Wow, you still look the same.'

Claire ignored the proffered hand and hugged her. She released her embrace and held her by the shoulders as she looked at her. 'Just look at you, Sarah Hughes. All grown up.' She turned to Tom quickly and said, 'You weren't doing her justice when you said she was beautiful.'

Sarah blushed. Tom slapped his forehead and dragged his palm down to cover his eyes while he shook his head.

Lynda looked at the boy closely. Tom was her half-brother. Some of their facial features were even similar. He looked like one of her own children. Lynda wondered if Claire had told him. Lynda's eyes raised for a second and she and Claire exchanged a knowing glance. He doesn't know. Claire's eyes said it all. Lynda gave a nod no-one else in the room noticed. The secret would remain between them. She'd like to get to know her half-brother, though. Maybe one day when this was all over she would.

'Er, we got the tube open,' Sarah said. Claire and Tom followed her over to the table. The Daves were examining the extremely small and faded writing with magnifying glasses.

'What is it?' Tom asked.

'Blueprints,' Dave answered.

Claire edged in closer and looked down at the finely detailed drawings. She tilted her head this way and that, but could make no sense of them. Finally, she asked the question on everyone's lips. 'Blueprints for what?'

the bishop's gait

Coleraine, 1782

The meeting hall was filled to capacity. A long table sat on the stage where, in happier times, travelling troupes would perform the popular plays of the day. Tonight there was no entertainment and fear was the only cost of admission. Three men sat at the table. The man in the middle got to his feet and banged a gavel on the table before him. The impatient mutterings of the crowd silenced.

'Some of you know me, some of you do not. My name is Vincent Hopkins, head of the Ministry of the Shield these fourteen years since the death of Oliver Dwyer. On my right is Frederick Hervey, Bishop of Derry and on my left, Charles O'Conor, historian and author of the book…'

'Who cares!' came the shout from the back of the room. Most of the crowd shouted their agreement.

'What are you going to do about her?'

'She killed my husband.'

'She doesn't stay around Ballycastle anymore, she goes everywhere!'

'My son! She killed my son, he weren't even of age and she killed him!'

'No one's safe from her!'

'What are you going to do?'

Hopkins held up his hands and quieted the crowd once more. 'I know of your concerns. I, too, have lost those close to me. It is my understanding that local lore forbids anyone from even saying her name aloud. Superstition tells you this will summon her, or curse your house. You call her the tempest. You think her a storm from hell? You believe her name cursed? No such nonsense is true. I defy her to come to me. I say her name without fear. Taisie.'

The assembled crowd gasped as one at his bravery. Some crossed themselves or rubbed talismans around their necks. 'Taisie, the fair of head,' he repeated, louder. 'I call out to thee. If you have the power to know when your name is said aloud then come to me now. Taisie! Come before me and feel my blade if cowardice does not impede you.' The assembled townsfolk were nervously looking around. A few pushed through the crowd and ran out the back doors.

Hopkins held out his arms. 'Your tempest has no power but the power of fear. The soldiers of the Ministry are searching for her this night and every night until she is killed or driven from our shores.' The crowd gave modest applause. 'To hasten her demise, we have a job for each and every one of you.'

A worried mumble passed between the townspeople.

'Fear not. I am not asking you to take up arms against her, or do anything that would endanger your kin. I will ask Mr O'Conor to continue.'

Hopkins sat down and O'Conor stood up. Obviously no stranger to speaking to large groups of people, he spoke in a loud, authoritative tone. 'In 1218 A.D. three knights of the round table were dispatched to our land to fight what were known then as "blood-drinkers." To help them on their quest, the sorcerer, Merlin, made a talisman in the form of an amulet and put at its centre a crystal imbued with magical properties. A crystal that was said to be able to bring sunlight during the night.'

The townspeople gasped and whispered quietly among themselves until O'Conor began again.

'The three knights never returned to their king and the talisman was lost. It never left Ireland. That means that somewhere in this land it is waiting to be found. I believe this crystal may be our best defence against... the tempest. We know these creatures shy away from the sunlight on fear of death. To bring forth sunlight during the night is something she would never expect. We have the chance to not only put an end to her, but to safeguard us from all of her kind in the future.'

The crowd gave a more enthusiastic cheer this time. O'Conor sat down and the bishop stood up. 'So we ask of you all, search. Wherever your travels take you, seek out the crystal talisman. It is a light blue stone embedded in gold, on a gold chain. Do not be tempted by its opulence. No one will pay you more for it than I, and by handing it over you may save your family, your friends, maybe even yourself. We have a plan to use the crystal in ways that will make us feared by the tempest and all her kind, but we must find it first. Tell everyone you know of our quest, and tell *them* to tell everyone *they* know. The more people who are looking for it, the better chance we have of finding it. You all know where I live; the villa at Downhill. If you happen upon the amulet, bring it to me, day or night. You will be rewarded not only by me, but by your fellow men, your country and God Himself.'

This time the crowd roared in its approval. The bishop said a short prayer for their safety and they all began to file out.

O'Conor addressed the two other men quietly. 'Do you really think they can find it after five-hundred and sixty-four years?'

'It never left these shores. It is here somewhere. It will be found, sooner or later,' the bishop answered.

'We have given them hope,' Hopkins added. 'Even without the crystal, that will give them courage and strength.'

'For a while,' O'Conor said. He turned to the bishop. 'Are preparations being made?'

'Shanahan has begun already. With any luck, it will be ready by the time we find the crystal.'

'Luck has not been on our side of late,' Hopkins said. 'Let us hope that changes.'

Downhill, 1784

The fire crackled beneath the arch of ornate marble. It cast a soft flickering light across the study. He had asked the servants not to light the lamps tonight. Instead he lit a single candle. He wiped the dribbles of last night's hardened wax away before setting it down on his desk. He checked the door was locked for a third time, then removed the paper from behind his bureau. He rolled it out gently on his desk and weighed it down with a polished stone from the beach, given to him by one of the children of the parish. He dipped the quill in the inkpot. The nib hovered above the page. He imagined a tether to his rational mind holding it there, trying desperately to stop him from writing any more. However, no tether could hold back what he had to say.

Even though his heart was racing, his brain was calm. Each phrase, each word, must be the exact word that best describes his feelings. Anything less would unworthy of the lady. He read what he had already written.

15 March, 1784

Ma chère cousine,

I hope you will excuse these writings if they do not compare to the practised hand of the poets that I know you do so admire, for love is a language never studied and barely understood by me. I can only hope that the honesty of my words will suffice where polished verse is lacking.

I hope the sentiment of this missive is not overly shocking to you. It cannot have gone unnoticed that when I have occasion to touch your hand in greeting I am loathe to release. Are my affections folly? Am I a fool to imagine that your eyes linger a fraction longer than is acceptable in polite society between cousins? If that look conveyed a fraction of the love I feel for you, I would take that sliver of time and trade it for eternity in Heaven.

Your husband is a fine man of commerce and good standing. His business dealings have made him a great fortune, though I fear he is ignorant of the priceless treasure that shares his bed.

I know of the absurdity of my actions. You are over three decades my junior, you are married and have a high place in English society, and if my intentions were ever discovered I would find myself expelled from the church. Though I care deeply for Elizabeth and our children, she no longer ignites the fire in me that she once did. Ours is a marriage in name only. It seems I make no better a bishop or husband than I did a barrister. All I can offer in my defence is that the laws of man and God seem petty if they mean I should ignore my love for you.

The bishop looked down at the words. There was growing fear inside him, but also excitement. Just to release these words from inside himself was liberating. He took a deep breath and continued.

I think of you often, dressed in your finery, your hair lightly powdered and wearing your favourite pearls. It is an image I believe will stay with me all my days. Frideswide, my love, if there is any part of you that believes me more than just a foolish old man coveting that which he will never have, then I implore you to make your feelings known to me, as I have to you.

I eagerly await your reply.
With love, F.

The bishop sat back and read the entire letter again. He held up the frame that carried the likeness of Frideswide Mussenden. The picture did not capture her essence or her radiance. He folded the letter carefully then heated the waxstick on the candle's flame and dripped it onto the fold of the letter. When there was an adequate pool he pressed the seal of the Bishop of Derry into the hot wax.

When he was sure it had set he got up and walked to the fireplace with the sealed letter in his hand. He rang the bell for a servant. He would send it immediately. He would instruct the messenger to wait for a reply, even if it took her days to compose one.

He would gamble everything. She was worth it. He had spent years filling his villa with paintings, sculptures and priceless works of art from all around the world, but what were pieces of stone and decorated canvas next to Frideswide. But what if she denied his advances? Not only would he never know her touch, but he might never again look upon her. If she told her husband he would surely never allow the bishop to cross his threshold again. The bishop looked into the dancing flames of the fire.

The door opened and his butler entered. 'You rang, your grace?'

The bishop turned and looked at the butler for a few moments then shook his head. 'I apologize. I rang by accident.'

The butler nodded and left.

The bishop dropped the letter into the fire.

The following morning the bishop was sitting alone breakfasting when the butler interrupted him. 'Excuse me, your grace, but a messenger has just delivered this.' He reached the bishop an envelope. The butler took two steps back and waited.

The bishop tore the paper open roughly. 'Probably from Elizabeth and the children. News of their holiday.' The butler said nothing. The bishop opened the letter and read:

Frederick,

I regret that I must trouble you, but a business deal of some import has come to my attention and I must make my way to the Far East on the first available ship. These linens I seek are not only of the highest quality, but the price at which they are being sold would lead you to believe they are fit for vagrants, not kings. It is my intention to buy a large quantity and return with them to England, where I shall be able to sell them at an astounding profit.

I will be gone several months at least. I do not wish to leave Frideswide alone for that length of time, nor does she wish to accompany me. You will remember the conversation we had when last we met concerning certain members of the local gentry making advances towards her. This is the burden of having a much-desired bride.

So I am sending her to you and Elizabeth. When last you visited she seemed most interested in your talk of the beauty and customs of Ireland, perhaps you would take this opportunity to indulge her interests. I do hope this is not an imposition, but there is no one else I trust to ensure her virtue.

I have instructed the messenger to ride ahead and deliver this. Frideswide's coach cannot be more than half a day behind him. I hope this gives you and Elizabeth adequate time to prepare for her arrival.

I am indebted to you.
Charles Mussenden

'We are expecting company,' the bishop said. 'Prepare a guest room immediately.'

The butler nodded. 'Any response for the messenger?'

'No, pay him the usual… no, pay him double, and make sure he and his horse are well nourished before he begins his return journey.'

'As you wish, your grace.' The butler left quietly, closing the dining room doors behind him.

It was only then that the bishop allowed himself to smile, and then laugh.

The bishop had finished his breakfast and was filling his pipe with tobacco when the butler opened the doors again. 'Mister Shanahan to see you, sir.'

'Michael,' the bishop boomed loudly. 'Come in. Are you hungry?'

'No, thank you.'

The bishop gestured the butler to leave and Michael to sit down, which they both did. Michael cleared his throat and then timidly began. 'It cannot have escaped your notice that we are nearing the end of our project, your grace. I estimate two to three more months for completion.'

'Indeed. When I hired you for this job I was assured of your skill as an architect, but your work is a revelation. What you have designed goes far beyond the remit of a mere architect. That such an instrument of death could look so beautiful is indeed confounding in a most agreeable way.'

'Thank you, sir. I thought, since you were good enough to let us build it on your land, on your doorstep almost, that it should be something as beautiful as the rest of the villa, to all outward appearances at least.'

'Capital idea, Michael. And those two fellows who have done the carvings...'

'The McBlains, David and James,' Michael said.

'I noticed just yesterday that they have finished my little Latin phrase. Exquisite work, just exquisite.' A cloud of smoke rose around him as he lit his pipe.

'You, ah...' Michael cleared his throat. 'You *are* going to release the funds to complete it, then?'

The bishop looked shocked. 'Well, whyever not?'

'It's just, there have been some rumours. You know, since the amulet hasn't been found. Two years now. Some people have been saying that...'

'The amulet will be found, of that I have no doubt. And when it is, I want our little project to be ready.'

Michael's shoulders relaxed as he exhaled. 'Thank you, sir.'

'I have a meeting with my banker tomorrow. I will make arrangements then for the remainder of the funds to be released. The price is as we agreed, still? You haven't incurred any unexpected costs?'

'No, no, sir. The price is what we talked about originally.' Michael got up and nodded to the bishop. He started towards the door.

'A master builder, an artist, an innovator, *and* you keep to your price; you are indeed a rare breed, Michael.'

Michael chanced half a grin at the bishop, nodded, and quickly left.

As soon as Frideswide stepped from the coach that evening, all thoughts of the bishop protecting his reputation left his mind. She was more beautiful than he remembered. She smiled coyly as he kissed the back of her hand in greeting. He took her arm and led her inside as the footmen unloaded her belongings.

The servants smiled as they passed. Some of them had been taking bets below stairs. The bishop's usual posture was hunched and slow, but they had noticed when he would visit the town twice a week by himself, taking a single horse and not the coach (and driver), he would return with not only a greatly improved mood, but also the bounce in his step and confident swagger of a man half his age. Since the servants had all been made aware of this, they now looked out for it and noticed this lightness of step also showed up when certain female guests would come to stay. Those who had bet that the bishop's posture would not improve with the arrival of Mrs Mussenden had just lost their money.

'I do hope this is not an imposition,' she said as they crossed the threshold.

'It is a surprise of the most agreeable kind, Mrs Mussenden. I regret that my wife and children are not in residence though. They are taking a holiday on the coast of Donegal.' He looked closely for her reaction. Was it just his imagination or did he detect the briefest smile on her lips? 'I hope you will not find the company of an old man too tedious.'

'Bishop Hervey, I have heard many things about you, but I have never heard anyone describe your company as tedious.' She turned and gave him a smile. Then, in almost a whisper, 'I'm sure we can amuse ourselves until your family's return.'

The bishop smiled widely. The butler entered and silently chastised the footmen who were grinning behind the back of the bishop and his guest. Their faces became solemn and the butler began directing them. They waited at the foot of the stairs to follow Frideswide.

'I'm sure you must be hungry from your trip,' the bishop said, in a voice the help could all hear. 'We will dine as soon as you are ready.'

Frideswide dressed for dinner in an ivory-coloured dress with a neckline that fully accentuated her womanly attributes. She wore her favourite pearls. The bishop wore his best dinner suit.

The talk during dinner was perfectly respectful. The servants waited by the walls, ready to refill any glass or add an extra portion of meat or vegetables. Frideswide ate little but seemed filled. The bishop ate heartily. They rarely made eye contact and when they did their eyes did not linger. The bishop knew there would be time to talk freely after dinner, out of earshot of the servants. Even if they didn't inform his wife of any untoward conversation or action, he knew they talked among themselves and to the shopkeepers when they went to town for provisions.

After dinner Frideswide and the bishop walked to the cliff edge, just a few hundred yards from the villa. They stood by the fence and looked across the ocean at the setting sun. Frideswide looked down at the beach far below on her left and remarked on its beauty.

'There is much beauty to be seen tonight,' the bishop answered. Frideswide blushed and again gave a little smile. The bishop still didn't feel confident that his affections would be returned. 'Frideswide is an unusual name. I don't believe I have ever met another. Do you know of its origins?'

'Frideswide was an Anglo-Saxon princess,' she began with the confidence of a story oft told. 'While still very young she founded a priory and took a vow of celibacy. Despite this, a Mercian king tried to court her. When she refused his advances he tried to ravish her, but she escaped him by hiding in a nearby wood. She returned to the priory where he continued his pursuit of her until he lost his sight. Frideswide felt compassion for him and prayed to St. Catherine of Alexandria and St. Margaret of Antioch who instructed her to hit the ground with her staff. When Frideswide did this the ground gave way and revealed a well. She used the water from the well to cure his blindness.'

'As good a parable as I have ever heard.'

'You think it a parable?'

'A man blinded by love is redeemed by the object of his affections? Yes, I believe it a parable.' He stepped closer to her. 'Many men have been blinded by love. To stare at great beauty too long is akin to staring at the sun on a summer's day.'

She turned and took a step away from him with a gentle laugh. 'You are all your reputation suggests, Frederick.'

It was the first time she had called him by his first name. He took it as an encouraging sign. 'You alluded to the fact that I had a reputation earlier. Pray tell, what gossip lies in my wake?'

'It is not my place.'

'Nonsense. I care not for the rules of polite society. We are just two people, talking. Two friends should be able to talk without censorship.' He edged closer again.

She turned to him. 'A common phrase I have heard is "When God created the human race, he made men, women and Herveys".'

The bishop laughed. 'And what meaning to you derive from those words?'

She looked unsure, but continued. 'Perhaps that the rules which exist for men and women do not apply to you. Is it true?' She stepped closer and looked him in the eyes. 'Do you disdain what most people would hold sacred?'

'On the contrary, what most people hold sacred, I would hold in equal or even greater esteem.' He raised his hands to hold her but she stepped back. 'What other rumours do you hear of me?'

'What of your meetings with Countess Lichtenau? Are those reports idle speculation? They have certainly angered the Prince of Prussia for, if rumours are to be believed, she is *his* mistress.'

'Wilhelmine and I have a friendship. I do not deny that.'

'A friendship like ours?' she asked quickly.

'That is yet to be seen,' the bishop answered carefully. He thought he detected the smallest hint of a smile as she turned away.

The sun had gone down a few minutes ago and there was now a chill in the air. Frideswide shivered.

'Do you wish to go inside?' the bishop asked.

'I would like to stay out here for a little longer. Perhaps I could trouble you for my shawl.'

'Certainly. Perhaps I should bring some wine out, too?'

'I believe I would enjoy that.' She smiled at him.

When the bishop turned they both saw the structure. He noticed the look of interest on Frideswide's face as she examined the round building with its domed roof.

'Magnificent, isn't it?'

'What is it?' she asked.

'There is a story behind its construction that will chill your bones. You are not easily frightened, I trust?'

She shook her head.

'Then I will tell you the story when I return.' He smiled and hurried back to the villa.

Once inside he made his way down to the cellar. It took him quite a long time to pick the perfect bottle. He believed wines to be like women; each with their own personality and each best enjoyed in a milieu reflecting that personality. Eventually he selected a youthful, fruity Burgundy. He quickly made his way back up the stairs to the kitchen and found two glasses. He carefully uncorked the wine and put his nose to the neck of the bottle. The scent of wine always had an affinity with romance in his life. This was the perfect bottle for tonight. He put on his topcoat and had a servant fetch Frideswide's shawl from her room. When the servant returned he grabbed it and said the staff could retire for the night. The bishop stopped at the back door and put the shawl to his face. He breathed in the scent of Frideswide and was intoxicated by it.

He ran out of the villa's courtyard towards the cliff edge, the bottle and glasses clinking in one hand, her shawl in the other. He was only a few yards from the walls of his villa when a voice stopped him.

'Freddie!'

The bishop stopped and turned. A beautiful woman walked from the shadows. Frideswide was equally beautiful, but in a different way. This woman was not coy. Everything from her dress to her walk suggested a brazen nature. She wasn't a lady.

'What are you doing here?' he spat. 'I am not in the market for company tonight. Miss Nancy should have told you that.' He looked her up and down. 'Though, perhaps, later in the week I could pay you a visit.'

'I'm not one of your whores, Freddie.'

'Who are you? Why do you feel you can address me with such familiarity?'

The woman stepped forward. 'I want your pursuit of me to end.'

'I do not...'

She grabbed him around the throat, lifting him off his feet. Her eyes glowed unnaturally blue and her incisors grew before his eyes. The bishop struggled in her grasp but was easily restrained. '*Now* you know who I am.'

'The tem... the tempest!' he managed to say.

'I prefer Taisie, but that little title has made me known the length of this land.' She dropped him to the ground. The bottle, which he had forgotten he was still holding, smashed on the ground. The blood of the vine seeped into Frideswide's shawl. When the bishop saw it, he became panicked to greater heights.

'Frideswide!' He looked behind him, but could see nothing. He scrambled to his feet, keeping a close eye on Taisie, then turned and ran to where he had left Frideswide. Taisie smiled.

The bishop stumbled to a stop before the building. His eyes grew wide at what he saw. He dropped to his knees. On one of the curved walls of the small building, Frideswide had been nailed up by her hands using the builders' tools that were lying all around. Her throat was ripped out and her once-ivory dress was soaked in red. Her head hung to the side, her facial expression as innocent in death as it was in life.

Another vampire, a male, leaned on the wall below where she hung, smiling. He looked at the bishop and nodded as he buttoned up his trousers. 'Don't worry, bishop. I didn't let all that anticipation go to waste. She had a lot of spirit. I like that in a woman.' The vampire laughed.

The bishop screamed at the sky, tears running down his face. When his vision cleared, Taisie stood before him.

She looked at the structure and read the Latin inscription: 'Tis pleasant safely to behold, from shore to rolling ship, and hear the tempest roar.' She turned to the bishop. 'You think this little... temple, a haven from my rage?' She knelt down before the bishop and whispered, '*Nowhere* is safe from my rage, nor no-one.' The bishop was still sobbing quietly. 'You will end your quest for this trinket you seek and you will cease building this... whatever this is supposed to be.' Taisie grabbed him around the throat and lifted him to his feet again. 'Do you understand me, Freddie? If you continue to irritate me, I'll nail a different member of your family to that wall every week until you stop. Am I understood?'

The bishop hung his head, shameful of what he was about to say. 'I will call off the search for the amulet.'

She nodded backwards. 'And this thing?'

'I'll dismiss Shanahan and the builders tomorrow. It can't be completed without my release of certain funds.'

Taisie dropped the bishop to the ground. He made no attempt to get up, but instead stared at Frideswide's defiled body. Taisie patted him on the head, 'Good boy, Freddie.' The other vampire joined her. 'See, Galen, I told you he was a reasonable man.'

The bishop heard their laugher disappearing into the night. He slumped over and lay on the ground, then cried openly.

The servants would cease taking bets on their master's improved posture in the coming months. He no longer took trips to town by himself. His dark mood seldom improved. Female guests still stayed on occasion but the bishop made no play for them. He walked hunched-over and slowly, the lightness in his step gone forever.

rek'd

Rek's phone rang for the eighth time and woke him. Not that he was sleeping exactly, but he was drifting in and out of consciousness. He looked at the screen. It was Sarah again. He let it go to voicemail again. He knew what she was going to say and he didn't want to hear it. His niece may be a dhampir, she may have strength and powers he didn't have, but nothing was going to stop him from killing the vampire that had killed his sister.

The police scanner crackled again. Rek sat forward. The dispatcher gave the code 11-54 and the address. Rek sat back in his chair. 11-54: Suspicious vehicle. Not what he was waiting for. He leaned forward and rested on the steering wheel. He was purposely trying to pick an uncomfortable position to keep himself awake, but somehow within a few minutes he had leaned back into his seat. His eyes were closing. He wasn't going to sleep. He couldn't. He had to be alert and ready to move on a second's notice. Maybe he would just close his eyes for a few seconds. Just to refresh himself.

The streets were empty. He didn't understand it. It was a scorching hot day, not a cloud in the sky and Portrush was deserted. He walked down the centre of the street that should be bumper to bumper with holidaymakers. The traffic lights still changed. In the distance he heard electronic pulses of music. He followed them to the amusements. Nobody stood at the video games. No-one tried their luck on the grappler. No-one rode the ghost train. He walked outside and looked up. The rollercoaster made its way up steep inclines then rocketed down, but no screams of excitement accompanied the cars.

He walked on down to the beach and looked the length of the golden sands and saw no-one. Not even a stray dog or even... He looked up. No seagulls. No birds of any kind. The air was as quiet as the ground. He looked at the windows of the hotels and B&Bs and saw they were all bricked up.

In the blink of an eye it was night. The moon had replaced the sun. Blue skies were now black. And there were people all around him. Everywhere he looked the streets were packed with... No, not people. Vampires. They were all vampires. They stood at the slot machines trying their luck. They were riding the rollercoaster. They were lying on towels on the beach. Hundreds of them, thousands maybe, all lying on the beach in the dead of night in swimming costumes and sunglasses. Something wasn't right. Something was off.

No children.

Of course. There wouldn't be. He watched the vampires play in the dark waters of the sea. One of them caught him watching and stared at him. The beach became silent as they all turned and looked at him. Rek turned and walked away from the beach quickly. He glanced over his shoulder and saw they were all getting up from their towels and getting out of the sea. They were following him.

He ran into a café. A vampire filling his cup at a vending machine turned and stared at him as he burst in. The vampire took a drink from his cup and walked back to his table. Everyone in the café was staring at Rek now. He took a few steps forward and saw Mand inside the vending machine, slumped over, pale. Her hands were cuffed to the bottom of the vending machine. A tube ran from her neck to the nozzle where the vampire had filled his cup.

'Mand!' He screamed and started pounding the glass front of the vending machine. She was so weak she could barely move her head and open her eyes. Her lips moved, trying to speak. Rek kicked the glass sheet on the vending machine but it wouldn't break. He turned around and grabbed a chair to swing at the glass. There was another vending machine behind him and Sarah was inside. She wasn't moving. Rek dropped the chair and pounded his fist on the glass of Sarah's cage. She didn't move. Rek looked at the LED readout above the coin slot. It said EMPTY. He bowed his head and felt his heart ache. He had failed Sarah. He had failed Anna. He could still save Mand. He could still use the chair to smash open the vending machine.

He looked up and found himself in a graveyard. Before him were the graves of everyone he knew; Sarah, Anna, Mand, Chloe, Tom, Dave1, Dave2. Rek fell forwards onto his belly and began to cry. Arms shot out of the ground and seized him.

His cries turned to screams as the vampire counterparts of his beloved dead rose all around him and attacked him.

He felt his blood draining. He felt his limbs being ripped off. With his last breath he screamed…

…and woke. He grabbed the steering wheel tightly. He panted heavily and looked all around. He got his bearings back in a few seconds and took deep breaths to slow his heart rate down. He pushed the sweat from his forehead back into his hair. He yawned. He didn't know how long he'd been sleeping but he guessed not that long.

His phone rang again. He lifted it and looked at the screen. DAD. Sarah had called her grandfather. The big guns. Rek set the phone back down on the passenger's seat and let it go to voicemail. He wasn't going to be talked out of this. No matter what Sarah, his dad, or his sub-conscious said about it.

The brief sleep had not rested him. He slapped his face a few times, but still felt himself drifting off. Four Harley Davidsons roared past his car. The bikers were all dressed in leathers and were racing through the quiet streets at crazy speeds. He smiled at them. He wished he had nothing else to worry about. Riding from town to town, getting drunk and putting up a tent on any deserted patch of grass sounded pretty good right about now. He wondered if Mand would like that sort of lifestyle, for a few weeks anyway. She might. They might do a lot of things if they got through this. He wondered how her mission was going. Mand and her plans. She was reckless but he had never met anyone so brave either. It was just one of the reasons he loved her.

The police scanner crackled. The dispatcher sounded panicked. *Code 11-54V. Repeat, Code 11-54V. All units please proceed with extreme caution.*

Rek brought his car to life as the dispatcher gave the address. This is what he had been waiting for. Code 11-54 meant an animal bite or attack. And the additional V? He knew only too well what that stood for. With a squeal of tyres Rek was heading towards the address.

The mother was hysterical. The policeman tried to hold a piece of gauze tightly to the wound on her neck, while another tried to hold her upright. She was struggling against them, screaming, crying. The most senior officer shook her by the shoulders and looked her straight in the eyes.

'Hey!'

She stopped shouting but her breaths were still shallow and her chest was rising and falling quickly. Tears streamed from her eyes.

'You have to tell us the situation in there before we can do anything.'

She swallowed then drew several short breaths, trying to find her voice. 'M… m… my daughter and h… her friend. Still in there. Th… th… that thing.' Her composure broke. 'It's going to kill them. You have to get in there!'

The senior officer, who was only slightly senior, looked at the other two officers. They looked scared. He imagined he looked scared too. Of course he knew the rumours, well, not even rumours. Cops didn't joke about things like this. But this would be the first time he had seen one of them in the flesh. What was he supposed to do? The cops in the area may know all about these creatures, but that didn't mean they came out on patrol prepared to fight them. He looked again at the whimpering woman before him. Her legs were giving way under her. She had already given up. She had already accepted that her daughter was dead. The officer wasn't so sure. If her daughter was dead then why was the creature still inside? Why hadn't it left? He could be fairly certain it wasn't staying inside because it was scared of the three police officers on scene.

OK. This was it. If he was going to lead, he was going to lead by example. He took off his cap and jacket and handed them to one of the other officers. He looked around and saw a yard brush propped against a wall. He ran to it and broke it over his knee. He now had half a shaft with a pointed end. All those years watching Hammer horror movies in his teens, just hoping for a glance of exposed breast, were about to pay off.

Another man came bounding down the street. It was the father of the other child. The officers restrained him and explained what was happening as best they knew. Then all eyes turned back to the senior officer. The makeshift stake was visibly shaking in his grasp. He gripped it tighter, took a deep breath and entered the house. Everyone held their breath and watched him disappear inside.

Rek saw the flashing lights up ahead and gunned the accelerator. He skidded to a stop alongside the police car. He jumped out and grabbed his backpack from the backseat. He started towards the door.

'How many inside?' he said to no-one in particular. Everyone was too stunned to speak. 'How many!'

One of the police officers cleared her throat and said, 'Two... two children and one police officer and the... the...'

Rek didn't break his stride and was inside within seconds. The hall was empty. The TV was on in the living room and a cigarette was still smoking in an ashtray, but there was no-one. No-one in the kitchen. Back out to the hall and up the stairs. The police officer's body lay on the landing with his throat torn out. A stake lay beside him. Rek took the Taser from his backpack. There was only one door off the landing that was closed. He moved towards it. He dried his palm on his trousers then reached for the doorknob. He turned it slowly and opened the door a crack. He could hear someone quietly sobbing. He wasn't too late. He took a deep breath and swung the door open.

They were in the corner. A little blonde girl, maybe seven years old, and a female vampire. The vampire hugged the little girl closer, like a favourite toy she didn't want to share. The little girl's face was slick with tears. Rek looked around the room and saw another girl with dark hair. She was lying face down and wasn't moving.

'Hey,' the vampire shouted at him. 'We is playing. No boys allowed.'

'Why don't you let her go and play with me?'

'Boys are yucky.'

Rek edged closer. 'Do you know someone called Kaaliz?'

The vampire combed the little girl's hair. 'You have nice hair. Me could braid it for you.'

Rek had reached the dark-haired girl. He knelt down and put two fingers under her jaw-bone, still keeping his eyes trained on the vampire. There was no pulse. 'Why don't you and I play? I'm not going until you do. You want to braid her hair, you'll have to get rid of the yucky boy first.'

The vampire took a baby rattle from her pocket and rattled it by her ear. She pulled the little girl closer and rattled the toy in her ear too. Rek could see the little girl was having trouble breathing. The vampire was holding her around the neck.

'How about we play Star Wars?'

The vampire shouted, 'No. Go away. Star Wars is for boys!' The vampire threw the girl aside and launched herself at Rek.

Rek pulled out the Taser and hit her with a full blast in the chest. As soon as the full charge was deployed Rek hurled the little vampire across the room. She smashed into the dressing table, shattering the mirror. Rek glanced over his shoulder and saw the little girl was still in the corner, but she now had her arms wrapped over her head. That was good. She didn't need to see this.

Rek dropped to his knees and pulled the vampire from the debris. He looked down at her. She was still dazed. He punched her face. Once. Twice. Again. Harder. Faster. She tried to cover her face but didn't have the strength. When Rek got control of himself again his arm was sore from punching and he was out of breath. He looked down at the vampire. She was crying. Audibly crying, like a child.

Rek steeled himself, remembering what she was and what she had done. 'Where's Kaaliz?'

From the bloodied mess below, a mouth opened. 'Me not know.'

Rek shook her violently. 'Yes you do! Tell me!'

She started crying again. 'Me *not* know.'

Rek got up and walked to the landing. He grabbed the stake lying by the policeman's side and walked back into the room. He dropped to his knees and raised the stake.

The vampire stopped crying for a few seconds and said, 'Me is sorry me was bad.'

Rek hesitated, confused. She started crying again. Rek looked round and saw the dark-haired girl's body. He turned back and drove the stake into the vampire's chest. She gave a short yelp of pain then her body shrank to that of a child, before shrivelling and drying up. Rek's eyes went wide and his mouth dropped open. He had never seen or heard of anything like this before. The body of a long-dead child lay before him. The body of a newly-dead child behind him.

He got to his feet and walked over to the corner. He knelt down and said, 'Hi. Let's get you out of here.'

Cautiously, the blonde girl lowered her hands and looked at Rek. 'Where's the bad girl?'

'The bad girl's gone.'

The blonde girl got up and put her arms around Rek's neck. He lifted her up and made sure her face was buried in his chest so she wouldn't see any of the bodies as they left. He lifted his backpack and they left the bedroom.

A large crowd had gathered outside. Rek walked outside with the little girl and the crowd cheered. The father who had come from down the street ran towards him and took the girl from his arms. He hugged his little girl tightly, then hugged Rek. Rek looked round for the mother. She met his stare. Tears welled in Rek's eyes as he very slightly shook his head. The woman dropped to the ground and wailed.

Rek walked over to the remaining police officers and addressed the woman who had spoken to him as he entered. 'I'm afraid your colleague...' The police woman wiped her eyes, sniffed and nodded quickly, trying to stay professional. 'It's safe now if you want to go in.' Rek turned and walked back to his car.

He threw his backpack inside the car and rested his arms on the roof. This had to stop. He couldn't look into the eyes of another wife, mother, daughter or lover of someone who had been lost to vampires. This little quest he was on was selfish. He had to look at the bigger picture. He should go back and make a strategy with the others. Kaaliz would die along with the rest of them if they worked together. He took a deep breath. This was the right thing to do. He had wanted so badly to be the one to execute Kaaliz, or at least to be there; to watch him die, but not being there seemed like a small sacrifice now. He looked back at the grieving mother being comforted by the police woman. Compared to what some people had lost it was nothing.

'You're not giving up that easily, are you?'

Rek turned slowly and saw Kaaliz standing before him. Instinctively Rek reached inside his backpack and brought out a Taser and a stake. Kaaliz looked into his eyes, grinning.

Rek held his stare but shouted, 'Get these people back!'

The police woman turned and saw Rek advancing on the attractive, though extremely pale man. The crowd seemed to notice him at the same time and were silent apart from a few gasps. A few pushed their way through to the back of the crowd and ran home. The two remaining police officers spread their arms and the crowd allowed themselves to be shepherded back a few steps. They all watched Rek approach Kaaliz.

They began to circle each other. 'You should have killed me when you had the chance,' Kaaliz said.

'Don't I know it.'

'You'll never have that chance again.'

'We'll see.'

'It took me a while to place her, your sister.'

Rek's blood boiled.

'Undertaker's daughter, right?' He nodded, smiling. 'She looked a bit different last time I saw her. I have got the right girl, haven't I? Prefers the man to be on top? Bit of a screamer? Struggles a bit, but secretly loves every minute of it?'

Rek raced towards the vampire and drove the stake into his chest. Kaaliz made no attempt to move. The crowd inhaled, ready to cheer, but stopped when the vampire kept smiling. The stake felt as if it had hit rock. Rek pushed harder but the point couldn't penetrate the heart of the creature. Kaaliz swung a punch and Rek flew through the air, landing on the bonnet of his car and shattering the windscreen. His back ached and he grabbed it with both hands. Kaaliz pulled the stake from his chest and the crowd whispered in awed amazement as the wound on his chest closed in seconds. Kaaliz tossed the stake aside.

An arrow plunged into his chest where he had just removed the stake. He looked around and saw Rek by the open car door with a crossbow. Another arrow, and another. A dozen arrows in all entered Kaaliz's body. He laughed as he pulled them out, one by one, like they were splinters.

Rek pulled his sword from the back seat and ran at Kaaliz. He landed a lot of blows but the wounds healed instantly – no vampire could heal that quickly! Rek noticed that Kaaliz would block the blows heading for his neck with his arm. That meant his neck was still vulnerable. He could still kill him if he took his head off. Rek hacked away with all his strength but couldn't get a clear shot at the vampire's neck. Eventually he began to tire and Kaaliz took the sword from him and tossed it aside.

Rek threw a punch at Kaaliz's face. Kaaliz caught it and twisted his arm around behind his back then pushed him. Rek flew full speed into the side of his car. Before he had time to get his senses back, Kaaliz grabbed him by the collar and threw him into the air again. Rek's back hit the window of the house he had rescued the little girl from and shattered it. He fell forward into the garden and Kaaliz was on him again. Kaaliz picked him up and punched him. To his body. To his face. To his body again. Rek hadn't even the strength to hold his arms up for defence. Kaaliz dropped him to the ground. He took three running steps towards Rek and kicked him just as he got to his hands and knees. The impact sent Rek into the air again and back out onto the street. He fell awkwardly on his left side and pain shot through his back again.

Kaaliz grabbed him by the throat and lifted him up. Blood was dribbling from Rek's mouth. Kaaliz pulled him close. He closed his eyes and breathed in deeply. 'Your scent is intoxicating. Your fear, grief and guilt are like a marinade your body is soaked in. Your blood carries it in every drop.' Kaaliz opened his mouth and his incisors grew to full length. He leaned in slowly. He was going to enjoy this.

'Hey!' The mother stepped forward and wiped her tears away. 'You leave him alone.'

Kaaliz turned and laughed. 'What?'

The father whispered in the little blonde girl's ear then set her down. She pushed her way through the crowd and ran home. The father stepped forward. 'You heard her, leave him alone.'

The police woman lowered her arms and threw off her cap. She stepped forward.

'And you mortals are going to make me, are you?' Kaaliz smiled.

Throughout the crowd children ran backwards towards their homes. The adults stepped forward. The father looked behind and was emboldened by the support of his neighbours.

He took another step toward Kaaliz. 'We're not going to tolerate your kind anymore. You've walked among us too long. Too many of our loved are in their graves because of you and your kind. No more.' He turned to the crowd and shouted, 'No more!'

The crowd surged forward as one. Kaaliz was dumbfounded. What were they *doing*? He dropped Rek. Suddenly there were hands all around him. Scratching, punching, ripping at his skin. Some had rocks in their hands. Others had makeshift stakes. Some stabbed him with knives. The police officers shot him in the face at point blank range. Mortals were all over him. He tried to bite them but couldn't get close enough. There must have been half a dozen people twisting his head, presumably trying to break his neck. He tried to punch and kick but had no room to draw back his limbs, which were also being held.

Rek crawled back to the car and found his revolver. His whole body ached but he fought through it. He loaded one bullet into the chamber and closed it. He looked back at the mob. He could see Kaaliz's head and shoulders struggling above the heads of the others. He was trying to escape into the air. Rek rummaged around in the backpack and eventually found the small black, pill-sized object. He twisted it and the LED inside started flashing. He dropped it down the barrel, holding the gun vertically so it wouldn't fall out.

Rek got to his feet and pain shot through his legs and up his back. He ran into the crowd. Kaaliz was waist high above the heads of the mob now. He would soon be free. Rek pushed aside the men and women and made it to the centre of the fray just in time to push the barrel of the gun into Kaaliz's stomach and fire. The bullet wound repaired before his eyes. A few seconds later Kaaliz broke free and flew into the air.

He hovered a safe distance above the crowd and looked Rek in the eyes. Rek stared right back at him, unafraid despite his injuries. They were both thinking the same thing.

We'll meet again, real soon.

Kaaliz flew away and the crowd cheered and hugged each other. Rek managed to stumble back to the car and collapse in the driver's seat. His phone was ringing on the passenger's seat. He picked it up and looked at the screen.

SARAH CALLING.

He pressed the button and answered it.

section zero

Nicholl awoke with a splitting headache. She sat up and looked around. It was dark, but there was some light coming through the curtains from outside. She was on a bed. In a bedroom. She was lying on top of the covers still wearing the orange boiler suit. She swung her legs off the bed and planted her feet on the floor. She fell back onto the bed on her first attempt to stand. Whatever drugs they had shot her up with were still kicking around her system. She looked around the room. It was clean but impersonal, like a hotel room. A stack of photos lay on the bedside table. She reached out and lifted them. They were all pictures of her family and friends. These were the pictures that had hung on the walls of her flat, taken out of their frames. She set them back. She scratched her itching palm then looked at it. There was a circle of redness with a pin-prick in the centre. The same mark was on her other palm. She grinned briefly; the Daves were right. She felt in control of her equilibrium and tried standing up again. This time she managed it.

She walked to the window and pulled back the curtain. The light was coming from a circle of lampposts about a hundred yards away. She could see figures moving, talking and... drinking? There were houses beyond the circle, in fact, as far as she could see the houses formed a larger circle around this communal area in the centre. She heard laughter. Was this really Section Zero? She needed to talk to those people.

She was heading outside when she noticed the wardrobe door was ajar. She stopped and opened it. All her clothes were inside. She went to the drawers and found her underwear, her T-shirts, jeans, jumpers, they were all here, but there was something off about them. They didn't smell right. She looked around for her brown suede jacket and couldn't see it. She walked out of the bedroom and barely looked at the little living room she was crossing. All her jackets hung on pegs on the wall by the door. She grabbed the brown suede jacket and checked the cuff, no missing button. She checked the left lapel, no cigarette burn. These weren't her clothes. These were new versions of all her clothes. They really weren't taking any chances about smuggling transmitters into Section Zero. She kept hold of the jacket and walked back to the bedroom.

She rummaged through her underwear drawer and found her favourite bra; the one with the dodgy clasp, and found it didn't have a dodgy clasp. Where did they find this stuff? She'd searched everywhere for another bra like this one. She took off her boiler suit and got dressed in jeans and a T-shirt: an original 1987 T-shirt from Def Leppard's Hysteria tour. She had this T-shirt but it had been washed so many times the print was barely distinguishable from the background. This one was pristine, the colours rich and vibrant. She had scoured eBay for years trying to find a new one! If the Ministry ever got out of the vampire business they could make a killing in the collectable clothing market, she thought. She pulled on the suede jacket and looked at herself in the mirror. She was quite nervous about what sort of response she was going to get here. Was this like prison; rival gangs, watch your back, don't drop the soap, or was it more like that old TV show with Patrick McGoohan? *I am not a number, I'm a free man!* Or woman as the case may be. There was only one way to find out. She looked in the bottom of the wardrobe and found all her shoes; none of them had a single mark on the sole. She pulled on a pair of Nike trainers that they stopped making at least ten years ago and headed for the door.

It was a relatively mild night. Spring seemed to be bullying winter away early this year. People said it was the Greenhouse Effect. Nicholl just thought of the sunlight as a weapon and the more she saw of it, the better. She walked towards the sound of conversation and laughter. There must have been twenty people at least. And they *were* drinking. It looked like some suburban garden party that had run on into the wee hours. When she was about twenty feet away someone noticed her and a ripple of taps and touches went through the crowd to attract their attention. They all turned and watched her approach. Several of the men licked their lips. Away from the main group Nicholl saw the silhouette of a woman sitting by herself, smoking. The woman seemed to turn briefly and look at Nicholl, then returned to the business of smoking and staring off into space. Excited whispers were now passing among the crowd. An older man pushed his way to the front and began applauding. Everyone else joined in.

Nicholl stopped on the edge of the communal circle and forced a smile.

The older man stepped forward. He was skinny with a gaunt face, wearing a loose peasant blouse and jeans, and was walking in his bare feet. His hair was grey, long and rather unkempt. 'Welcome, Welcome! You *did* sleep a long time.'

'You knew I was coming?'

'Yes, we all get a notification when someone new is joining us. We like to throw a little party to welcome them and introduce them around. I am Joshua.'

'Nicholl.'

'Oh, we don't hold to that old Ministry dictate here. We're all on a first name basis in our little community.' He smiled widely, waiting for an answer.

'Amanda. Mandy.'

'Mandy, welcome.' The rest of the assembled crowd echoed his greeting. 'Would you permit me entrance into your comfort zone for the purposes of an informal, non-verbal display of greeting and love?'

'What?'

'Can I give you a hug?'

'Oh. Right. Well, er, sure.'

Joshua stepped forward and hugged her tightly. He smelled of hemp and smoke. The crowd applauded again. Joshua smiled and ushered Nicholl into the centre of the circle where chairs and tables of finger food and drink had been set out around a large, circular stone plinth.

Joshua made a sweeping gesture towards the tables and looked to Nicholl for approval.

'Very nice. Thank you. Nicest prison I've ever been to.'

Joshua laughed and shook his head. 'We don't think of this place as prison.' He offered her a glass of wine. Nicholl shook her head politely and lifted a bottle of beer from the table and popped the cap. She wasn't drinking anything that wasn't coming from a sealed container. 'Didn't you watch the Introductory DVD before you left your domicile?'

'No, I... I guess I just wanted to get out and have a look around.'

'Quite understandable. You really should have a look at it though; it does explain the basics of living here. How to order food, clothes, recreational activities.'

'Wait a minute. You're saying they give us whatever we ask for?'

'Yes.'

'What's the catch?'

Joshua smiled. 'The catch is obvious; you have to stay here and you can have no direct contact with the outside world.'

'So where are we?' She tried to make it sound like a throwaway sort of question.

'No one knows. We all have our theories of course, but no one really knows. My guess is up north. Somewhere off the coast of Scotland.'

'How do you figure?'

'The weather. Gets very cold in the winters. Although they say this greenhouse thing has messed up the Earth and its cycles. Winters are longer and more intense, summers are earlier and shorter. So maybe the south is just as cold as the north these days. You would know better than I. You'll be inundated with questions for the next few weeks, I'm afraid. Try to take it in good humour.'

'Questions about what?'

'The world. What's happening, what's changed, what's the same? We get newspapers here, but it's the little things that people seem to miss the most; that social domesticity that we all took for granted while we were in the other world.'

'How long have you been here, Joshua?'

'Thirty-seven years. First ever resident of Section Zero. I was alone for the first two years.'

'Jesus,' Nicholl whispered.

'Yes, it was tough.' He turned to her and smiled. 'I don't mind telling you, I had quite a few conversations with potatoes in those early days.'

Nicholl giggled and Joshua smiled. 'Can I ask what you did? Why you got sent here, or is that not the done thing?'

'No, no, it's fine. We all know everything about each other in here. You'll find when you live in this close proximity, you soon run out of things to talk about. What got you sent here? is always one of the first topics when someone new arrives. I tried to free a vampire from HQ. She was beautiful and I was in love, or thought I was. I was so young then.' Nicholl saw his eyes glass over. 'I think I would have let her bite me if it meant being with her. She said if I released her she wouldn't hurt anyone, but she killed four Ministry staff before the agents brought her down. I'll remember those four names until I die. I killed them. By my own selfish actions, I killed them. So they sent me here. I think I got off lightly.' He forced a smile and rubbed his eyes. 'And what about…?'

'Aren't there any guards here?'

'You're thinking about escaping.' He gave a thin smile and nodded. Nicholl gave him a neutral look. 'Which direction are you going to go?'

'What do you mean?'

'This island is one point three miles across at its widest and two point three miles at its longest. I walk all the way around it every day, and even on the clearest summer day, I can't see land in any direction. So if you're thinking of swimming…'

'Are you saying there are no guards?'

'I've only seen them twice. Last time was a few years ago. This fella we had here. He was some kind of engineer or designer for the Ministry but in his youth he had won several awards for kite design. He built a glider in secret.' He pointed past the smoking girl towards the cliff edge. 'Came out one morning ready to launch himself off there. They came out and stopped him.'

'Where'd they come from?'

Joshua nodded his head at the plinth.

'That opens?'

'Lowers. That's where we get all our deliveries. Food, clothing, games, whatever. There's a little computer in your living room, you just type in there whatever you want and in a day or two you'll find it sitting on the plinth. It lowers down, they set the stuff on it and raise it up again. That day Ted tried to escape they raised themselves up, Tasered him, burnt his glider and lowered themselves down again. Never said a word to any of us.'

'So they're under us,' Nicholl said, almost to herself. 'And they can see what we're up to, so they must have…'

'Cameras, yes,' Joshua nodded. 'Dotted all over the island.'
'What about the living quarters?'
'No.'
'How can you be sure?'
'That's where Ted built his glider.'
'Maybe after his attempt they installed them.'
'When? While we were away on our holidays?'
Nicholl nodded and smiled. Good point. 'How many of them were there?'
'Two.'
Nicholl thought it through. Two, plus they'd need at least another one in the control room to bring the plinth down again. There could be as little as three guards on this island. 'How do they bring these deliveries in?'
'By boat, at night. You can hear it sometimes. No running lights so you can't see what direction it comes from or leaves in. Probably how they change the personnel down there as well when their shift is over.' Joshua could see the cogs moving behind Nicholl's eyes. 'You thinking about taking the boat?'
'Been tried?'
'Many times. It *is* the most obvious escape route.'
'No one ever managed it?'
Joshua shook his head. 'You can try it if you wish, most of us have, even me.'
'And what happens?'
'You get close, then you wake up the next morning back in your domicile with a tranquillizer dart hangover. And your computer won't let you order anything for two weeks afterwards.'
'*You've* tried to escape?'
'Why does that surprise you?'
'I... well, I know I just met you, but you seem pretty settled here.'
'Even a cage with all the luxuries this one has is still a cage.'
'Haven't you monopolised our new inmate long enough, Joshua?'
Joshua turned and smiled. 'Mandy, may I introduce the island's top chef, Donna.' Nicholl shook her hand. 'She's the one you go to when you get tired of microwave food.' Donna

was an attractive woman with long, black hair and a curvy figure.

'I'm in number twenty-two. Drop by anytime.' She still had hold of Nicholl's hand. Nicholl noticed a hungry look Rek sometimes got after a few drinks. She removed her hand as politely as possible.

'I'm in... Oh, I didn't look when I left the house.'

'You're in number six,' Joshua said.

'Right.'

'Twenty-two is more like the island's restaurant. Donna's making you a welcome dinner tomorrow. We'll all be there. About one o'clock, Donna?' She nodded to Joshua.

'Come on, then,' Donna said. 'Let me give you the full SP on this place.' She put her arm around Nicholl's waist and led her away. Nicholl waved to Joshua over her shoulder.

'You were talking to Joshua about escaping.' Donna smiled to herself. 'I know you'll have to discover this for yourself, but there really is no way off the island. The sooner you accept that, the sooner you'll settle here.'

'Haven't you ever tried to escape?'

'Of course I have. And I had a lot more inventive ideas than stealing the supply boat.'

Nicholl was interested. 'Like what?'

'I tried overdosing once. I wasn't trying to kill myself; I just thought they'd take me to a hospital.'

'They didn't?'

Donna shook her head. 'I did it right there in the communal circle, too, so they definitely saw me. Joshua eventually made me vomit and I was OK after a few days' rest.'

'So in a genuine medical emergency they just leave us to die?'

'Fifty domiciles on this island and they never get full. That's why. There's a diagnostic program on the computer in your living room and some of the people here have some medical background. If you can figure out what you have, you can order the drugs for it, but if you can't, you roll the dice. I saw a guy called Ted collapse and die in the communal circle. Heart-attack. No-one came out of the plinth to save him.'

Ted. The guy who had built the glider.

'We put his body back in his domicile and it was gone the next day.'

'How many are here at the moment?'

'Your arrival brings our population to thirty-two.'

Nicholl let it sink in for a moment, then asked, 'What else have you tried? To escape, I mean.'

'Getting pregnant. I figured they wouldn't let a baby grow up on the island, so I started having unprotected sex with everyone, as often as possible.'

'But you didn't get pregnant?'

'No one on the island does and no one uses protection. I thought they were putting something in the water to start with, so I only drank bottled stuff for six months. Still nothing. I don't know what they did, or are doing, to us, but it works.' She gave Nicholl a gentle nudge. 'Still, I keep trying.' She smiled and winked.

Donna kept a discreet distance from the crowd but they were still close enough for her to pick out individual faces and give them scores.

'Bosco. What an asshole. Still, if you ever just want a quick – and I do mean quick – shag with no questions asked, he's your man. The guy's a walking hard-on. Four out of ten; all for enthusiasm, none for technique.' Nicholl looked at the moustachioed man with his shirt open halfway down his chest. He saw her look, wiggled his tongue and winked at her.

'Now, Ralph, on the other hand, is all about the technique, but he is somewhat lacking in confidence and does tend to burst into tears when he comes.' Ralph glanced at Nicholl then blushed and turned away so quickly he toppled a table of hors d'oeuvres.

Nicholl winced. 'He cries?'

'Not out of dismay, out of... gratitude, I think.' Donna shrugged at Nicholl in a I-just-work-here kind of way. 'It's the quiet ones you have to watch, though. See that guy reading by the plinth?' Nicholl looked over and saw an older man, engrossed in a novel. 'That's Rex Stevens. Did Joshua tell you about him? He was going to expose all the Ministry's secrets in a book he wrote; that's what got him sent here. He writes horror novels now and gets special dispensation to send them out into the world. He uses the pen-name... Oh, I won't spoil it; I'll let him tell you. But you *will* have heard of him. So, if you want a scary story or an orgasm, he's the man to see. He makes me squeal in three octaves. Like Mariah Carey or something. Every time. I don't know how he does it.'

Nicholl didn't bother to ask if he made her squeal with fright or delight.

'Oh, you'll end up screwing them all, I imagine. We all have. Even an asshole like Bosco, after a while you begin to wonder if you're missing anything. Sometimes I do him just to kill the boredom.'

'You've slept with everyone here? Even Joshua?'

'Joshua's not half bad since he started on Viagra. I'd give him a solid six out of ten.' Donna looked at Nicholl's puzzled face. 'Hey, I'm not a slut! It's not like I can go bar-hopping and find some stock-broker with a Porsche. What you see is what you've got to choose from. So you may as well try before you buy.'

'Right. That seems fair.'

Donna stepped closer and lowered her voice. 'You might find yourself trying a lot of things you never tried before after you've been here a while.' She raised her hand and gently stroked it across Nicholl's cheek, pushing a strand of hair behind her ear.

Nicholl smiled and stepped back. 'OK.' Nicholl looked behind her and saw the crowd was breaking up and heading back to their living quarters. Some alone, some had paired off. She turned back and saw Donna blow her a kiss and walk off towards domicile twenty-two.

Nicholl walked back across the circle. She stopped and looked at the plinth for a while but could see no panels or wiring she could mess with. She was alone when she looked up again. She started to walk back to her domicile. She noticed an orange speck of light in the darkness. The smoking girl was still up. Nicholl knew she was way too pumped up to sleep, so she wandered over to the girl.

'Hi, I'm Mandy.'

'They don't talk to me. If you want to stay tight with them, you'd best go back to your domicile.' The girl pulled her coat and scarf tighter around her.

Nicholl sat down. 'It's got a bit chilly, hasn't it?' She looked at the girl now, head on. She was beautiful. Long, brown hair, piercing blue eyes and voluptuous in all the right places. 'I didn't catch your name,' Nicholl persisted.

The girl smiled. 'It's Eileen. Eileen Brown.'

'How long have you been here?'

'Four months.'

'Trouble making friends?'

Eileen smiled, shook her head and took another drag on her cigarette.

'Everyone else I've spoken to has tried escaping. You tried it yet?'

Eileen looked off across the dark waters. 'There's only one way you leave here. Feet first in a body bag. I'm starting to think that maybe it isn't such a bad idea.'

Nicholl looked down, unsure of what to say. She saw a photograph clutched in Eileen's hand. 'What's the photo?'

Eileen glanced down then handed it to Nicholl. It was a picture of two children, a girl and boy. They were holding ice-creams and seemed to be trying to push each other out of shot while laughing. 'Yours?'

Eileen nodded.

'I guess they don't allow you to...'

'No phone calls, no letters, no emails. I don't even know what they've told them. Probably that I'm dead, right? That would be the logical thing to tell them since I'll never see them again.'

'How old are they?'

'Geraldine's ten and Luis is eight.' Eileen sniffed back the tears and changed the subject. 'I know you.'

'You do?'

'We've never met, but everyone always talked about you at HQ. Never thought you'd end up here.'

Nicholl said nothing. Eileen flicked her cigarette into the ocean and got to her feet. Nicholl got up and walked back with her to the domiciles.

They stopped at number twelve. 'This is me.'

Nicholl nodded as Eileen opened the door.

'You're in...'

'Number six, I know. The irony isn't lost on me.'

Eileen smiled.

The door was just about to close when Nicholl said, 'Hey.' Eileen paused. 'That escape plan of yours, don't try it just yet. Give me a day or two, I might come up with something better.' She gave her a smile and walked away. Eileen looked puzzled, but also, for the first time since she got here, hopeful. If anyone could escape from Section Zero it was Agent Nicholl.

Nicholl got back into her domicile and went straight to the bathroom. A few minutes later the toilet flushed and she was washing the pill-sized device in the sink. 'The things I have to do to save the world,' she mumbled under her breath. When it was clean she got a sharp knife from the kitchen and cut the rubber cover off. She took the metal and plastic device from its casing and twisted it. An LED started pulsing inside it. She slipped the device into her ear.

'Hey, you guys hear me?'

There was a few seconds of ominous silence, then, 'Yeah, we're here.' It was one of the Daves.

'You got a GPS location on me yet?'

'Just zooming in now.' The seconds ticked by slowly.

'You were right by the way,' Nicholl said, looking at the circular burns on her palms. 'They did electrocute me while I was unconscious.'

She heard the other Dave in the background say, 'See, the rubber coating *was* necessary.'

Nicholl smiled.

'OK,' Dave said slowly. Nicholl could hear the rapid clicking of a keyboard. 'We've got you... that's weird.'

'What?'

'Well, according to the maps online, there's no island where you're standing.'

For a few seconds Nicholl panicked. The Ministry had discovered her transmitter and found a way to re-route the signal. Her throat went dry. Was she really going to be stuck here for the rest of her life like everyone else?

'Wait a second.' It was Chloe's voice. 'I've got an old Atlas here from the 1950s and your island's in it. Týndi Island. The Ministry must have erased it from all modern maps.'

'Where am I?'

Dave spoke again. 'You're kind of halfway between Ireland and Iceland, but over to the left a bit.'
'Did everything go as planned at your end?' Chloe asked.
'Oh, yeah,' Nicholl said. 'I think we've found our warriors.'

pale riders

Hal was almost too ashamed to go back to the house. He was burned and his clothes were soaking after an impromptu dip in the ocean to extinguish himself. Added to which, he had come back without the thing the Master had sent him for. He wasn't going to like that one bit. Hal thought back to the guy the Master had tortured for three years and a shiver went up his already cold spine.

He closed the door and looked into the darkness of the living room. He couldn't see anything or hear anything, but then he never could.

'Hello?' There was no reply. Hal turned to go upstairs and find a change of clothes.

'You have failed me.' The voice cut through the dark like a laser.

Hal swallowed hard. 'I couldn't touch it. The cardboard tube. The priest, dirty scumbag, carpenter-follower that he was, must have worked some mojo on it. Plus, they sent someone for it, too. The Ministry. They got it. And Jacqui, she was no fuckin' help at all. She...'

'Jacqui is dead.'

Hal began to seriously worry now. The Master had some kind of special affection for Jacqui. She was a child in a woman's body and he had some kind of paternal need to protect her. Was Hal going to be blamed for Jacqui's death too? Tortured for three years. He might even try to break his record. Maybe he'd manage five years this time, or ten.

'You saw her die?' Hal asked.

'I felt her presence disappear. I have a connection with all my children, even you.'

Hal knew the Master could sense his guilt; he could tell by the tone of the silence. Why the hell was he feeling guilty? *He* hadn't killed her.

'Your anxiety is misplaced.'

He *had* been reading Hal's mind. Hal briefly thought of making himself a hat out of tinfoil. Isn't that what the crazies in Sycamore Acres do to stop aliens reading their brains? He was so scared that the words the Master had said hadn't been processed in his brain for what they actually meant. He replayed them and this time he understood, and hoped he was telling the truth.

'I have no reason to lie.' His voice had moved in the darkness again. 'I mourn Jacqui's passing like I would mourn any of my children, including you, Harold, should a stake find you. I know you were not responsible for her death. Whoever was will pay for what they have done. That I guarantee you.'

Hal took a deep breath and tried to be brave. 'What about that cardboard tube? What was in it?'

'That I don't know. I only sensed its importance to the Nazarene's slave who carried it. His mind was filled with vengeance and he regarded that cardboard tube as a mighty weapon.'

'You could read his mind, even before he was in the country?' Hal asked.

'His presence created a ripple that I sensed. Like a stone dropped in a lake, it's quite easy to trace the ripples back to their source.'

'Can I do that?'

The voice had moved again. 'Maybe you'll develop the talent if you live as long as me. Anyway, we will soon see how the mortals use this weapon. The riders have come. It was prophesied that they would be here when the world of darkness began. There is no doubt. The time is at hand.' There was excitement in the usually flat voice. 'Long have I waited for this season of evil.'

Hal wanted to ask. He wanted to know how old the Master was. What had he seen in his time? World War I? Maybe he saw Shakespeare's plays performed while the ink was still wet on the parchment. Shit, maybe he was even a day-labourer at Stonehenge. The Master must have known what he was thinking but didn't answer. Hal took that as a sign that he shouldn't ask. 'I'm going to go upstairs and change.'

The darkness said nothing. Hal went upstairs.

There were a lot of clothes in the house. All the vampires who had used this house over the years had one thing in common: they had all fed on tourists. And with tourists came luggage (and cash). Most of the clothes were horrible, garish shirts, unbecoming of a vampire looking to establish an image at first sight. Still, after a fair amount of rummaging, Hal found himself a black suit and black shirt that were a passable fit. He discarded his burned and sodden clothes on the floor and was about to leave when he went back to the mound of rags.

He looked behind himself, ashamed of his actions. He found the photo of him and Sarah. He took it out of his pocket gently so it wouldn't fall apart. It was soaked through and flopped in his fingers.

He meant to spend eternity with her and one way or another, it was going to happen. Sure, she had set him on fire earlier that night, but all good couples fought; it showed there was passion in the relationship. Maybe when vampires overran the Earth she would feel differently about him. Maybe if she *were* a vampire she would feel differently.

Hal smiled and put the photo into his dry pocket.

Tom sat in the huge house alone. Lynda had gone with Sarah to find Rek. With Lynda being married to a doctor she had picked up enough knowledge over the years to serve as a good field medic. He had shared a coffee with Lynda earlier. He liked her. Not like he liked Sarah, but there was definitely a connection between them. Hollywood folk would call it chemistry maybe. She was easy to be around and had a lot of great stories.

His mum, one of the Daves and Chloe had gone to get Agent Nicholl back from Section Zero. The other Dave had gone to Mussenden Temple. After deciphering the architect's name on the blueprints as Michael Shananhan, it didn't take long on the Internet to match the drawings to the local landmark. The Daves had been very excited about what they thought they had found, but neither of them wanted to say. They had even rock-paper-scissored for who would get to go to the temple. It gave Tom hope. If the Daves' excitement wasn't misplaced, maybe, just maybe, they might win this thing after all.

They all had their assignments. They were all out there being brave. And he was sitting here… twiddling his thumbs. He wondered if his mum had secretly spoken to the others and arranged this little exclusion to keep him safe. Chloe had said they were leaving him behind to guard The Fist of Merlin. Even though it was locked in her safe she said she still wanted an extra layer of security should someone come looking for it. She said that was why their strongest warrior had to stay and protect it. As Tom replayed the conversation in his head now he was amazed he had fallen for such an obvious line of bullshit.

The phone rang. Tom lifted it quickly; expecting some of the others needed his help.

'Hello?'

'Yes. Chloe knight, please,' the voice said impatiently.

'She's not here at the minute,' Tom said. 'Can I take a message?' Now he really felt useless. Everyone else was out there fighting the forces of evil and he was at home doing the admin.

'Uh… I don't… I mean, are you…?'

'Yes, I'm Ministry if that's what you're asking.' It would take too long to explain what he really was, and Tom wasn't even sure he knew himself.

'OK. This is Portrush Police Station. We've got a serious situation at Kelly's.'

'The nightclub?'

'Yeah. Four… of *them*…'

'Vampires?'

'Yeah. Four of them showed up on Harleys, now they've locked the place down. We can't get in, but we're getting hundreds of phone calls from the people trapped inside. They're killing them all. We don't know what to do!' The young officer sounded almost hysterical, but he calmed himself down with several deep breaths before adding in a pleading whisper, 'My younger sister's in there.'

Tom grabbed his sword. 'Sit tight. I'm on my way.'

He slammed the phone down and ran out of Chloe's house, slamming the door behind him.

There was blood on the dancefloor.

Lance was spinning doughnuts in the crimson pool. Behind his bike he was trailing a clubber who he had decided was way too old to be dressed the way he was. Lance kept a three-pronged abseiling hook for such occasions. He hooked it through the clubbers neck and out through his mouth, then dragged him around by it. He'd once used it to drag an unhelpful gas station attendant all the way across the Nevada desert.

The burning rubber of his Harley's back tyre was mixing with the smell of searing blood, exhaust fumes and the decomposing dead to create a nauseating smell. His three companions watched and laughed while the captives huddled against the walls. Some were throwing-up from the noxious fumes in the confined space. Lance rode off the dancefloor, parked his Harley by the bar and killed the engine. He unhooked the corpse and tossed it aside.

'Damn, D, you should try that, man,' Lance said, between swigs of whiskey. 'Need to re-wet the floor though; I think I done dried it all up.' Lance's drawl matched his slovenly appearance. Unlike most vampires, he was not vain in the slightest and was proud of the fact that he hadn't changed his clothes or bathed in forty-seven years. The result being that even if you didn't have a supernatural sense of smell, you caught his scent from thirty feet away.

'Maybe later. We need to get organized first, afore sun-up.' D (or Big D as he was more widely known) stood up and stretched. He looked good in his black leathers and his muscular frame gave him an aura of solidity; like punching him would be like punching granite, which is why few ever tried. He was the leader of this gang and no-one ever challenged his authority. He looked to the remaining members of his gang. 'Warren, Minnie, separate the cattle.' He sat back down and returned to his drink.

There were fresh screams as Warren and Minnie approached the clubbers in their short dresses and best shirts. Their make-up ran with tears now, their hair gel sweating down their cheeks.

Warren approached the women, most of whom looked too young to meet the eighteen year age limit imposed by the club. He was an intimidating figure; six foot five, his hair shaved short and wearing a camouflage jacket. He had broad shoulders and an upper torso that was about as close as evolution could get to creating a living battering ram. He had been a soldier in his mortal life but not guns, bombs or even knives, had given him the killing intimacy of biting. The sensation of drinking someone else's life-force and making it his own was unique and incomparable. He still employed some of the more sadistic torture techniques he had learned in the army, but these days they were not to obtain information; they were just for fun.

Minnie was the only female in the group, though her femininity was not immediately apparent. She had a flat chest and no ass to speak of. She was thin, painfully thin. The eating disorders she had had in her mortal life had carried over to her vampiric existence. She ate just enough blood to keep herself alive and no more. Her appearance had suffered because of it. Not in *her* eyes though. She still believed what the magazines told her: thinner was better. But she had taken this belief to extremes that would have killed any mortal woman. Her skin hugged her skeleton tightly. When naked she could see almost every bone in her body and in *her* eyes this was the ideal she had been trying to achieve her whole mortal life. Back in the 1980s she had cut herself open and removed her two bottom ribs in an attempt to make her stomach flatter and her already tiny waist even smaller. As a consequence she now had trouble finding any clothes to fit her. She mostly wore children's clothes, but even then she needed a belt to hold the trousers up. Her face was as close to looking like a skull and still living as anyone had ever got. Her cheeks were sucked in, her eyes set deep in their sockets. She imagined herself (and her protruding cheekbones) the envy of every female who looked at her. Despite her emaciated appearance she was still stronger than any human, though probably weaker than any other vampire.

Big D and Lance watched from the bar, laughing as Warren and Minnie threw unworthy specimens over their shoulders like they were emptying a sock drawer. They herded the worthy into the SYNK, a smaller room where people who didn't like the constant thump-thump-thump of dance music could go and listen to live music performed by a real band.

The band was still on stage – as per Lance's instructions – when Warren and Minnie brought the worthy in. Lance had spared the band when the vampires had initially taken the club because they did a passable rendition of *Sweet Home Alabama*. Since then, the guitarist had effusively thanked the bass player for talking him into learning the Lynyrd Skynyrd classic and kept his fingers firmly on the D chord, ready to crank it out again at a moment's notice.

The club's DJ had not been so lucky. When Lance grilled him on classic rock trivia and found his knowledge severely lacking he had become the main source of the red stain on the dancefloor. In Lance's opinion, someone who didn't know their Creedence from their Jefferson Airplane had no right wasting oxygen other people could be using.

There were maybe a hundred people in the SYNK (including the band who were poised like a music video on pause, waiting for a cue to resume playing) when Warren and Minnie were finished driving the worthy inside. They stood at the doors looking hungrily at the assembled mortals who were quietly crying and holding each other. Big D walked up behind his two companions and put a hand on each of their shoulders, parting them and taking a few steps inside the SYNK.

'You can all relax,' Big D shouted.

The guitarist played the first few notes of *Sweet Home Alabama* then stopped. He mouthed the word sorry at Big D and then released his tensed hand from the fretboard and stretched it.

'You're the lucky ones,' Big D continued. 'Those ones we left in there, they're the ones who should be worrying. We're going to eat them.'

The crowd gasped as one and fresh tears broke out from many of the girls.

'But you lot, you're going to live. And live. And live.' He took another couple of steps inside and lifted someone's drink from the bar. 'You see, things is going to change. Mankind's time is up. You've had your shot and you've fucked it up. So now it's our turn. In twenty-four hours vampires will take ownership of this planet and it all starts right here. Tell 'em what the Corpora says, Minnie.'

Minnie stepped forward. She knew the passage by heart. She spoke loudly. 'A door opened by grief will loose the children of the new age. And the blood of mankind shall be the milk of their infancy.' Minnie bowed and stepped back again.

Big D had the floor again. 'You're going to be the first children of the new age. You may think us monsters now, but I guarantee you, in a week, you'll be thanking us.'

Big D watched the assembled crowd. The girls quivered, crying. Some of them collapsed to the ground. Boyfriends held tightly to their girlfriends. Some of the braver males looked around the windowless room for any chance of escape.

'There's nowhere to go. And no-one can save you,' Big D shouted triumphantly. 'This is our world now!' A strong but familiar smell stopped him from continuing his speech. He sniffed the air. Familiar, yes, but there was something different about it, too. He couldn't quite place it.

Something rolled along the floor and hit the back of Big D's ankles. He looked down behind him and saw Lance's head (looking very surprised) age a few hundred years in a matter of seconds. He looked back into the main dancefloor, where Warren and Minnie were already staring and saw Tom standing with his sword pointing at the ground after a successful decapitation. Tom raised his head and looked into the furious eyes of Big D.

Warren looked around. The room was empty. Where were all the clubbers they were going to eat? Where were the unworthy?

Big D pushed his rage deep down inside and spoke to the child who stood before him in a more controlled tone. 'This world is ours, boy. You gots balls but you're no match for us.'

Tom drew his sword behind him and adjusted his stance to attack. 'Guess again, asshole.'

The three vampires charged at him.

Tom needed to take them one at a time. He grabbed the skinny one around the throat and swirled her behind him. She flew into the air and slammed into the back wall of the club in a classic Wile E. Coyote pose. Tom spun around and readied himself for the other two. The one in the army jacket put a hand to the other's chest and said, 'You mind if I have this dance, D?'

The bigger vampire smiled and took a few steps back. 'Be my guest, only leave something for me.'

'I make no promises,' Warren said with a smile. He drew out a large hunting knife and threw it from hand to hand, spinning it occasionally around his fingers.

Tom held his sword up to the circling vampire.

'You gonna put your eye out with that, boy. Ain't got much 'sperience, have you? I's surprised you's pointing the right end at me if truth be told.' He laughed to himself. Tom kept his gaze concentrated on the vampire. The taunts wouldn't distract him. Warren lurched forward with his blade at incredible speed. Tom parried and brought his blade down hard towards the vampire's neck. Warren jumped back quickly... but not quickly enough. He took a couple of steps back and put a hand up to his bleeding face, just to confirm what he was seeing on the ground was real.

They both looked down at Warren's nose, lying on the dancefloor.

Tom couldn't resist. 'That's to spite your face.'

'Motherfucker!' His voice sounded different without a nose. He turned to his leader, and Tom thought he detected a noticeable shift in the confidence of the leather-clad biker. 'He cut off my fuckin' nose, D!' Warren threw down his knife and charged at Tom, all training and tactics forgotten in blind hatred. Tom leapt over his head and landed behind him. Before Warren could turn Tom had swung his sword and a second head was rolling across the floor.

Tom turned to the one they called D. 'Your turn.'

The skinny vampire jumped on Tom's back and locked her arms around his neck like a noose. Tom had to drop his sword to stop her from biting him. He ran backwards with her and slammed her into a bar. She released for a second but then tightened her grip again. Tom grabbed a bottle of whiskey from the bar and smashed it in her face. All he needed now was a match. He looked for the ashtrays on the bar and saw none.

Shit. Fucking smoking ban!

She wrapped her bony legs around his waist and squeezed. His lungs constricted, he could only take shallow breaths. He would lose consciousness soon and then it would be all over. He imagined kissing Sarah. Tom could feel the vampire's bones pressing into his flesh. He looked around for anything he could use as a weapon. There was nothing. The vampire's bones ground into him like iron railings. He had an idea. There were three steps down to the dancefloor. He had one chance.

He launched himself at the steps and turned mid-air. He fell hard on top of the vampire. She loosened her grip with the pain and Tom used that second to drive his elbow as hard as he could into her left ribs. He heard a loud snap and she released him. Tom spun around, on top of her now and saw the broken rib sticking up under her skin like morning glory under a duvet. He grabbed the rib, twisted it, directed it towards her heart and then slammed it with the heel of his hand.

She screamed and then shrivelled to a state not unlike her living appearance. Tom stood up and faced Big D. His sword was lying at the vampire's feet. Big D kicked it behind him, out of reach.

'What's say we do this without weapons?' Without waiting for an answer the vampire charged at Tom. Tom countered by throwing himself at the vampire, hitting him in the chest with both feet. Tom dropped to the ground. The vampire was unhurt and unmoved. Tom felt like he'd just tried to punch out a building. He scrambled backwards and got to his feet.

'You can have that one for free. Next 'un 'll cost you.'

Tom punched the vampire as hard as he could in the face. Big D swiped his arm like he was annoyed at a fly. Tom went careening through the air and smashed into the bottles behind the bar. He fell to the ground followed closely by a rain of spirits and glass.

'You see, you'll never beat us 'cause we're stronger,' Big D said, taking off his jacket and hanging it over the nearest chair. 'That Darwin guy, he'd be proud of us. Survival of the fittest n' all. Humans… you're just the modern dinosaurs. Time to step aside and let someone else have a go at being top o' the food chain.'

Big D heard a scuttling on the other side of the room. He walked over and peered behind the bar he had thrown Tom at: he wasn't there.

Big D took a deep breath and addressed the room. 'You ain't gonna makes me play hide n' go seek with your dumb ass, are you boy? Shit, I thought you had balls as big as watermelons.'

Big D walked slowly around the whole perimeter of the club, checking anywhere big enough to conceal one scared mortal. He couldn't find him. He walked back over to the SYNK and looked in. Everyone took a step back. The guitarist on stage started playing *Sweet Home Alabama* until Big D waved him to stop.

Big D walked out again and then it came to him. 'Of course! Where else would someone who's shitting himself go!'

Big D walked out into the lobby and into the toilets. He checked all the cubicles and found nothing. He did the same in the ladies'. When he stepped back out into the lobby again, he heard the sound of a Harley coming to life. He stared across the large lobby into the dancefloor and saw a single headlight come on. Tom revved the bike.

'You can knock me down as many times as you want, sonny. I'll still get up. 'Cause I'm stronger, see? An' I will always be.'

'Maybe,' Tom whispered to himself. 'But I'm smarter.' Tom dropped the bike into gear and raced towards the vampire. Big D opened his arms to brace himself for the impact. At the last second, Tom changed course and flew past Big D's left shoulder leaving only a three-pronged hook in his wake.

The vampire saw it only a fraction of a second before it ripped into his neck and then jerked him backwards. Tom twisted down on the throttle and aimed for the doors.

The Harley smashed through into the dawn light dragging six feet of kicking and screaming flames behind it. The policemen all drew their guns and took cover behind their cars as Tom skidded to a stop in the middle of the car park. A few seconds later the shape stopped twitching, but continued to burn. They all let it.

Tom got off the bike. The assembled clubbers that he had already evacuated through the fire door in the VIP lounge (his entry point) applauded and cheered loudly. Police officers waited for him to give them the nod before they ran in and rescued the hostages in the SYNK.

One of the senior officers brought him his sword back and thanked him.

Tom had run from Chloe's place, which was only a mile from the nightclub, but he didn't fancy walking back after his night out. He ushered the policeman closer and said, 'This Harley belonged to one of them. I don't suppose...'

The policeman looked back at the club and then turned and smiled. 'I don't think they'll be needing it. Godspeed to you, son.'

Tom smiled and nodded his appreciation. He unhooked the tow-line from the back of the Harley, brought it to life and raced out of the car park.

the last day

Kaaliz got into the elevator and descended towards Project Redbook only minutes before dawn. His anger still raged that the humans had attacked him. The thought of their hands touching him made him sick. He had tried to take out his frustrations on a couple of early-morning joggers on the way home. He had fed from them and then ripped them limb from limb, but instead of sating his anger, killing them had just energized him even more. He felt like a human might if they had just downed several dozen caffeine drinks in a matter of seconds. He was buzzed. Full of energy and ready to fight. And now he had to spend the next few hours by himself without even a woman to…

Ping!

The doors opened and the Che'al charged at him. He'd forgotten that he'd set one of them free. He dived into the air, avoiding its grasp by millimetres. He waited on the ceiling as the Che'al mindlessly jumped up trying to catch him. He'd seen this act before and he didn't fancy spending all day watching this thing do some half-assed Riverdance below him.

He felt so powerful, so invincible.

He flew at her at full speed and began landing punches faster than even he believed he was capable. The Che'al could do nothing but put up its arms and try to fend off the attack, but Kaaliz was too quick. He must have easily landed hundreds of punches in just a few minutes. It was only when his hands started to hurt from pounding the coarse skin of the Che'al that he slowed down. The Che'al grabbed him around the throat and tried to unscrew his head. There was no tactic in the creature's assault; it was just pure, blind animal rage. Kaaliz was food and the only way the Che'al was going to be able to eat him was if he stopped moving. Its arms swung at him, knocking him off-balance. Kaaliz twisted himself from its grip and kicked it hard under the chin. It dropped onto its back and Kaaliz grabbed its cowboy boots.

Kaaliz laughed. 'Eenie meanie minie mo…' He started spinning the Che'al. It was totally confused by the rotating world. It grunted in primal fear. 'Catch a Che'al by the toes,' Kaaliz continued. He increased his speed. There was now just a five-foot blur moving around Kaaliz's waist, like the rings of Saturn. The Che'al's cries became more panicked. 'If it screams, let it go.' Kaaliz released his grip on the cowboy boots and the Che'al shot across the room and smashed head-first into a brick wall. It fell to the ground. Blood leaked from its skull. It wasn't moving. Kaaliz looked at it with contempt. 'Eenie meanie minie mo,' he concluded.

Kaaliz walked over and grabbed it by the heavily embroidered collar. He could sense it was still breathing. Sin had said these things would be hard to kill. Kaaliz dragged it across the floor. He didn't want to have to worry about this thing attacking him while he slept. He took it to the *Raiders* room. It was the only room that was air-locked with a thick steel door. He guessed it wouldn't be able to escape. He spun the circular release on the door then opened the latch. Like a bank vault, the door slowly swung open with a sigh as air rushed in.

Kaaliz threw the Che'al inside and heard it make a faint groan as it hit he floor. He looked around and could hear Sin's voice in his head. He closed his eyes.

'Wow, look at this place. It must be three or four hundred yards long. I'll bet it runs the whole length of the reservoir above.'

His eyes still closed. 'It's just a big, empty room, Sin.'

'No way, baby. This is no ordinary room. Look at these sheets scattered on the floor. Everything's blacked-out but the pro-nouns. This is where the army stored all their secret stuff I'll bet. This is their Raiders room.'

Whispered tenderly. 'Their what?'

'At the end of Raiders of the Lost Ark, the place where they store the ark. This is the British equivalent. Boy, I'd have liked to have a rummage around here when this place was full. I wonder where they moved everything to.'

'I daresay you could find out with your computer.'

'I daresay I could.' They kiss. *'There'll be time for everything later.'* She rubs the crotch of his trousers. *'Except this.'* She smiles. *'This needs delivered immediately.'* They drop to the floor of the *Raiders* room and give themselves completely to one another.

The Che'al grunts, snapping Kaaliz from his reverie. He considers killing it just for disturbing him, but refrains. He feels his cheek and finds a tear. He scoops it off with his middle finger and holds it before him. He curls his fingers and the tear runs into his palm. He closes his fist tightly around it. He pushes the rage deep into his stomach.

He gives the stirring Che'al one more look before leaving and locking the door behind him.

He goes into the Overnight Room and lies on the bottom bunk. He tries to sleep but cannot. He feels exposed. So much space. Ten years buried with a quarter-of-an-inch's wiggle room will make you agoraphobic apparently. He goes to the filing cabinet. He rips out the drawers, lies on the floor and covers himself with the metal shell. He feels safe now and sleep finds him quickly.

Melanie arrived for work that morning and found yellow police tape cordoning off the Bishop's Gate. Her key wouldn't work in the lock. She got back in her car and drove around to the Lion's Gate entrance. It was open. Her mouth dropped in disbelief. Vans and lorries were driving up towards Mussenden Temple and delivering what looked like building supplies. There were workmen. She ran towards the temple.

'Hey! Who's in charge here?'

Dave walked over and shook her hand. He saw her National Trust fleece and knew the same story he had given the early morning dog-walkers wasn't going to work here. 'Hi there. My name's Dave and you are?'

'Melanie. What the hell are you doing here?'

Dave looked shocked. 'What, you didn't get the memo?'

'What memo?'

One of the workmen ran over to them. 'Hey, Dave, we canny get that back wunduh oot. Fuckin' things built right on the edge. There's nay way to get behin it.'

Dave looked at Melanie. 'Any idea how they got the window fitted in the first place?'

'The cliff edge used to be a hundred yards away; it's erosion over the years that brought it right to the back of the temple. The Trust had it underpinned so the temple wouldn't fall off the cliff.'

Dave nodded and smiled to Melanie. 'Right. Well. You learn something new every day.' He turned to his workman and put his hand to his mouth to shield it from Melanie. 'Just smash it and put the other one in from the inside.' The workman ran off.

Melanie grabbed Dave's arm. '*What* did you just tell him to do?'

'Look, why don't you take the day off?'

'I am not moving from here until I make damn sure you have permission to be doing this.'

'OK, OK.' Dave put his hands up and took a deep breath. 'You're right. We don't have permission to be doing this.'

A look of total terror crossed Melanie's face. 'Are you insane? That's a Grade 1 listed building! Stop them, stop them right now.' Melanie started to run towards the temple but Dave stopped her.

'Listen, haven't you ever wondered what those spherical alcoves are for? We've found Shanahan's original plans for the temple and we're just altering it to his specifications.'

She considered this. 'That sounds like a great idea, but you have to apply for permission. You can't just barge in here one day with a cement mixer.' She shook herself free of his grasp and started towards the temple again.

Dave shook his head. He was hoping it wouldn't come to this. 'I don't suppose you know anything about the vampire problem in this area,' he shouted after her.

She stopped, her back to him. Dave prepared his best I-know-you're-not-going-to-believe-this-but wince. She turned to him. Her face was serious.

She walked back to him and looked him square in the eyes. 'Go on. I'm listening.'

Sarah got out of the car and stretched. It had been a long night. Lynda beeped the horn as she reversed and drove off down the lane. Sarah unlocked the door and stepped inside. Tom was standing beside a roaring fire.

'What are you doing here?' she said with mock surprise.

'I wanted to make sure you were OK.'

'You could have called,' she said coyly.

'I didn't want you to be alone. How's Rek?'

'Lynda and I took him to A&E. They patched him up then he skipped out on us.'

'He just left without saying a word?'

'Lynda thinks he might have gone back to Chloe's but I doubt it. He's out for revenge, but he can't beat Kaaliz and he knows it. I don't know what he thinks he's doing. I wish Amanda were back. She'd know how to find him, and knock some sense into him when she did.'

'He should be safe in daylight,' Tom offered. Sarah shrugged.

She closed the door and walked over to him. She gently touched the fresh cuts on his face. 'You've been fighting.'

'Yeah, where was that spider-sense of yours that lets you know I'm in trouble?'

'There's so much going on right now, Tom. I feel like I'm being pulled a dozen different ways.' She hung her head, exhausted.

'Hey, I was only joking. Anyway, I can handle myself. There are four dead vampires who'll testify to that.'

'Four, eh? That's pretty good going, slick.'

'Got a free Harley out of it, too.'

She looked him in the eyes. She whispered. 'Let's go to bed, Tom.'

He took a few seconds before replying, 'Shit, they weren't joking about Harleys being babe-magnets, were they?'

She smiled. 'It's not the Harley... well, not completely.' Tom smiled. Sarah looked at him seriously. 'I love you, Tom. I always have.'

'I've always loved you, too.'

Sarah took his hand and they walked to the bedroom.

Seven minutes later...

'We should do it again.'

'Yeah, I think I'll be able to last longer next time,' Tom said. 'It's just, you're my... well, you know.'

'You're mine, too.'

'We don't *have* to do it again,' Tom said.

'Oh, listen, I can do it better than that, too. I've seen videos.'

'No, I don't mean I don't *want* to do it again. I'm just saying...' He turned to her and looked in her eyes. 'This isn't our only chance. We're not going to die tonight.'

Tears welled in Sarah's eyes.

'We're not, Sarah. I won't lose you. And if I have to save the world to hold onto you, then that's what I'll do.'

Sarah smiled and ducked under the duvet.

After a few seconds Tom said, 'Wow, you *have* seen videos.'

Sarah giggled. Tom ducked under the duvet with her.

Nicholl slept late the next day. Probably because she had been too wired to sleep most of the night and ended up watching *Heathers* and *Amelie* from her DVD collection. When she did finally go to bed she didn't sleep immediately. She lay there, planning. Trying to cover all the angles of how this escape was going to work. It must have been sometime after dawn when she finally fell asleep.

She awoke just after midday. Dinner at one left her plenty of time for a shower and to try to work out what she was going to say to them all. She had gauged from the people she had met last night that no-one was happy here, but there's a hell of a difference between not liking a place and being willing to die for the chance to leave it. It only took one person to chicken out and the whole plan would be compromised. One person too scared to leave, and at the same time not wanting to be left on the island alone, would sound the alarm and bring extra security from HQ. It had to be all of them.

12:51

Nicholl looked out her window. Donna had set up tables in front of her house. People were milling around with drinks in their hands. Nicholl left her domicile and walked over to the assembled crowd. The closer she got the stronger the smell of a home-made roast dinner with all the trimmings got. She smiled and nodded to a few familiar faces, shook hands with a few more that hadn't waited up for her last night, and edged inside Donna's domicile.

Joshua ran over to her. 'Ah, here's the lady of the hour. Now I thought I'd introduce you before dinner and then maybe you could say a few words?' He raised his eyebrows hopefully.

'Is this everyone?'

Joshua did a quick look around. 'Yes, I think everyone's here.'

'I'll speak to them now if you don't mind. Can you bring everyone inside?'

'In here? It'll be a bit cramped. We have tables outside, the weather looks like it's...'

'Please, Joshua. Bring them all in.'

Joshua looked concerned but went outside. He shepherded everyone in and Nicholl closed the door. She looked at the expectant faces before her. They were all standing shoulder to shoulder in the small room. Donna stepped from the kitchen and looked at Nicholl, too.

She took a deep breath and said, 'The Endtime is here.' The facial expressions of six or eight of the assembled people turned to stone. 'I see some of you know what that means. For the rest of you: it means the final battle. It's tonight.' A gasp went through the crowd. 'Humans versus vampires. And only one side is walking away from it. If we fail tonight, vampires take over the world and we become nothing but their unhappy meals.' She let it sink in for a few moments. She looked around the crowd and couldn't see Eileen. She wasn't there.

'So what do you want us to do about it? We're locked up,' someone shouted from the crowd.

'You all worked for the Ministry. You all know more about vampires than anyone else I could recruit.'

'Recruit?' the same man shouted.

'I didn't get thrown in here by accident. I came here because I need soldiers. I need you all. I can get you off this island, but the price of your freedom is your service in the battle tonight.'

'And if we refuse?' a different man asked.

'Then you take your chances. Maybe we triumph tonight without you, maybe we don't. Best case scenario; we win and you spend the rest of your life here, worst case, we lose and vampires find this island eventually and kill you all.'

'What's the Ministry doing?' A woman.

Nicholl hung her head. 'Nothing. The ministry's policy on prophecies is...'

'They don't believe them until *after* they happen.' Someone finished for her.

The crowd were looking at each other in a stunned silence.

'You can stay here, prisoners,' Nicholl said. 'Or you can do what you all chose to do with your lives when you joined the Ministry. Fight vampires. Tonight we go into battle and with your help we'll be victorious, and no-one ever needs to lose a loved one to a vampire ever again. I don't know about you, but I think that's worth dying for.'

Joshua stepped forward and faced Nicholl. Tears were streaming down his face. 'You can really get us all off this island?'

Nicholl took him by the shoulders and held him tightly. 'I can, Joshua. Are you with me?'

'You're goddamn right I am,' he whispered. Joshua turned to the crowd and wiped his cheeks. 'Anyone want to stay here?' Everyone looked at each other but no-one spoke up or raised their hand. Joshua nodded, smiling. 'I'm proud of you all.' He turned back to Nicholl. 'We're all with you.'

They all looked at her, awaiting orders. 'OK. Everyone act normally. I suggest we all eat this beautiful meal, then discreetly go back to our domiciles. Pack anything you want to take with you – only what you can carry. We're going to have to move very fast, so be prepared.'

Everyone stood still, hanging on her every word. Donna clapped her hands together and everyone turned. 'OK, you heard her. Let's get something to eat.'

The crowd started to move slowly towards Donna's serving table.

Nicholl patted Joshua on the shoulder and said, 'I'll be back in a minute.'

Joshua was about to speak, but she ran out.

Nicholl ran across the communal circle to number twelve and knocked the door. 'Eileen! Come on, wake up!' She banged the door again. 'Eileen, come on. I have to talk to you.'

Nicholl tried the doorknob and found the door unlocked. She opened the door and stepped inside. Eileen was walking towards the door with her arm extended for the doorknob when Nicholl entered. The sunlight rushed in and scorched

Eileen's exposed arm. She jumped back into the far corner of the room, holding her smouldering forearm. Nicholl looked at the girl cowering in the darkened corner.

'Holy shit,' Nicholl said quietly.

They sat opposite each other in Eileen's darkened kitchen, each holding a cup of coffee. 'I worked in Research and Development. We had brought a vampire up from level six to run some tests. We all thought it was sedated, but it was just playing possum. We were scientists, we couldn't fight it. It killed my two colleagues and tried to use me as a hostage to get out. When the agents showed up there was a lot of posturing and macho banter, but despite all his tough talk the vamp realised they weren't ever going to let him out. The threat of killing me carried no weight with the agents. They only see the big picture.' She smiled. 'Look who I'm telling. It's in the small print in all our contracts you know, if that situation arises, you agree to being killed. Did you know that?'

Nicholl shook her head. 'There seems to be a lot of shit in the small print that no-one ever reads.'

'So the vamp knows he's beaten, but just as a final "fuck you" to the Ministry, he rips open his wrist and shoves it in my mouth.' She looked down into her coffee. 'Next thing I remember is waking up on the wrong side of the plexi-glass.'

'Why send you here though? Why don't you...?'

'Why don't I kill all these nice people?'

Nicholl nodded.

'One of the projects we were working on was a bloodlust inhibitor. It's a drug that basically stops a vampire craving blood.'

'And it works?'

Eileen smiled thinly. 'There's the rub. It only works if you administer it before the vampire kills anyone. After it makes its first kill, there's no going back.'

'So they shot you up with this inhibitor and sent you here?'

Eileen nodded. 'I told you I've only been here four months, but they had me locked up in HQ for six months before that. When they realised I wasn't a threat they let me out. I was able to walk around HQ like normal while they decided what to do with me. I was sort of hoping I could keep my job.'

'Why didn't they let you, if they decided you weren't a threat?'

'Kyle said there were too many unstable elements. He thought another vamp might have been able to work mind mojo on me and make me do stuff. He thought I might try to leave to see my children. My fault for asking him so many times. So four months ago, after I'd tried calling home, he decided it was in the best interests of everyone that I be sent to Section Zero.' Eileen sniffed back the tears. 'I never even got through. It only rang twice before they cut me off.'

Nicholl sat back in her chair and tapped her teeth with her thumbnail. 'Can you fly?'

'I can, but...' Eileen opened the neck of her bathrobe and showed Nicholl a plastic collar around her neck.

'What's that?'

'It's my leash. I get more than two hundred yards away from the perimeter markers on the island...' She looked up. '...in *any* direction, this little ring of C4 blows my head off.'

Nicholl was silent but Eileen could see she was deep in thought.

'I heard what you said over at Donna's.'

Nicholl gave her a questioning glance.

'I could hear you from here. I would have liked to fight with you, but you'll just have to leave me here.'

'You would fight with us? Even though...'

Eileen nodded. 'I know. If you win, it's the end of vampires and I'll die, but at least my children will be safe. If you lose tonight... I don't even want to think about what could happen to them.'

Nicholl pondered for a few seconds more, then got to her feet quickly. 'I'm not leaving you behind.'

'You have to.' Eileen pulled at the plastic collar around her neck. 'I can't leave.'

'Bullshit. We'll find a way.'

Eileen was close to tears. 'Really?'

Nicholl nodded. 'Really.' Eileen hugged Nicholl. 'You be ready to go on a moment's notice.'

'I will be,' Eileen said, smiling. She wiped her cheeks.

Nicholl nodded for Eileen to step into the shadows before she opened the door and left.

She walked back across the communal circle towards Donna's domicile. She was really hungry. She hoped they had saved her some. She fished the device from her pocket and stuck it in her ear. She spoke as discreetly as possible.

'Chloe, are you there?'

There was a loud burst of engine noise in the background but she heard Chloe clearly. 'We're on our way. Should be there in about an hour.'

'Stop where you are.'

The engine noise lessened and then died. 'What's wrong?'

'Nothing. We're going to wait until nightfall.'

'That's going to cut it damn close.'

'I know.'

'Amanda, why are we waiting until nightfall?'

'We've got a couple of complications this end. Let me speak to Dave.'

razed

Downhill, 1851
The butler already had the door open when the coach stopped. He opened the coach's door and lowered the step.
'Lord and Lady Moore?'
'Yes,' the man answered.
'I'm afraid we had given up on you. Dinner has already begun.'
'One of the horses threw a shoe.'
'Please follow me through to the Dining Room. There may still be time to join the meal.'
'Wait,' the man commanded. He stopped just inside the doorway and carefully removed his topcoat and hat and handed them to the butler. He took the woman's shawl and bonnet. 'Don't try to hurry gentry, my good man. We do everything at our own speed.'
The butler bowed.
The woman hooked her arm around the man's and they walked slowly behind the shuffling butler. The butler thought he heard them snigger behind his back but ignored it dutifully. The butler opened the doors and entered.
'I apologize for intruding, sir, but Lord William and Lady Margaret Moore have arrived.'
'Wonderful. Show them in.'
The butler ushered the last two guests inside. The long dining table was filled with various meats and vegetables, though it seemed most of the other diners had already cleared their plates. The butler showed them to their seats, just two from the head of the table. They sat beside each other. The butler discreetly left.
'So we finally meet, Lord Moore.
'The pleasure is ours, Lord Hervey.'
'Please, call me Frederick.'
'Then you must call me William. I must say, I expected an older man.'
'It's the family name: Frederick. I am Frederick William, my father was just plain Frederick and my grandfather was

Frederick Augustus.' He looked at the newly arrived couple. 'In fact I was just telling my other guests before you arrived how my grandfather came to build the structure behind the house.'

'Then please continue.'

Frederick glared at them for a moment, then smiled. 'My grandfather named it Mussenden Temple, though no worship was ever held there as far as my knowledge goes. It was named for Frideswide Mussenden, a close friend of the Hervey family who was tragically killed while visiting these shores. She was twenty-two years old.'

'How terrible.'

The waiters filled the plates of the late arrivals. 'Please, eat. I will be offended if your bellies are not filled to capacity,' Frederick said. There was a gentle laugh from the table. 'You must be hungry from your journey.'

'My wife and I thank you for your hospitality.'

'Not at all.' Frederick addressed the table again. 'My grandfather used the temple as a library. My earliest memories of childhood are of him sitting out there by himself with his books, and a wee nip of something to keep the cold out.' Gentle laughter again. 'Though sometimes he would just stare out the windows, across the sea. Lost in his own thoughts, I suppose. Even at that young age, he struck me as a man carrying many a burden.' He took a drink from his wine glass and many of his guests aped him. 'I'm sorry to say the temple has fallen into disrepair since his death. My father never used it and I rarely open its doors. I have tried to find the original blueprints, but for some bizarre reason the architect sent them to the Vatican, or so his grandson tells me.'

One of the men cleared his throat loudly and said, 'Frederick, I think we should discuss our most pressing problem.'

'Of course.' Frederick nodded to his wife at the other end of the table.

She stood up and placed her napkin on her plate. 'Ladies, I believe that is our cue to leave. We shall retire to the West Drawing Room while the menfolk discuss their business. Lady Moore, please do not rush your dinner and join us when you can. I will trust my husband to keep the conversation light in your presence.'

Lady Moore nodded and Lady Hervey returned the gesture. The ladies quickly left the dining room. When they had all left a boy no more than twenty years entered the room and closed the doors behind him. He remained silent, standing at the threshold.

'Lady Moore, would you rather we wait until you have eaten? The business we have to discuss is not for those of a delicate disposition.'

She dabbed the sides of her mouth with her napkin before answering. 'If I may be so bold, Frederick, I would have you know that I have read the complete works of Mister Poe and am not easily frightened.'

The men laughed heartily as they lit their cigars.

'Then I shall continue,' Frederick said with half a bow. 'We are plagued in this area by vampires. Two in particular. These godless creatures kill without remorse, to satisfy their own unnatural and monstrous thirst for blood.'

'I have heard legends of such creatures, of course. I believe one was known as the tempest. Tales of her infamy have spread the length of Ireland.'

'Yes, Lord Moore, it is her we still seek. Some say she is hundreds of years old. She and her partner have been a blight on this land as long as anyone can remember.'

'She is married?'

He gave a short humourless laugh. 'I would not call it marriage. Certainly no priest or minister has blessed the union. And stories tell of them both having their way with locals while the other watches. I apologize for my language, Lady Moore. It seems they will do anything to fly in the face of what is right and proper. They have no respect for God, or for each other it seems. They are merely animals with human faces.'

'And speaking of which, what *do* they look like?'

Frederick studied them before answering. 'That's simple, they look like you and your good lady.'

Lord Moore dropped his knife and fork and got to his feet, throwing his napkin aside. 'How dare you, sir!'

'Save us the theatrics, Galen. That is your name, isn't it? And the whore at your side is Taisie.'

The two men locked eyes.

Frederick continued, 'News reached us two days ago of the death of William and Margaret. We were well acquainted for many years. Last night you used his name to gain entrance to the home of Sir Woolsey and today gravediggers make space for his family in the local cemetery. So when I received your RSVP this afternoon, I took the liberty of replacing my guest list with agents of the Ministry of the Shield. You're familiar with the organisation?'

Galen glanced around the hardened faces of the men and swallowed hard. Taisie looked at the door and saw the boy.

'What's this? Taisie. Taisie the Tempest looking for an escape route? Before you decide the boy is your best chance of escape, let me tell you who he is.' Frederick refilled his glass. 'Even back in my grandfather's day, it was quite clear that we were not going to beat you with strong hearts and broad shoulders. You move too fast and heal too quickly for us to do enough lasting damage. So my grandfather secretly commissioned a new area of the Ministry to find out all they could about your kind. Every story. Every myth. Every legend. We recorded it and then tried to check it for authenticity.' He took a long gulp of wine.

'Tell me, have you ever heard the legend of the dhampir? It is first recorded in Eastern Europe. It happens when a vampire male mates with a human female. The offspring becomes a dhampir, with the strength and power of a vampire, but none of the aversions to sunlight or crosses. A dhampir is a fighter for good. That boy standing at the door is your son, Galen. He's waited his whole life to meet you. You killed his entire family except his mother, who you left pregnant and so badly disfigured that no man would ever look upon her with desire again.'

The boy stepped forward and drew a sword from behind his back.

'Your sins have found you out, vampire. Now, finally, you will both pay for your murderous ways.'

Taisie flew at the boy. He leapt into the air and drove his sword into her chest as she passed. Galen was upon him in a second. The boy fought him back with combinations of punches and swipes with the sword. Galen was cut and bleeding. Taisie got to her feet. Her wound was closing, but very slowly. She needed to drink. She had starved herself all day in anticipation of a huge feast on the nobility tonight. She pulled on the doors. The women would be much easier to overpower, and if she picked the right hostage she and Galen could walk out of here. The doors wouldn't move. She pulled again, harder. It was no use; the doors were barred from the other side.

Galen and the boy were fighting it out. Galen's hands and arms were getting badly hurt because he had no sword to defend himself with. The men stood watching the fight, laughing, still smoking their cigars. Taisie flew at them. One of them pulled a bottle and threw the liquid in her face. The water burned her flesh like fire. She screamed and jumped back. She flew at the nearest window and smashed the glass. There were iron bars every three inches down all the windows. She grabbed the bars and pulled on them but they were set deep in the stone and wouldn't budge.

Taisie hovered in the air, helpless. The boy was beating Galen into submission. The men laughed, drinking their whiskey and smoking their cigars.

She flew down and grabbed a bottle of whiskey from the serving table and hurled it at one of the men who was relighting his pipe. The bottle smashed and the man went up in flames. Taisie grabbed all the flammable spirits from the table and started hurling them, encouraging the fire in all directions. Soon the dinner table was engulfed in flame. The curtains took the fire to the ceiling. Taisie threw a couple of bottles at the doors and soon they burned too. The men had at first tried to extinguish the flames by beating them with their jackets, but now they saw that it was useless. They ran around the dining room screaming for the doors to be released, while trying to avoid the worst of the fire.

No one was watching the fight anymore; they were all too concerned with saving their own lives. Taisie flew at the boy and punched him as hard as she could on the back of the head. The boy lifted from the ground and was stopped by the nearest wall. Taisie took Galen's bloodied arm and helped him to his feet. She led him to the other side of the room, opposite the doors but on the other side of the table from all the choking men kicking and screaming at the burning exit.

'As soon as that door opens we fly the hell out of here.'

Galen coughed and blood ran from his mouth, but he managed to nod.

'And, no offence, but I think I've had it with these dinner parties.' Taisie smiled at him. She was still as beautiful as ever.

'No argument from me. This was a bad idea. Next thing we try is your choice.'

'Really?'

Galen heard the clunking of bolts being removed on the other side of the door. They would soon be free. 'You have somewhere in mind?'

'I've always wanted to see the Americas.'

Galen smiled a bloody smile and nodded. 'Me too.'

The doors swung open and the coughing men surged forward as one.

Taisie put her arm around Galen's waist. 'OK. Let's go.'

Galen saw the boy running up behind them and drawing back his sword a fraction of a second before Taisie's head rolled across the burning table. Her frame shrivelled to a skeleton and dropped by his feet.

Galen screamed, 'No!' He turned on the boy just as he swung again. Galen grabbed the blade of the sword before it hit him and held it tightly. The blade dug deep into his palms as the boy twisted and pulled on the hilt, but Galen wouldn't let go. With all his strength he jerked the sword from the boy's grasp.

The boy held up his palms in surrender and took a couple of steps backwards, always keeping his eyes on the vampire. Galen turned the sword around and grabbed it by the hilt in both hands. He squeezed the metal with all his rage. He took two steps quickly forwards, swung with all his might and sliced the boy in two below the rib cage. The boy fell to the ground and Galen watched as his arms flailed for his missing waist. The boy screamed until, seconds later, choking on his own blood, death found him.

Galen walked out of the burning room, the blood of his son still dripping from the sword, and left the villa unnoticed.

The whole house was filled with smoke now. The fire had spread beyond the Dining Room and was climbing the stairs.

Galen sat on top of Mussenden Temple to watch the building burn. He still held the sword, determined to make an example of Frederick Hervey, but then a more appropriate punishment presented itself.

The women were led from the house and huddled together while the men formed a chain bringing buckets of water from the well. Money was offered to the servants, some of whom took it and ran back inside to return with a painting or sculpture in their grasp.

No-one was watching the women.

Dawn was just breaking. The fire had completely taken the house leaving just its outer walls standing. It was only then that the men went to find their wives. And find them they did. Neatly lain in a row on the grass, each with their head sitting in their lap.

jailbreak

Nicholl looked at the horizon and watched the orange sun sink into the sea. Two litre bottles of vodka sat open on the ground at her feet. She missed Rek. She might die tonight. He might die tonight. A lot of people might die tonight. Her platoon, which someone had named Zero Squadron, was full of enthusiasm, but she sensed that was more about leaving the island than going head-to-head with the undead. Most of them weren't field agents, and those who were would have been retired by now if they had still worked for the Ministry. They all had basic combat training when they joined, but for some of them that was a long time ago. She hoped it all came back to them very quickly.

Was she doing these people a favour? If they lost tonight, if vampires took over the world they might not find this island for years, if ever. Though those boatloads of luxuries that arrived to satisfy their every desire would stop coming. Yes. This was the right thing to do. Besides, they all wanted to leave and fight.

She didn't want to look around. She knew they were all watching, waiting for her signal. In the distance she heard the sound of a boat's throttle, fully opened. Getting louder. This is the point of no return. She closed her eyes and took a deep breath.

She took a handkerchief out of each pocket and knelt down. She pushed a handkerchief into the neck of one vodka bottle, then the other. The boat's running lights came on. Nicholl turned the bottles upside down, soaking the handkerchiefs with the liquid. She flicked open the lighter and lit them. She dropped the two bottles off the cliff edge onto the beach below. The boat immediately altered its course and started heading towards the flaming markers.

Nicholl turned around and shouted, 'Everyone down to the beach!'

The doors of all the occupied domiciles opened immediately. They had all been waiting for this, some of them for a very long time. They all came running towards her.

Eileen landed beside her. 'Anything I can do?'

'Get to the boat.' People rushed past them and down the slope to the beach. The boat was in as far as it could come now and the first people were starting to swim out to it.

'As soon as everyone's safe...'

Nicholl turned to her. 'What?'

Eileen nodded; where the plinth had stood was now an empty hole.

'Shit, they're on their way.' Nicholl pushed the people running past her. 'Hurry! Faster!'

Two men in black uniforms raised quickly out of the plinth carrying guns. They took aim at Nicholl and opened fire. Eileen jumped between them and turned her back to the gunfire. The bullets ripped into her back as she stood face to face with Nicholl.

Nicholl winced. 'Doesn't that hurt?'

'Stings a bit.'

The guards stopped firing when their clips were empty. Nicholl turned and ran down the slope to the beach. Even the slowest of the prisoners was in the water now. Eileen ran after her until a harpoon burst from her stomach. She and Nicholl locked eyes.

Eileen shook her head and said, 'Go.'

The cable attached to the harpoon yanked Eileen backwards and dragged her back towards the plinth. Nicholl looked at the people being helped onto the boat, the others swimming. She turned and ran towards the plinth. The two men were holding Eileen as she struggled. The plinth started to descend with all three of them on it. By the time Nicholl got there it was twenty feet down. She jumped into the hole and fell into the darkness.

Everyone was throwing punches in the dark. Nicholl felt around and found a chest that definitely didn't belong to Eileen. She held tight to it and started landing punches as hard and fast as she could to the head attached to it.

The plinth stopped and the doors opened. All four of them fell out, fighting. The controller got up from his computer and ran to the wall where he hit a large red button. Alarms started going off all over the island.

Now that she could see, Nicholl kicked as hard as she could at the guard's most sensitive area. He fell to the ground, vomiting. She grabbed the other guard that was fighting with Eileen from behind and introduced his face to the nearest wall. He collapsed.

Eileen pulled at the harpoon through her stomach. 'Get this fuckin' thing out of me!'

'Hold on, hold on.' Nicholl examined the cable and saw it was attached to the harpoon by something similar to a climber's hook. She unscrewed the clip and then unhooked it. She walked to the front of Eileen. 'OK, it's going to have to come out the front.'

Nicholl took hold of the end of the harpoon and put one foot on Eileen's stomach just below the wound.

Eileen nodded and swallowed. 'OK, on three. One...'

Nicholl yanked the harpoon out of her stomach in one fast movement.

Eileen grabbed the bleeding hole. 'Ow, you bitch,' she said through clenched teeth.

'Sorry, honey, we didn't have time to count to three.' Nicholl dropped the harpoon and looked around the huge underground room. The huge rock walls rose up on all sides, the blackness of their surface defying the fluorescent lights hanging everywhere. It looked like a small warehouse. Behind her were hundreds of boxes filled with god-knows-what. In front of her was a bank of about thirty monitors, showing the feeds from the cameras all over the island. A few desks and computers formed a rough semi-circle before them. The operator who had pushed the alarm button still stood frozen to that spot. His eyes were wide, watching the two women. Nicholl walked towards him and he looked the other way (hoping she wouldn't notice him?).

Nicholl stopped face to face with him. 'OK, what's your... shut that fuckin' alarm off, will you?'

The operator twisted the button he had just pressed and it popped out again. The alarm ceased.

'Thank you. Now, what's your name?'

'Operator four.'

'It's no wonder you ended up in a job like this if your parents called you that.'

'They're still coming. Even if I shut off the alarm, they'll still be coming.'

Nicholl nodded. 'Yeah, I thought so. How long before they get here?'

'I don't know. This has never happened before.'

'OK, four, I want to know how to get that collar off her neck.'

'I don't know.'

'Do I have to grind your nuts like I did with the other guy?'

'I *really* don't know. They put that thing on at HQ. Please don't squash my nuts.'

'OK, I believe you; you can hold on to your nuts.'

Operator four grabbed his balls with both hands and gave a deep sigh of relief.

'I didn't mean that literally, four. How do we get out of here?'

'I can send you back up on the plinth or you can take the back exit.' He nodded to a large set of metal double doors.

Nicholl ran over and hit the release. The doors parted and she saw a small beach outside. There were high rocks on both sides trailing out into the sea. A secluded cove the residents wouldn't be able to get to very easily. Two jet-skis sat on the sand. 'Eileen, come on.' Nicholl pulled the transmitter from her pocket and stuck it in her ear. 'Chloe, is everyone on board?'

'Yes, where the hell are you?'

'Get going, we'll catch you up.'

'But…? How…? Are you sure?'

'Yes, get going.' She took the transmitter out of her ear and put it back in her pocket. She and Eileen walked out onto the sand and started pushing one of the jet-skis towards the water. They turned at the sound of the doors closing behind them. Operator four stood there smiling. Just before the doors closed he said, 'Give my regards to the perimeter guards.' The doors slammed shut.

Nicholl and Eileen turned and saw two men standing up on the rocks. They opened fire and the two women dove to either side, finding shelter behind rocks. The jet-ski was pulverised with gunfire.

Nicholl looked at the other jet-ski. They still had a chance. She could hear Chloe's boat gaining speed somewhere in the distance. The gunfire paused as the guards reloaded. Eileen flew from the safety of the rocks and slammed into one guard with her shoulder, then the other, knocking them both into the water. Nicholl was already pulling the other jet-ski towards the water.

The two of them heaved the jet-ski into the water. 'Why are we bothering with this? I could just fly us out of here.'

'You're weak. You've lost a lot of blood. I don't want you dropping me in the middle of the fuckin' Atlantic.'

Eileen guessed the unsaid part of that answer was: *Plus, your head might explode at any minute, then where would I be?* She said nothing and got on the jet-ski behind Nicholl. She brought it to life and they raced out of the cove and into the open sea.

Chloe saw the jet-ski approaching and stopped. Nicholl pulled alongside and she and Eileen climbed up the ladder and on board. Everyone stood shivering in wet clothes. They were all staring at Eileen.

Nicholl broke the silence. 'Where's Dave?'

'I'm here.'

Nicholl found Dave sitting in the aft fiddling at some electronic device with a screwdriver. 'Dave...'

Dave held up his screwdriver for a second to silence her then continued doing whatever he was doing. He mumbled to himself, 'First you drag me all the way out here and make me float in the middle of nowhere all day with nothing to do but play I Spy.' He raised his head and glanced at her, still twisting and screwing. 'And let me tell you, there wasn't a whole hell of a lot to spy. Then you tell me I'll have to disarm this high-tech collar thing without any of my tools. Then we get there and the girl with the collar doesn't even show. She's the last to leave of course...'

'Sorry,' Eileen said quietly.

'You expect miracles and give me nothing to work with.' The device in Dave's hand came to life and a light started pulsing on it. 'And still I deliver.' Dave got to his feet and walked over to Eileen, offering her the device.

Eileen looked at Nicholl first, then at Dave. 'Thank you. What is this?'

'Your collar explodes if you get beyond two-hundred yards of a perimeter marker. You weren't there so I couldn't disarm your collar. So I took a perimeter marker and hooked it up to this battery. You might want to keep that close. At least until I get back to my tools.'

Eileen smiled and hugged Dave. She dropped the perimeter marker into her pocket and zipped it shut.

'Sorry about being a bit ratty with you,' Dave said to Nicholl. 'It's been a really long day and I could desperately use a doobie.'

Nicholl smiled and patted his shoulder as she passed him. 'Don't worry about it, Dave. You're a star.' She headed for the cabin.

Dave exhaled. Joshua approached him. 'Hello, Dave, is it?'

'That's right.'

'I just wanted to thank you.' Joshua opened his jacket and took out a water-proof bag full of joints.

'My man!' Dave hugged him and they walked off together.

Nicholl walked in to the cabin and greeted Chloe and Claire. 'OK, let's go.'

'Has Dave finished his little project?' Claire asked.

'Yeah.' Nicholl laughed and shook her head. 'That guy's a genius.'

'Yes he is.' Chloe brought the boat to life and took off at full speed.

'How long will it take us to get back?'

Chloe didn't answer. She was staring out the window, dead ahead. Claire looked, too. Nicholl stepped forward and followed their gaze. They all saw the helicopter heading straight towards them.

'Shit.'

'Kill the running lights,' Chloe shouted. Claire turned and flipped a switch. The helicopter turned on its spotlight and they were all momentarily blinded. The helicopter opened fire and bullets ripped up the sea on all sides of them. Chloe brought the boat to a full-stop. 'That was a warning, we won't get another one.'

Chloe charged past Nicholl and out onto the deck. 'Where's the vampire?'

Eileen stepped forward. 'That's me.'

Chloe looked around. 'Any of you guys handy with your fists?'

A tall man in his forties stepped forward. He looked like he was still in good shape. 'Carson. Ministry boxing champion three years running.'

'Great. You'll do. The rest of you, put your hands up.'

The boat had stopped. The helicopter pilot manoeuvred closer. They were all standing on deck with their hands up. 'OK, I think they're surrendering. Stand down the weapons.' The two men in the back obeyed, put the safety catches on and sat back. Eileen threw Carson into the back of the helicopter and disappeared. The pilot turned and saw his two men getting thumped by a guy who looked twice their age.

The pilot's door opened and Chloe was there being held by Eileen. Chloe sprayed mace into his face. The pilot screamed and put his hands to his stinging eyes. Chloe reached in and undid his safety harness. The helicopter banked left, then right as the pilot struggled. Chloe grabbed him and pulled him out. He dropped into the sea, which was a relief for his eyes if nothing else. Chloe climbed into the pilot's seat and turned around. She saw Carson sitting in the back by himself, smiling.

'What sort of pussies is the Ministry churning out these days?'

Chloe laughed and tuned the radio to her boat's frequency. 'Claire, are you there?'

'Right where you left me.'

'Think you can handle my boat?'

'No problem, lead the way.'

The helicopter flew overhead to the delighted screams of the freed prisoners. Claire started the boat and followed it into the darkness.

The pilot and his two men were left treading water, screaming for the boat to come back. When it had disappeared into the distance they stared at each other.

The pilot tried to sound confident. 'OK, everyone huddle together. We'll need our combined body heat to...' He looked at his men and they all knew the same truth.

'It's been a pleasure serving with you, sir.'
'Yes.'
'Thank you, lads.' The pilot winced. 'Er, listen, I don't feel right going to my grave without telling you that I slept with both your wives.'
'What?'
'You bastard!'
He turned to one of them. 'And your sister.' He turned to the other. 'And your mother.'
The two men looked at their superior, open-mouthed.
'What a complete bastard.' The three men turned and saw Eileen sitting on the jet-ski. 'I think you guys have a lot to talk about when you get back.' She patted the jet-ski and pointed. 'There's plenty of fuel and the island's that way.' She flew into the air, smiled at them, then took off after the boat.

intruders

The Master watched Tom and Sarah through the window. Their bodies were almost glowing in the wake of their exorcised virginity. A simple pleasure long-forgotten to the Master. They lay in each other's arms, blissfully smiling in silence. Each holding back everything they wanted to say for fear that it broke some 'law of cool' – a phrase from Sarah's mind. She had friends who had lost their virginity before her and they all said not to come on too strong afterwards because boys didn't like it. You had to be aloof no matter how much you wanted to scream your love from every rooftop. It wasn't the done thing. The done thing was to say little. One of her friends had offered the advice: *'If you have to say anything, compliment him on the size of his thing, no matter what size it is. It's the one thing that it's never wrong to say.'* There was also some debate about how long to wait before calling him. Two days seemed the absolute minimum. Sarah thought, under the circumstances, these rules shouldn't apply to her and Tom. This was war. Either one, or both, of them could die tonight. Wasn't it better to say everything just in case? She glanced at Tom out of the corner of her eye for a sign that he was thinking the same thing.

The Master changed his focus and concentrated on the boy's thoughts.

Just like Kyle Reese and Sarah Connor in *The Terminator*, Tom thought. They only get one night together because he dies in the big fight at the end. If someone were writing this, that's what they'd do. They'd let us have sex once, just to make my death hurt her more. And Sarah – ooh, there's a spooky coincidence – will love me forever in a quiet, tortured way. Of course, another writer might consider losing my virginity as the transition into manhood, and that I need to be a man in order to face my destiny. Do I feel more like a man? Yes, I think I do. That last time was pretty special. If we had more time to practise, I'm pretty sure I could get our minute-count into double figures.

Sarah's phone rang, distracting all three of them. The Master listened intently but could only hear Sarah's responses. Sarah hung up and turned to Tom. 'That's the bat-signal. Everyone meet at Chloe's.' Sarah started to slide out from under the duvet and Tom stopped her.

'Sarah, I really love you.'

Sarah shook her head slightly. 'Don't say goodbye, Tom.'

Tom looked into her watering eyes. 'I'm not. I'm saying I love you.'

She smiled. 'That's OK, then. I love you, too.'

They kissed. Sarah got out of bed and started pulling on her clothes.

'Do I have time for a wash?'

'If you're quick,' Sarah said, hopping out of the bedroom pulling a sock on.

The fire had gone out in the living room. She raked the last heat from the embers with the poker. There was a knock at the door.

She got up and answered it.

The Master stood before her.

'Oh, it's you.' She paused. 'You'd better come in.'

'Thanks.' The Master walked into the living room.

'I've been trying to contact you for days,' Sarah said. 'I was just about to put the kettle on, do you want a cup?'

'No thanks,' the Master said. 'Are you heading out soon?'

Sarah nodded. 'Tonight's the big night. The Daves think they've come up with something, out at Mussenden Temple.'

'A weapon?'

'Yeah, maybe.' Sarah hung her head. 'Sorry. I'm avoiding the subject. Look, there's no easy way to say this…'

Tom walked out of the bedroom pulling a T-shirt over his head.

Sarah walked over and hooked her arm around him for support. 'Tom, this is Alec. Mum's boyfriend. I told you about him. He's been away on business in Eastern Europe. I've been trying to call him to tell him…' Sarah dropped her head.

Tom stared at him. Something was off about this guy. Something not quite right. Instinctively, Tom glanced around for his sword. He couldn't see it. Was it still sitting on the Harley?

'Thing is…' Sarah started, gathering her courage.

'Don't waste your tears, Sarah. He already knows. Who the fuck are you?'

The Master smiled. 'The boy's instincts are better than yours,' he said to Sarah. 'Not as easy to fool as you and your gullible mother. That *is* unusual. Maybe you *are* the chosen one after all.'

Sarah was glancing back and forth between the two of them, confused.

'I said, who the fuck are you?'

'Don't try to scare me with fake bravado, boy. I've seen inside your head and your heart. I see the fear that you hide from everyone, even her.' He smiled at Sarah, then looked them both up and down. 'So this is the competition? Forgive me if I don't go weak at the knees. I've been around long enough to see stronger and braver warriors than you die by my hand.'

Sarah held tighter to Tom. 'You're the leader, the one the Vampyre Corpora speaks of. The first vampire.'

'In the flesh, so to speak.'

'You're the vampire from the Garden of Eden? The one God cursed to live in darkness?' Tom asked.

'The Bible.' He shook his head and exhaled deeply. 'Five thousand years of good intentions rewritten dozens of times by whoever is in power, edited another couple of dozen times by those with their own agenda. What's left is nothing but an ancient tabloid filled with inaccuracy, exaggeration and invention. And the Vampyre Corpora suffers from the same failings. But you are right about one thing; I was there at the beginning. I know how it all began. I've walked this Earth longer than any other living creature and over the millennia only one thing has remained constant: mankind destroys all he touches. Well, no more. Your time is over.'

'What are you going to do tonight?' Tom asked.

The Master smiled. 'That's the funny thing! I don't know any more than you what's going to happen tonight. Prophecies, they're all so vague. That's why I'm not going to kill you now. You made it this far, which I didn't expect, so maybe you're part of how it all comes to pass. Maybe it's one of you who does something, or fails to do something, and that starts off the whole vampire reign. And I wouldn't want to fuck that up.'

'It's never going to happen,' Sarah said, finding her strength in anger.

'I think it is,' the Master said. He took a couple of steps towards them. They pressed their backs against the wall. He looked into their eyes. 'And I think, deep down inside, you know it's going to happen, too. I smell defeat on you already.'

Tom looked into eyes that were as old as mankind and saw pure evil. Every trace of humanity was gone, deadened by thousands of years watching humans at their worst, from the darkness. A resident of the world, but never a part of it.

The Master turned and walked to the door. 'When this is over… if you're still alive, I *will* come looking for you. I have a connection to all my children. You've killed many of them and I've felt them die. That won't go unpunished.' He stared at them, showing the merest hint of the hatred he had inside. 'I'll see you on the battlefield, kiddies.' He opened the door, laughed to himself and left.

Rek woke with a start. It was night. He had fallen asleep again. He shook the heaviness from his head. It must be the painkillers they gave him at A&E that kept making him pass out. His clothes were wet and he was cold to the bone. He pulled out a pair of night-vision goggles from his backpack and looked around the reservoir. There were no signs of movement.

He must be underground.

When Rek had given Sarah and Lynda the slip at the hospital he had used his GPS tracker to locate the transmitter he had shot into Kaaliz's stomach. It had led him here, to Ballinrees Reservoir. Rek had searched, but the signal seemed to be coming from under the reservoir. He thought Kaaliz must have found an underground cave below the water. If he had, it was a hell of a big cave. Rek had watched him move two-hundred yards in one direction, then back. There was something down there, something big. Kaaliz didn't need oxygen but he couldn't imagine him lying on the bottom of the reservoir during the daylight hours.

It was still early, so Rek had decided to visit one of his more disreputable contacts and pick up some supplies. He was still back two hours before sunset with his backpack bulging. He had picked a spot in some tall reeds with a good view of the whole reservoir, and waited. Wherever Kaaliz was, he would come out as soon as the sun went down.

Now he wondered if he had missed him. He rummaged in his pockets and found his GPS tracker. Kaaliz was within 30 yards of him. Somewhere. Rek looked around the darkness again. The goggles highlighted everything in shades of green. A low hum came from his left. He turned and saw something rising from the ground. Some kind of box. A coffin? No, too big. He checked his GPS. Whatever it was, Kaaliz was inside it. Rek grabbed his backpack and ran across the grass towards the rising box as quietly as possible. Kaaliz rocketed up into the night sky, not even noticing him. Rek got to the box and ran to the front of it. It was an elevator car. The doors started to close. He jumped inside.

The doors opened and Rek found himself in a large room. He fumbled for a light-switch and found one. Fluorescents flickered on the length of the room. The light also brought with it an orchestra of screams and growls. Rek cautiously approached the room with the cages. They were hybrids. Nicholl had killed one years ago on Dempsey's Island and they had taken it back to HQ for analysis. It turned out to be a vampire/Che'al hybrid. It had taken Nicholl and a team of soldiers to kill *one* of them and there must be... He looked around. There must be at least forty or fifty in here. So Mand was right; this had been Sheridan's work.

There was no doubt in his mind now. Killing Kaaliz had been his objective, but he couldn't let these things live. If they ever got loose they would be virtually unstoppable. He dropped his backpack and started unloading the C4. He would wire the whole place with plastic explosive, wait 'til Kaaliz got back and then bury the whole fuckin' place. Whatever magics Kaaliz had working for him that allowed him to instantly heal wouldn't do him much good under a hundred tonnes of concrete and earth. It would at least hold him. Rek wasn't about to make the same mistake he had made before. He would bury him and then get the whole might of the Ministry here as soon as the sun came up. With that tracker buried in his gut, they would be able to pinpoint him easily and drag his worthless ass out of there and into a box at Ministry HQ. Forever.

Rek grabbed the GPS tracker to make sure Kaaliz wasn't on his way back. He saw the dot cross the screen at incredible speed then slow down and eventually stop. It took the GPS a few seconds to catch up with him and map his location, but when it did Rek recognized the street he had landed on. He knew what house the vampire would approach, and he watched on the screen as he did. It was Mand's sister's house.

'Too late, asshole,' Rek mumbled to himself. 'Nobody's home.' Rek smiled. Even a small victory at this point was something to celebrate. He set down the GPS and started attaching the detonators to the first block of C4.

He didn't notice the dot on the GPS screen was returning the way it had come at considerable speed.

Nicholl ran into Chloe's house first. 'Rek?' She shouted louder to be heard over the sound of the helicopter landing outside. 'Rek, are you here?' she shouted up the stairs. Claire was ushering Zero Squadron off the bus outside. Chloe had hired a luxury coach with a bathroom and had bought several dozen changes of clothes. They had all taken their turn in the bathroom on the return journey, getting out of their wet clothes. Claire had also taken an inventory of who everyone was and what special skills they might be able to bring to the fight. She was heartened by what she heard. They might just see tomorrow after all.

Nicholl ran into the living room. The picture was hinged backwards. Nicholl ran towards it. The safe behind the picture was open. The Fist of Merlin was gone!

Nicholl ran to the front door. Chloe was just getting out of the helicopter. She ran towards Nicholl as the rotors began to slow. Nicholl grabbed her by the arm and ran her into the living room.

She pointed at the empty safe. 'Please tell me you moved it.'

Chloe's mouth dropped open. She stepped in closer and looked at the empty steel box. 'I don't believe it.'

Nicholl dropped into an armchair. She took a few deep breaths, staring straight ahead.

Claire ran into the living room. 'OK, do I bring this lot inside or are we going straight to...' She saw the empty safe and the looks of despair on Nicholl and Chloe's faces. 'Oh, shit.'

Chloe leaned her back against the wall and slid to the floor. 'Our whole plan was based on this. Without it... we can't...'

'Don't say that!' Nicholl shouted. She exhaled deeply. 'Just give me a second to think,' she said quietly.

Claire and Chloe watched her.

Nicholl got to her feet. 'OK, here's what we do.'

'I know what you should do.' Dave and Lynda walked in from the kitchen. Dave was wearing The Fist of Merlin around his neck. 'You should buy a safe that isn't so easy to break into.'

Chloe, Claire and Nicholl started laughing with relief.

'What took you guys so long anyway? I'm out at that bloody temple all day rebuilding the feckin' thing. I get back here and everyone's gone. Then Lynda shows up but she doesn't know the combination of the safe. Then it got dark and still no one's shown up.' He nodded at Lynda. 'We thought we were going to have to go to Mussenden Temple ourselves.'

'We ran into a few snags. I'll explain later. Right, let's get the bus loaded. Any idea where Rek is?'

'He ditched Sarah and me at the hospital. Haven't seen him since,' Lynda said.

Nicholl looked concerned. 'I'd better give him a call.'

Rek looked through the window in the door to the *Raiders* room. It was a huge space and he would need to set charges, but there was one of those things running around in there periodically trying to smash through the door, wall and floor. He didn't think it was going to be easily distracted. He looked up and saw vents in the roof of the room.

He climbed up and pulled the grating off the vent outside the room. He shone a torch inside. The vent seemed to run the whole length of the room. He clambered inside and quickly shuffled his way down to the far end of the room, pushing his backpack in front of him. The creature smelled him. He could hear it below, jumping up at the ceiling that it had no chance of reaching.

When he reached the end of the vent, he took out a block of C4 and armed it. He began to scuttle backwards, leaving another block every ten yards or so. When he reached the vent he had climbed in, he still had three blocks of C4 left. He armed them and pushed them into the vent as well. He didn't know how much reinforced concrete was up there, but hopefully that much plastic explosive added to the pressure of the water above, should be enough to bring the roof down on this place.

He ran around the corner towards the elevator and found Kaaliz standing there, a struggling teenage girl in his grasp. Rek stopped in his tracks. The two of them faced each other, twenty feet separating them.

Kaaliz shook his head. 'Just can't keep a secret hideout secret anymore? How did you find me? Some computer gizmo probably, right?'

'Let the girl go.'

Kaaliz smiled. 'Why? Because this is between us? Because she has nothing to do with it? You're a walking cliché, my friend. But you're also my guest, so I'll oblige.' Kaaliz hurled the girl across the room. She slammed into the wall and fell unconscious on the floor. Kaaliz turned back to Rek. 'Pretty cute, eh? She's going to be my new bitch.'

Rek started to edge toward the girl. 'Doesn't seem too keen to me.'

Kaaliz shrugged. 'Give her a hundred years, she'll come around.'

Rek knelt down beside the girl and felt for a pulse. He closed his eyes briefly, then turned to Kaaliz. 'She's dead.'

'Oh, what a pity,' Kaaliz said flatly. 'I suppose there's no point in me staying here, then. Now that the word's out about this little subterranean getaway.' He took out a swipe card and walked to a terminal that said EMERGENCY on it. 'I guess there's nothing left to do but let the kids out to play.' He swiped the card through.

Every door in Project Redbook opened simultaneously. The cages too. Though it seemed none of the hybrids had noticed yet. But it wouldn't take them long.

'I'll leave you to it.' Kaaliz smiled. He turned toward the elevator. Rek pressed a button on the keypad in his hand and the elevator exploded, blowing Kaaliz back against the wall. Kaaliz got to his feet as the smoke started to clear. Rek looked at him and saw Kaaliz's burned flesh becoming new before his eyes.

'If I'm going to die down here, so are you,' Rek said. He heard a growl from behind. He turned and saw the first of the hybrids had realised their cages were open. They charged towards him. Rek ran down the corridor he had just come from. At the end of the corridor the door to the *Raiders* room slammed open and a hybrid jumped out. Rek tried the office door to his left and jumped inside. The door wouldn't lock. He pushed an empty filing cabinet against it, then a desk.

He sat down on the floor and put his back against the desk. The door was being slammed from outside. His barricade wouldn't hold for long. He looked at the keypad in his hand. All the rest of the C4 was wired to go off at the same time. One blinding flash of light and it would all be over. He put his finger to the button.

Beep, beep, bop, buh, beep, beep, buh, bop, bop.

Rek reached into his jacket and pulled out his phone. It was Mand. He took a deep breath and answered it.

'Rek, where are you? We're ready to go here at Chloe's.'

'Your plan worked, then? You got the zeros?'

'Of course it did. Zero Squadron are right here. Where are you?'

'I'm not going to make it, Mand.'

'What do you mean?'

'I've got him cornered... and ironically, he's got me cornered, too. Only thing to do is to take him with me.'

'What? No, Rek! Where are you?'

'I'm sorry, Mand.'

'Don't do anything! Tell me where you are. I'll come and get you.'

'This has to end.'

'I agree, but there's another way. I've got a plan.'

'I love you.'

'Rek, tell me where you are.'

'Bye, Mand.'

secret weapons

'Shit!' Nicholl ran back into the living room. Claire had brought in one of the women from Zero Squadron. She was a slim woman with short, black hair. She stood nervously in this company.

Claire raised her finger like a shy pupil trying to attract the attention of a busy teacher. 'Ah, Agent Nicholl?'

Nicholl held a quietening finger up to Claire. 'Dave, that program you used to find me on the island, could you use it to track a mobile phone signal?'

'Er, sure. If I had the number.' Dave dropped into a chair and opened his laptop. She showed him the screen of her phone. He read the number off it and typed it in. In a few seconds he had bypassed the phone company's security and was overlaying the signal onto a local map. He turned the screen to Nicholl.

'Ballinrees Reservoir? What the hell's he doing out there?'

Tom and Sarah ran in. Claire hugged her son. They turned and joined everyone else, looking at Nicholl.

'OK, who took stock of our zeros?' Nicholl asked.

Claire stepped forward. 'I did. I think we're in pretty good shape. Five of them are ex-field agents and two of them were specialist sharp-shooters.'

'I'm not sure what good a sharp-shooter is…'

'They're crucial,' said Dave.

'We're very lucky to find two of them,' agreed Dave. 'We've brought some weaponry that we've been working on, but without sharp-shooters, things would be a lot harder.'

'You've… *invented* some weapons?' Nicholl asked.

The Daves looked at each other and smiled. 'Oh yeah,' they said in unison.

'Don't they need to be trained how to use them?'

'What's to train?' Dave asked. 'Point the dangerous end at the bad guys. Works for most things.'

'We'll give them a crash course on the bus,' Dave added.

'OK, you better start loading your gear into the luggage compartment.' The Daves nodded and left. 'OK, Claire. Who else have we got?'

'Another eight of them have some kind of hand-to-hand combat training. And of course they all had basic sword skills training when they joined the Ministry.'

'I've got enough swords for everyone,' Chloe offered.

Claire smiled. 'And then there's Lee-Anne,' she said, ushering the slim girl forward. The girl blushed as everyone looked at her.

Nicholl waited but the girl didn't speak. She cleared her throat. 'And what was your role at the Ministry?'

The girl looked around all the anxious faces before answering, 'I was the Delegation Secretary.'

'What does that mean?' Sarah asked.

'Well, basically there was the problem of everyone wanting to use the Slayer for every little thing and she couldn't be everywhere at the same time, so all the requests came to me and I decided where to send her, you know, where she was most needed.' She looked around the shocked faces in the room.

Lynda managed to speak. 'There's an active Slayer around?'

'Yes. She lives a couple of miles from here.'

'A couple of miles away?' Lynda asked. 'Anyone else get the feeling everything's playing out exactly as it's supposed to?'

'Is that a good thing?' Tom asked.

'Not according to the Vampyre Corpora,' Chloe said.

'OK, never mind about that, we're going to change it.' Nicholl turned to Lee-Anne. 'Go on with what you were saying about the Slayer.'

'She got so fed up with people calling her that she changed her mobile and moved here so no-one could find her. Except me, of course. I'm the only one who has her number.'

'Is she hot? Like Sarah-Michelle hot?' Tom asked. Sarah slapped his chest playfully. 'What? I was just interested, so I'll recognize her.' Sarah shook her head, smiling.

'She's gorgeous,' Lee-Anne said. 'Abs to die for, a cleavage that has made grown men weep and a backside you could crack walnuts on.'

Tom smiled and said, 'Good to know.' Sarah slapped him again, grinning.

'Wait, the Ministry must have tried to get her number out of you,' Nicholl asked.

'Damn right they did,' Lee-Anne said. 'But see, I knew they were coming to arrest me so I erased all my phone records and burned my Rolodex before they got there so that the only record of her number left was in my head. Six months they interrogated me for before they gave up and sent me to Section Zero.' She hung her head and mumbled, 'All they had to do was reinstate me and I would have given it to them. One silly little slip-up should not condemn a person to Section Zero for the rest of their life.'

'Why were they sending you to Section Zero in the first place?' Sarah asked.

'They were doing this research with different levels of ultraviolet light, to see what effect it had on vampires. Turned out at a certain frequency it temporarily disrupted their brainwaves and made them act... well, sorta drunk. Everyone was emailing the video footage around HQ – it was hilarious. So I... well, I... posted it on YouTube.'

'Won't the Slayer think it odd that no-one's contacted her in – how long since you last called her?' Nicholl asked.

'Almost two years. I doubt it. She'll probably be glad of the rest. She's been inactive for long periods before.'

Nicholl looked around the other shocked members, then handed her phone to Lee-Anne. She took it with a smile and walked out to the kitchen for some quiet.

'OK, Tom and Sarah, I want you to take The Fist of Merlin out to Mussenden Temple.' She threw the amulet to them and Tom caught it. 'You know what to do when you get there?' They both nodded. 'It might take a while to fit so get going. We'll swing by and get this Slayer, then pick up Rek and meet you there. Whatever's going to happen tonight is probably going to happen close to that stone, so be careful.'

Tom hugged his mum. Lynda stepped forward and hugged Tom too. He looked at her, a little confused, then smiled.

'Be careful,' Lynda said and kissed his forehead. She turned to Sarah. 'Both of you.' She kissed Sarah's forehead too.

'We will,' Sarah said. She took Tom's hand and they ran outside. Lynda and Claire exchanged a look full of unsaid fears they both understood.

'Chloe, take one of the sharp-shooters and follow them in the helicopter. Are you OK for fuel?'

'Getting refilled as we speak.'

'OK, everyone else on the bus. Let's go pick up the ultimate vampire killer.'

Everyone shuffled out. Chloe and Lynda were the last to leave.

'You don't need to do this, Lynda.'

'Neither do you.'

'You have a family. You don't have your dhampir powers anymore. I don't want to have to tell your kids you aren't coming home.'

'Like I said before, I think we're all supposed to be here, me included. I'm not a big believer in coincidences. And whether that kid knows it or not, he's my little brother, and I'd like to get to know him. So anything I can do that might help keep him alive… I'm going to do it.'

Chloe nodded. 'OK, I see your mind's made up.'

'Chloe.' She let the word hang for few seconds before continuing, 'If someone has to… call Frank and the kids. I want you to do it.'

Chloe nodded. Lynda forced a smile and walked out.

Chloe walked over to the sideboard in the hall and opened the drawer. She looked down and saw her Last Will and Testament. She left the drawer open and walked out the door.

Deirdre Goose sat slouched in her favourite armchair before her favourite late night TV debate show. During the commercial break she had slid down the chair so far that she was now peering over her stomach to see the screen. It was the most comfortable she had ever felt in this chair but the obstruction before her was ruining it. The 'few extra pounds' she had admitted to carrying had taken advantage of all the exercise that she hadn't got around to. She looked at the landscape of her torso; it was dominated by a belly that had sprung up in the last two years to become the major feature of her physique. The valley between her bosoms had widened to such an extent that her breasts looked like they were suffering from subsidence and falling into her armpits.

Fugitive Wotsits and M&M's were dotted over her T-shirt like sheep on a hillside. She didn't remove them because she didn't intend moving for the foreseeable future, so what was the difference in setting them on the side of the chair or letting them sit where they were? She decided they could be free-range snacks and she would let them roam until she was hungry. The commercials were over and she returned her attention to the important issues being discussed.

The show's title was: *'No one will hire my transsexual puppeteer boyfriend!'* The exclamation point said it all: the American public was furious that this problem had been ignored for so long. It was, after all, fundamental to their way of life that these people were not discriminated against.

The poor Patsy-in-a-suit they had dragged up onstage to take the flak was doing just that. He had refused to hire the man for a church social in response to the concerns of parents who found his appearance 'confusing and scary.' He took the insults from everyone with quiet good humour until an elderly, skinny woman with sharp, unforgiving features suggested that he was, 'Worse than Hitler!'

With that, the man calmly got to his feet, buttoned his jacket and said, 'The average IQ in this room is about the same as a warm day in the Antarctic.' He walked off to a largely silent audience who were wondering if they had just been insulted.

A huge, angry woman in an equally huge T-shirt bearing the legend: *I'm with Stupid* decided to pick up the baton and waddle with it. She asked the heavily made-up performer, 'Why don'ts you gets a real job?' The fickle crowd roared its approval of this, before unthought-of, suggestion.

'Because I'm an entertainer – that's who I am! I am a joy-bringer!' was his riposte, and then he broke into an overly melodramatic fit of sobbing and hugged his partner (whose gender was anyone's guess).

Deirdre wondered why Americans seemed so obsessed with defining who they were and, once they decided who they were, were so defensive about anyone suggesting they do something other than their dream job. Just because this guy was a 'joy-bringer' did that mean he was physically incapable of flipping burgers or washing cars?

Deirdre stretched her legs out and ploughed a furrow in the empty crisp packets, sweet wrappers, kebab containers, pizza boxes and Diet Coke cans that surrounded her chair. By chance, her stretch made her catch sight of the framed photo on the sideboard. It showed her, four years before, wearing cycling shorts and matching top with a large gold medallion around her neck. Her belly was flat - more than flat - it was well toned and rock-hard. She slapped her hand on her stomach (hoping it was just her T-shirt that was making her look fat), and the resulting ripple caused a free-range M&M to plummet to the ground.

The picture had been taken after she was given the David Award for Crucial Service to Mankind. The award, named after Goliath's executioner, was a long held tradition of the Ministry, given to the person who made the biggest difference in the fight against evil. They had surprised her with the award while she was out jogging, which is why she wasn't in a long evening dress and adorned with jewellery. The picture had even been published in the local paper the following week with the single line below saying: *Deirdre Goose: winner of the CSM award.* They couldn't publicly announce what the CSM award was; most people assumed it was some kind of sports trophy, but those in the know knew better. She had been proud that day, proud of what she had accomplished and proud of who she was – The Slayer.

The trouble nowadays was she had no motivation. Two years without a single call-out! It was hard to run yourself ragged at the gym every day in preparation for a night watching TV. The Slayer had always been the financial responsibility of the Ministry, so even if she lay at home all day and did nothing they would still pay her a generous lump sum every five years. It was like a retainer, so she would always be close at hand if they needed her. But no one had needed her in a very long time.

In the first few weeks of staying at home she was restless. She was used to being up all night fighting vampires and resting all day, but now her days *and* nights were free.

She had always steered clear of anything that might turn out to be a long-term relationship. She might be needed in New Orleans, or Peru, or Auckland, and might not be back for months or years. Boyfriends wouldn't understand that so (apart from a few brief but enjoyable one-nighters back in her slimmer days) she didn't try to find one.

Deirdre waited at home, busying herself with the minutia of daily life. She trained in the beginning, keeping herself physically alert and ready to fight a murderous cult of vampires on a moment's notice. But as the months went by and the call never came, her enthusiasm for training waned. She put on weight and watched TV from morning to night. Friends and family suggested that she needed to find something to do. A job, any job. It didn't matter what it paid because the Ministry were paying her anyway, just something to get her out of the house. Deirdre had scoffed at the very idea. She was The Slayer, what did they expect her to do; flip burgers or wash cars?

Deirdre was suddenly stirred by two knocks on the door. Two knocks? Who used two knocks? The pizza guy was four, the kebab guy was three and the Chinese take-away guy was a rapid seven. Who was two? She couldn't remember ordering any food, though she had so many standing orders she rarely knew what was coming to the door and just ate whatever arrived. But it was three-thirty in the morning – nothing was due at this time. It was an intriguing mystery. It was almost worth getting up and going to the door to see who it was – but only almost. She continued watching her show. The door was banged five more times. Five? What were they trying to tell her? It was a puzzle all right. She'd mull it over later and try to work out who had been at the door. She cursed the poor design of her peephole, which you couldn't see through if you were sitting ten feet away with your back to the door. She thought briefly of getting a window put in the door and carefully positioning a mirror above the TV, which would enable her to see mysterious callers with erratic knocking patterns from the comfort of her chair.

'Deirdre,' a female voice shouted from outside.

'She knows my name,' she said. 'The plot thickens.'

The doorknob was tried and the door opened. She'd forgotten to lock it again. She was usually in such a rush to get the food delivery back to her armchair and start enjoying it, things like home security often took a backseat.

Lee-Anne stepped in and was almost pushed back out again by the stench of the fast-food graveyard that lay about Deirdre. Taking a deep breath she walked in.

'Holy Christ! Is that you, Deirdre?'

Deirdre couldn't tell by the smell what this girl was delivering so she was forced to crane her pudgy neck around. 'Who are you? Why aren't you carrying any bags of food?'

'Deirdre, it's me, Lee-Anne. From the Ministry? Why didn't you answer your phone?'

Deirdre kicked her feet and rolled back and forth until she had gained enough momentum to get off her chair. She stood up and brushed the food from her T-Shirt. She stood as straight as her belly would allow and put her hands by her side. 'Sorry. I must have forgotten to charge it. Slayer Goose ready for duty.'

'Ready for duty? I've got a busload of people outside and our ace-in-the-hole, our secret weapon is... what the hell happened to you?' Lee-Anne pushed the door closed behind her.

As the door clicked back into its latch, the heap of junk-mail that had been displaced by the door opening slid back to its original place under the mouth of the letterbox. Lee-Anne walked over and looked at Deirdre. She was wearing a T-shirt that would have been loose-fitting on the Slayer she knew. It was now skin-tight over her round belly and straining to reach her waist but only making it part of the way – it looked like a giant eye trying desperately to close. Loose grey jogging pants that were stained with tomato puree, curry sauce and at least a dozen other patches of dried food, emerged from somewhere under her stomach. Lee-Anne looked at the food spillages on the carpet beneath her seat and thought she could probably camouflage herself quite well in those pants. Her hair looked like it hadn't been washed in weeks and, if Lee-Anne wasn't mistaken, there was part of a chicken-wing hiding in it just below her right ear. The Slayer looked embarrassed so Lee-Anne tried not to stare.

Lee-Anne looked around the room for a place to sit. There was only one other chair and it had three unopened boxes of crisps stacked on it. She edged backwards, perched herself on the sideboard and lifted the framed photograph.

'You need me?' Deirdre asked timidly.

Lee-Anne turned the frame to her and showed her the photo. 'Actually, I need her,' she said.

'The Endtime?'

Lee-Anne nodded.

'I thought it was getting close. I had this feeling, but wrote it off as gas.' Deirdre was excited again. She had made the best of this humdrum life but now she was going to get back to what she did best. She missed the glory of heroism and the satisfaction of helping mankind. She missed how every guy had wanted to shag her and every girl had wanted to be her (and some of them wanted to shag her too). 'OK,' she said brightly, 'In just a few weeks...' She grabbed a handful of belly in each hand. '...this will be gone. I guarantee it. I'll be back to...'

'It's happening tonight,' Lee-Anne said solemnly. 'We're on our way there now. You think you're up to it?' she asked, subtly nodding at Deirdre's belly.

Deirdre tried to pull the T-shirt down but there simply wasn't enough material to cover the area, so she pulled her jogging-pants up and bridged the gap. 'I'll be fine,' she said confidently.

'OK, let's go,' Lee-Anne said, with as much enthusiasm as she could muster. She was not looking forward to the looks she was going to get when she marched Deirdre onto the bus.

A curious blend of fear and excitement were being mixed in Deirdre's belly as she pulled her trainers on (were her feet *always* that far away?). She pulled on her jacket and looked at herself in the full-length mirror. She sighed, disappointed with the reflection, and wondered if there was any chance the mirror wasn't working properly. It was a long-shot.

She shrugged and said, 'Oh well, at least the butterflies in my stomach have plenty of space to fly around.'

Lee-Anne gave her a flat smile.

Deirdre looked in the mirror again and winced. She wasn't even dressed like a Slayer, but none of her sexy, tight Spandex outfits would consider stretching to such extremes. That was a shame because she used to look so good in them. Her mentor had told her that a moment's distraction can give the chance for destruction (roughly translated: give the vampire the horn and stake him while he's looking at your tits). Deirdre realised she was going to have to fight this fight without sex-appeal, without the agile acrobatics she was known for and... without any new puns! She was badly unprepared. She cursed herself for not watching Comedy Central more often.

'You ready?' Lee-Anne asked.

'Yep, just need to... where did I?' She ran into the bedroom and came back wiping the dust off her samurai sword with the sleeve of her jacket. She held it up to Lee-Anne. 'I had my pants hanging on it in front of the radiator.'

Lee-Anne nodded and walked out the door. Deirdre took one last look at her apartment, then followed her.

into battle

Tom and Sarah roared towards Mussenden Temple on their motorcycles. The night was unusually quiet. Not just free from traffic, but it seemed the whole world was holding its breath, waiting. Sarah took the lead, as Tom wasn't sure where they were going. The full-moon hung over them, ever-watchful.

Something seemed to move in the air. Tom looked around. He couldn't see anything. He looked at Sarah's tail-lights. She wasn't slowing down or looking around. Maybe it had just been his imagination. Though what were the chances on a night like this? This was the night when everything you feared would probably happen. Tonight every movement in the trees *was* a monster lying in wait. He felt it again. Something in the air. He had to warn Sarah. He twisted down on the throttle and started to move closer to her.

A dark shape flew from the sky and plucked Sarah off her motorcycle. Tom raced forwards and grabbed her sword from the bike. A second later the front wheel wobbled and the bike collapsed and skidded across the road amid a hail of sparks. Tom looked up and saw Sarah fighting with the vampire. It was carrying her higher and higher.

Chloe saw what had happened and raced forwards in the helicopter. The sniper in the back slid open the door and took aim. 'Get closer!' he shouted to Chloe over the wind noise. Chloe pushed on the cyclic stick and dove towards the struggling pair. The sniper hadn't held a gun for six years but it was all coming back to him. He turned on the infra-red sight and took aim. Sarah was punching furiously at the vampire holding her. He just needed her to be still for a second. Just one second. He took a deep breath and held it. Sarah twisted in mid-air and exposed the vampire's back to the sniper. He smiled and fired.

The vampire burst into flames and dropped Sarah. Tom looked up and saw her falling. He twisted the throttle and lined himself up under her. Sarah slammed into his lap. The bike wobbled but Tom managed to keep it upright. Sarah smiled at him then climbed behind and put her arms around his waist.

The shrivelled corpse of the vampire dropped onto the road as the helicopter flew over. The sniper reloaded and said to Chloe, 'That worked great.' Chloe raised a thumb above her head. The sniper turned the ammunition over in his hand. Glass bullets filled with holy water. How come no-one at the Ministry ever thought of that? Those Daves were geniuses.

Sarah tapped Tom on the shoulder. He turned and looked up into the sky. At least a dozen vampires were flying above them. Sarah grabbed her sword and turned around, now sitting back-to-back with Tom. A vampire swooped down at them. Sarah raised herself up, standing on the exhaust pipes and lopped its head off.

These vampires are stupid, she thought to herself. Newly-Made. Inexperienced. She had told the Master they had a weapon out at the temple. He must have gone out and Made as many as he could to stop us getting there. How could he sire so many by himself? It was impossible. What the hell *was* he?

Another vampire swooped in. Sarah grabbed it by the throat and landed a few punches to its face before taking its head off, too. The sky above them was being illuminated by puffs of fire. Sarah winced but couldn't see what was going on. Another vampire came straight at her. She raised her sword.

The vampires were bombarding the helicopter. The sniper was firing as fast as he could and Chloe had managed to dice a couple with the rotor-blades. The sniper was reloading when a vampire flew inside the helicopter and grabbed him. He was cool. It wasn't the first time he had fought a vampire with his bare hands. He held it by the throat and landed punches as hard as he could. He'd forgotten how strong these fuckin' things were. Chloe banked left and right, trying to stop any more from flying inside. The sniper and the vampire got tossed from one side of the helicopter to the other.

Glass bullets were rolling around the floor. The sniper grabbed one and shoved it up the vampire's nose as hard as he could. The vampire recoiled with pain and raised his hands to his face. The sniper kicked him hard in the face, smashing the bullet in his nose. The vampire screamed as the inside of his head started to burn. The sniper gave him another kick and knocked him out of the helicopter. Another vampire flew towards him. The sniper grabbed the rifle and brought it around just in time to shoot the vampire in the face at point blank range.

    He looked outside and saw vampires circling the helicopter. They were everywhere. He started to reload, heavily.

Tom raced through the Lion's Gate and up the grass towards Mussenden Temple. Still a couple of hundred yards away, he skidded to a stop.

    'What are you stopping here for? Go all the way up to…' Sarah stopped as she turned around and saw what Tom was seeing. A line of thirty vampires stood before them. 'Oh, shit.'

    Tom turned off the motorcycle and dropped the kickstand. They both got off. Tom grabbed his sword and they faced the vampires.

    Hal stepped forward from behind the line. 'It was always going to be you and me, Sarah.'

    'Jesus Christ, Hal. Think about what you're doing.'

    'Oh, I have. My friends and I are going to dice your little playmate, then you and I are going to be together, forever.'

    'It's never going to happen, Hal.'

    'You'll feel differently when you're one of us.'

    'No, I won't. Hal, if you ever loved me…'

    'I do love you! This new age begins with us, Sarah. I've done this all for you. So we can be together.'

    Sarah hung her head. She reached out and took Tom's hand. She looked up again and faced Hal. 'I'm sorry. We have to do this.'

    Hal's blood boiled when he saw them touch. He took a few steps back, behind the line and shouted, 'Disarm and restrain her. Kill him.'

    The vampires surged forward. Some taking flight, others just running, but all headed towards Tom and Sarah. They released their hands and raised their swords. When the vampires were close enough they both launched themselves into the air and came down in the middle of the swarm, hacking for all they were worth.

Nicholl wasn't slowing down as much as she should on the corners. Everyone on the bus was getting thrown across their seats. Dave poked Eileen's cheek with his screwdriver for the fifth time.

'Sorry, again.'

The cut healed in seconds. 'Don't worry about it,' she said. Dave continued to work at the collar around her neck. He had got it open. Now he just needed to bypass the tamper switch so it wouldn't explode when she took it off. He twisted two wires together and then nodded to Eileen. Cautiously she pulled the collar apart. It didn't explode. She took the perimeter marker from her pocket and set them both on the seat beside her. She rubbed her neck, glad to finally be free of it. She smiled at Dave.

The other Dave walked up and down the corridor of the bus giving basic training in the weapons they had brought. 'Most of them are ordinary things that have been adapted to be used as weapons. Don't spend a lot of time wondering if it's going to work or not. We've already done that thinking. You just need to point and fire. Most of the weapons have a trigger and the ones that don't, don't take a lot of working out. Also, if you look at the casing of your weapon you'll notice we've included puns and cool things to say after you use them.' Everyone looked blankly at him. 'You know, for morale.'

The bus took a sharp left and Dave had to grab hold of the overhead luggage rack to stop from falling. Nicholl sped through the tiny car-park and smashed through the fence. Some of them saw the sign for Ballinrees Reservoir before the bus flattened it. Nicholl steered the bus through the narrow walkway, the trees on either side slapping the bus. They came out into the clearing and she skidded to a stop.

The bus doors opened with a hiss. Nicholl ran outside into the night and shouted for Rek. Lynda ran out after her. The surface of the reservoir was still. Nothing moved. No-one answered her cries. Everyone on the bus watched as Nicholl shouted repeatedly for Rek.

She didn't understand. The GPS had led her here. Where the hell was he?

Rek had finished sending all his farewell emails. He set his phone down. The screams and growls outside the door were becoming more and more angered. His door blockade was disintegrating and some of the hybrids were smashing their way through the plasterboard wall. Not long now. He looked around the ceiling of the office. He hadn't put any C4 in this room. Still, he had put a shitload of it everywhere else. Hopefully it would be quick. Worst-case scenario: he would be trapped in here as the room slowly filled with water and he drowned. He couldn't think about things like that now. He had to do this. He had to finish this and avenge his sister.

He lifted the detonator and put his thumb to the button. He took a deep breath. He closed his eyes.

'Maybe he dropped his phone in the reservoir to throw us off,' Lynda said. 'You know he didn't want us to find him.'

'No, wherever he was he said he was trapped. He couldn't have got out to ditch his phone. Rek!'

Lynda walked over to her and took her by the shoulders. 'Nicholl. Amanda. We have to go. Tom and Sarah need our help. We need to get the zeros to them.'

Nicholl shook her head.

'We can come back,' Lynda said. 'We'll look for him after the night is over. As soon as the sun rises…'

The ground shook beneath the two women. They put out their arms to keep their balance. A huge section of the reservoir seemed to drop all at once. The water sloshed and splashed around, finding its own level again. The women stared at it. Things started to bob on the surface of the water. Papers. A phone. A chair. Two more chairs. A printer.

Two arms broke the surface of the water. Lynda and Nicholl both jumped. Then a head appeared. Nicholl recognised the deformations immediately. She had fought one before and it had been very hard to kill. A vampire/Che'al hybrid. It walked towards the shoreline. Two more heads popped up. Then three more. Then more. Nicholl counted ten. Now twelve. And they were still coming.

Lynda stood, shaking at the sight she was witnessing. 'Oh, God.'

Nicholl turned to her. 'Come on, we don't have much time.' Nicholl ran towards the bus and shouted, 'Everyone off, quickly! Dave, break out the weapons. We can't let these things loose. If they make more like themselves we don't stand a chance.'

Lynda took a step back, watching the creatures emerging from the reservoir. A dark sense of certainty rose up inside her. They wouldn't be able to stop them. She spoke in barely a whisper, 'This is it... This is how the world ends.'

war

The remaining vampires backed away and formed a rough circle around Tom and Sarah. Their hearts were racing. They were running on adrenaline, their senses sharper and more attuned. Tom did a quick three-hundred and sixty degree scan. He counted eight left. Plus Hal made nine. He and Sarah had hacked their way through twenty-two vampires. Their bodies littered the ground and Tom and Sarah were both heavily stained with their opponents' blood.

The remaining vampires looked to Hal, who looked furious that Tom was still alive. 'Well, what are you waiting for? Kill him!'

Tom and Sarah put themselves back-to-back, poised to attack the approaching vampires. One of them leapt forward and burst into flames. The vampires looked at each other, confused. Another one burst into flames. Hal looked up and saw the helicopter hovering. He shot up into the air at incredible speed. The rest of the vampires charged at Tom and Sarah as one.

Hal flew into the back of the helicopter at such speed that he couldn't stop in time and slammed himself and the sniper against the opposite door. The sniper struggled to free himself but Hal bit into his neck. He screamed as Hal drained him. He managed to fire the rifle. The bullet hit the roof and shattered. A fine mist of holy water sprayed Hal and he jumped back. The sniper raised his hand to his neck and tried to staunch the bleeding. Hal grabbed him by the foot and hurled him out of the helicopter. Chloe looked out and saw him screaming all the way to the ground.

In a second Hal was at her throat. He bit into her neck. Chloe yelled, then gritted her teeth in anger. She reached backwards and grabbed Hal's head. She held onto him tightly as he drank from her. She pushed the cyclic stick full forward and the helicopter started to dive towards the ground. Hal stopped drinking. He could see what she was trying to do. He tried to break free of her grasp but couldn't. The instruments in the cockpit were bleeping and buzzing every kind of alarm.

The trees were rushing towards them. Chloe closed her eyes and held on tight to the struggling vampire. She smiled as the helicopter hit the tree-line. The rotors first chewed, then smashed on the treetops. Chloe and the vampire were thrown forward and smashed into the glass and the cockpit. The rotor blades were sent shooting in all directions. The forward momentum of the helicopter kept it going forward for a few seconds, then it dropped. The branches smashed and threw the occupants all over the inside of the metal shell until it crashed down on the ground.

Both occupants lay battered, bruised and bleeding, and perfectly still.

Tom beheaded the last vampire and followed Sarah up the hill towards the temple. They got there breathing heavily, but took no time to rest. Tom handed Sarah The Fist of Merlin then knelt down and laced his fingers together. Sarah put her foot into his hands and he launched her onto the domed roof of the temple. Sarah clambered up the smooth surface and put her arm around the apex. She prised the stone from its gold surroundings and held it in her hand. The hole in the apex was exactly the right size. Nicholl needn't have worried about taking a long time to fit it. She placed the stone into the hole on top of the temple. It was almost as if the temple gripped it. The stone was firmly lodged and not likely to move.

Tom walked inside Mussenden Temple and looked around. It was amazing how much Dave's men (and Chloe's money) had accomplished in one day. He looked up and saw the small circle of night sky disappear as Sarah put the stone in place. The narrow channel was mirrored all the way down. Eight spherical alcoves around the ceiling now contained concave mirrors. Dave had said there were mirrored channels cut through the roof leading to each of the alcoves. Tom walked to the windows and felt the convex glass. The windows were basically huge lenses. Sarah dropped to the ground outside.

Tom stepped through the door. 'OK, now we just have to figure out how this...' Sarah turned and saw what had stopped Tom. The Master was standing on the path before them. The moment of inspiration hit them both at the same time.

I have a connection to all my children.
They turned to each other, unable to suppress a smile and said,
'I know what…'
'…we have to do.'

Joshua climbed out through the skylight on the bus, closely followed by Dave. He checked the rifle and opened the loading chamber. Dave opened the blue box and handed him the glass bullet. Joshua loaded it and took aim on the closest creature. The bullet hit directly over the heart. There was a small flame that lasted about three seconds. Joshua turned to Dave.

'OK, don't worry. Plan B.' Dave brought out another box, this time red. He opened it very carefully. 'Looks like the holy water isn't making too much of a dent. That's OK. We've heard about these things and we came prepared.' He very gently handed Joshua another glass bullet.

'How are these different?' Joshua asked.

'These aren't holy water. These are Dicyanocetylene. It burns with the hottest flame of any chemical; four thousand, nine-hundred and ninety degrees centigrade. There's a little igniter in the tip of each bullet. Let's see if that slows them down.'

Joshua took aim and fired. The bullet hit the heart again, but this time the whole creature exploded in flames, screaming. Joshua turned to Dave, smiling. 'That was so fuckin' cool.'

Dave patted him on the back and said, 'Go nuts.' Dave jumped off the roof of the bus as Joshua reloaded.

Everyone was holding a weapon. Joshua ignited another hybrid. Dave addressed the crowd. 'OK, everyone, remember to let them burn for a little while first.' He thumped his chest with his fist. 'Gotta destroy the armour before these weapons will do any good.' Joshua ignited another creature. Everyone readied their weapons. 'And people,' Dave added. 'Let's not forget the puns.'

One of the zeros ran forward with a modified nail-gun, which had the cartridge of nails replaced with pencils. He shot several pencils into the hybrid's heart. The hybrid collapsed and died. The zero read off the side of the nail-gun, '2B or not 2B.'

A female member of Zero Squadron ran forward and fired an arrow from her crossbow. It hit the hybrid dead on the heart, but the creature kept coming. The woman turned to Dave.

Dave smiled and whispered, 'There's a little motor with a wooden drillbit attached inside the arrow.'

They both turned round and heard the faint sound of whirring. The hybrid started to shake, clutched its chest and dropped to the ground. The woman smiled and read off the side of her crossbow, 'And people say my work is boring.'

Another zero stepped forward and threw a wooden ring with a razor-sharp edge at an incoming hybrid. The ring cut through the air like a lethal Frisbee. The hybrid's still flaming body soon found itself without a head. 'Stick around,' the zero said. He turned to Dave. 'I don't get that.'

'It's a stick and it spins around… god damn it.' Dave shook his head and walked away, feeling unappreciated.

Nicholl counted fifteen dead hybrids lying on the shore. This wasn't proving as hard as she thought, thanks to the Daves' weaponry.

Another zero stepped forward with bolas. He built up speed, spinning the balls on the end of the thin wire, then flung them at the neck of the nearest hybrid. The three balls magnetized behind the creature's neck. The motors inside the balls all started drawing the wire back inside the balls. The hybrid stopped, choking. Suddenly the wire heated up to red hot. The creature screamed as the wire was pulled tighter, burning through its neck and eventually cutting its head off. The zero ran and retrieved the bolas and said, 'Feel the burn,' to the dead hybrid.

Kaaliz raised his eyes above the waterline. They were laughing. Those Ministry fuckers were laughing as they killed the hybrids. He moved slowly through the dark water and got out on the opposite side to where all the fighting was going on. He observed their tactics for a few moments and decided the sniper should be the first to go. He hovered into the air and then charged full speed to the other side of the reservoir.

Joshua smiled and reloaded. He didn't even see the vampire coming. Kaaliz ripped at his throat. Joshua was screaming. Everyone turned around. No one dared to fire for fear of hitting Joshua. Kaaliz dropped Joshua and lifted his rifle. Before anyone could react, he was firing indiscriminately into the crowd. Zeros were bursting into flames all around Nicholl. She ran towards the bus and drew her sword.

The rifle was empty. Kaaliz dropped it. He looked down and saw the box of glass bullets. He hurled it at Nicholl. She jumped to the side at the last second. The box exploded when it hit the ground. The blastwave knocked everyone off their feet.

Dierdre stood at the back of the bus trying to get a foothold on the bumper, but she couldn't get herself lifted. She turned when she heard screaming. Another wave of hybrids were out of the water and were feasting on the stunned zeros. Deirdre waddled across the smoke-filled battlefield and began hacking at the hybrids. More were emerging from the water, unchallenged. Dierdre saw Nicholl fighting one behind her. Two more were to her left, ripping apart members of Zero Squadron. Dierdre threw her considerable weight behind her sword but couldn't penetrate the creature's outer skin.

'Stand back,' Lynda shouted. Deirdre jumped to the side. Lynda lifted a torch and pointed it at the hybrid's heart. The ultraviolet beam burned at its flesh slowly. Deirdre walked backwards as the hybrid advanced on her. Thirty seconds cooking looked about right. Deirdre lifted a branch from the ground and drove it into the hybrid's heart. It stopped, wobbled for a moment, then dropped.

Lynda had been waiting to say what was written on her torch, so she said it loudly. 'Ultra-violent, ultraviolet.' No-one turned. There was probably too much other stuff going on.

Deirdre ran over to Lynda. 'Thanks.'

'No problem.'

'I think you're our best shot now that the sniper's gone. As soon as they come out of the water take out their eyes first, then go to work on their heart armour, or even better, their necks.'

Lynda nodded and followed Deirdre towards cover. Something hit her on the way and she dropped. Lynda woke up with one cheek on the ground. The torch was lying beside her, the beam pointed at an approaching hybrid's ankle. She could see the smoke rising from it. The hybrid was coming for her. Deirdre was behind it shouting her name. Her head was heavy, her thoughts disordered. The beam was still pointing at the hybrid's ankle but it was much closer now.

Deirdre ran up behind it and sliced the burning ankle off. The hybrid screamed and turned around, now balancing on one foot and one stump six inches shorter. 'Lynda,' Deirdre shouted. Lynda shook her head and managed to get her eyes to focus on Deirdre. 'Get your shit together. I'll keep it busy.

The hybrid took another faltering step towards Deirdre and screamed when the stump hit the ground. Deirdre held up its missing foot and wiggled it before its face. 'Got your foot, dude.'

The hybrid screamed and took off after Deirdre like a pirate with a wooden leg. The fat girl was easily keeping ahead of it.

Maybe it was the situation, or maybe it was just the concussion, but Lynda started laughing.

Eileen landed on the roof of the bus and punched Kaaliz. He dropped to his knees, then lunged at her. They rolled around the roof of the bus exchanging punches.

The hybrid Nicholl was fighting had been burned, though probably not for long enough. Its skin was yielding, but slowly. With one powerful swipe it sent her flying across the grass. Nicholl looked up and saw the nail-gun lying on the ground. She scrambled towards it and grabbed the handle. She turned just as the creature was bearing down on her. 'Eat lead, you son of a bitch!' She unloaded the remainder of the clip into its heart. It teetered. Nicholl jumped to the side as it fell forward and hit the ground with a solid thud.

Unsteadily, she got to her feet and surveyed the fight. They were getting annihilated. The pudgy little Slayer was running around with a foot in her hand while a hybrid chased her. Claire and a zero were attacking a hybrid together but not doing much more than annoying it. From the corner of her eye Nicholl saw something floating on the reservoir. She recognized the jacket. 'Rek?' She ran to the water's edge. He was way too far out. Another hybrid stood up out of the water before her. Nicholl ran back, out of its reach.

She looked around and saw Eileen and Kaaliz fighting on top of the bus. Eileen grabbed him and hurled him into the trees. 'Eileen!' She turned and looked at Nicholl. Nicholl pointed out to the middle of the reservoir. 'It's Rek!'

Eileen took flight and raced over Nicholl's head. She flew over the surface of the water and grabbed the pair of shoulders that were gently bobbing up and down in the water.

From the darkness of the trees, Kaaliz shot into the air and towards Eileen. Nicholl saw him and grabbed her sword from the ground. Kaaliz flew straight into her blade and fell to the ground, rolling to a stop. Nicholl ran over to him, the deep gash she had made in his face was almost healed. Kaaliz shot a foot out in her direction. It caught Nicholl squarely on the chest and sent her hurtling backwards through the air. Her back slammed hard against the side window of the bus, shattering it. She was aching all over. Her body was hanging half in, half out of the bus. The little shards of broken glass were digging into her back.

Kaaliz walked over to the pair of legs dangling from the broken window. 'You can't kill me,' he shouted. 'I am immortal!' Kaaliz grabbed her legs and started to drag her out of the bus. Nicholl leapt forward and snapped Eileen's collar around his neck.

'I wouldn't bet on that,' Nicholl said as she kicked him in the chest and dropped to the ground.

Kaaliz took a few steps backwards and pulled at the collar around his neck. 'What the fuck is this?'

Nicholl held up the perimeter marker with the battery attached. She grabbed the battery tightly with one hand and the perimeter marker with the other. 'Say goodnight, asshole.' She pulled the battery from the perimeter marker and the collar exploded with a loud crack. Kaaliz's head dropped to the ground. His hands and body twitched for a few seconds, before they too, dropped to the ground.

Eileen landed a short distance away with Rek in her arms. Nicholl got up and ran to them. Nicholl pumped hard on his chest and then gave three deep breaths into his mouth. She repeated this sequence four times.

'I'm sorry,' Eileen said. 'I think he's dead.'

'Can you do CPR?'

'Only the chest massage. I have no breath to breathe into his lungs.'

Nicholl took Eileen's hands and placed them on Rek's chest. 'OK, keep his blood circulating. I'm going to see if there's a first aid kit on the bus.' Nicholl stood up and watched Eileen pumping Rek's chest. She took a few steps backwards.

Claire and the zero were exhausted. The two of them had done little or no damage to the hybrid. They started taking steps back as it closed on them. Then a light hit its face and its eyeballs exploded. Claire turned and saw Lynda standing upright, though a little shaky, with a UV torch in her hand. Claire smiled.

Lynda said, 'Ultra-violent,' and smiled back.

By the time Claire looked back at the screaming hybrid, its neck was already smoking from the focussed beam. Claire drew back her sword and lopped its head off.

Deirdre came running towards them, still carrying the foot and still being pursued by its owner. Lynda focussed the beam on the hybrid's neck. By the time it reached them it was ready for a nearby zero to take its head off. Deirdre was out of breath from running. Between gasps she said, 'OK. Looks like we've got a system. Let's do it!' They obeyed her and ran off towards the nearest hybrid fight. Deirdre threw the foot over her shoulder, took a few deep breaths, and ran after them.

One of the zeros was crawling on his back along the ground. A hybrid stood over him. He fumbled around the ground and found a crossbow. He lifted it and fired. The arrow ricocheted off its skin without leaving a mark. He screamed as the hybrid dropped on him.

Lynda burned at the hybrid's neck. They were too late to save the zero, but they could still kill the thing that had killed him. Lynda turned off the beam and nodded to Claire. Someone screamed behind them. Lynda ran towards them with the torch. Claire raised her sword above her head. The hybrid turned around and pounced on her.

The stray arrow bounced off the hybrid and ripped through Eileen's neck as she leaned over Rek. Blood ran from her neck into his mouth. Nicholl saw what had happened and ran back to Rek. She put her knee to Eileen and pushed her off to the side with more force than she had intended.

Rek coughed, his mouth full of Eileen's blood. He licked the blood around his mouth and swallowed. Nicholl stepped back and grabbed her sword. Rek rose before her. Eileen yanked the arrow out of her neck. She held her hand to the entry and exit wounds as they closed.

Nicholl looked into the face of her lover. 'No, Rek. Not you.'

Rek opened his mouth and she saw his incisors grow to full length. He smiled at her.

She raised her sword. Tears welled in her eyes. She whispered, 'Please, Rek. Don't make me do this.'

sacrifice

Tom and Sarah were exhausted. They had been fighting the Master with every ounce of strength they had but he was just too strong. He blocked their swords with his arms. They just couldn't seem to damage him. They could barely lift their swords now after what seemed like hours of attacking him.

Tom glanced at the sky behind him.

'Is that what you're waiting for?' The Master nodded across the sea to the horizon. 'The sunrise?' He smiled. Sarah charged at him from behind. He grabbed her and threw her aside like a ragdoll. Sarah held onto her ribs when she stopped rolling. She'd heard something snap when she hit the ground. Something was wrong. She was weak. Really weak. She looked at Tom. He was bent over, hands on knees, breathing hard, but still keeping his eyes on the Master.

The Master continued, 'Back in the mid-seventeen-hundreds I was in love with a woman named Rosalind. In all the thousands of years I've lived I've only been in love three times. You believe that?'

Tom didn't answer.

'One of your little posse got hold of her one night and hung, drew and quartered her. It was the preferred form of torture at the time. They left her parts hanging from a tree where I would find them. And I did find them. And believe me when I tell you that every single man involved in her death lived to regret what he had done.' He stared into Tom's eyes with that unnaturally long, piercing gaze. 'Point is, even after I'd taken my revenge on them all, it didn't bring her back. I still missed her. So one day, I suppose I was feeling especially melancholy, I just walked outside into the sunlight.'

He knelt down next to Sarah, writhing on the ground. 'Now I'm not saying it didn't hurt. It definitely pinched a bit. But I *wanted* to die, so I stood there for about half an hour before I came to my senses.'

He got up and turned to Tom. 'What happened to me was probably on a par with a bad sunburn. My skin had fried and crackled and it took a while to come good again, but it didn't kill me.' He stood facing Tom. 'So, chosen one, what are we thinking here? Sun's almost up. I guess whatever happened to bring about the age of vampires happened somewhere else, eh? Kinda makes you wonder why the rest of your little gang didn't show up at some point.' He smiled.

They both heard a noise and turned. Hal was walking down the gravel path towards them. The Master laughed and clapped his hands. 'Harold, my boy. You made it!'

As Hal got closer they could both see what poor shape he was in; scarred and bleeding, holding one arm close to his torso and limping on one leg. 'Did we win?'

The Master shrugged then looked at Tom and Sarah. 'Well, *they* certainly didn't. I think the world's going to be a lot different when we rise again tonight.' The Master tilted his head and looked at Hal. He winced. 'You could really do with feeding. Do you still want to save her?'

Hal stopped beside the Master and looked at Sarah on the ground. Sarah shuddered as she felt a shiver go through her brain. 'She doesn't love me and she never will,' Hal said. 'I just saw everything that was important to her.' He glared at Tom.

The Master put his hand on Hal's shoulder. 'Do you want her?'

Hal was still glaring at Tom. 'No, I want *him*.'

'Then you don't mind if I have her? Dhampir blood is such a delicacy.'

'No, go right ahead.' Hal walked towards Tom. The Master walked towards Sarah, lying on the ground. Tom raised his sword and Hal knocked it from his grasp. Hal grabbed him and pulled him close. Tom tried to struggle but every muscle and bone in his body hurt. Hal whispered in his ear, 'I told you it would come to this.' Hal bit into Tom's neck and began to drink.

The sun broke on the horizon. Hal stopped drinking for a second to drag Tom into the shade of Mussenden Temple. He would have to make a quick getaway before the sun got to full strength, but he wasn't going to rush this pleasure.

The stone on the top of the temple started glowing, then pulsing brightly. No-one seemed to notice.

Hal moved in to bite Tom again, but caught a glimpse of the Master and Sarah, which stopped him. The Master was drinking from her neck but she was looking at Tom. Hal hadn't even noticed that Tom was looking back at her and using what little strength he had left to stretch out his hand to her.

The stone on top of the temple was pulsing at an almost blinding intensity now.

Hal looked down at Sarah being drained; blood running from her neck, tears running from her eyes. Still she looked at Tom. The way Hal had always wanted her to look at him. The way *he* had looked at *her*. The way he *still* looked at her.

Hal dropped Tom and charged at the Master. He grabbed him and was inside the temple before the Master knew what was happening. Hal threw him to the floor, slammed the door and locked it.

'What the hell are you doing, Harold!' The Master got to his feet. Harold walked to the window and looked out at Sarah. Tom had managed to crawl over to her. Sarah turned and looked at the window. Tears were running down Hal's face.

The Master slammed into the door but it was solid. 'Give me the fuckin' key, Harold.' Hal put his hand in his pocket. He felt the photo of him and Sarah and clutched it tightly in his fist. The Master looked at the boy standing at the window and strode towards him, determined to make him suffer for his betrayal.

The sun cleared the horizon.

Sarah saw Hal mouth the words, I love you. A second later the whole temple filled with light.

Inside, the sunlight was funnelled down the mirrored channels and into the alcoves where they shot the light, intensified many thousands of times, in concentrated beams into the temple. The windows magnified the suns rays and also added to the solar execution. Hal had been disintegrated in an instant, but the Master was screaming.

Tom and Sarah managed to get to their feet and hobble over to the window. They saw the Master in the centre of the room, held in every direction by beams of light. His skin was blackened with veins of orange breaking it from below. He gave one final, agonizing scream then his whole body exploded.

The stone on top of the temple powered down and the lights inside faded. A thick layer of dust on the ground was the only evidence anyone had been in there.

Tom held Sarah close as she wept in his arms.

Nicholl raised her sword and took another step back. Eileen took to the air. She saw the sun coming up. The trees would offer some cover but she would have to be careful. She couldn't go too high. If Nicholl wasn't ready to decapitate the love of her life, Eileen was ready to dump him into the reservoir and give her some time to prepare for it.

The blood streams from Kaaliz's body and head had found each other. They were pulling towards each other, almost guiding. Kaaliz's hand twitched. His eyes opened. He saw his body lying close to him. He really *was* immortal, much more than any other vampire. He was eternal. His fingers dug into the dirt and pulled his body closer to his head. The blood on the ground started circulating; going into his head, coming out of his head. Across the ground. Going into his torso, coming out of his torso. It seemed to pump faster the closer he got to joining the two pieces together again.

Kaaliz's hand dragged his body closer to his head.

Rek lunged at Nicholl and she punched him with the hilt of her sword. He fell to the ground and landed on his front. His back was exposed to her. This was her chance. For the good of all mankind, she had to do it. She pointed the sword downwards over his back and grasped the hilt in both hands.

Eileen screamed and dropped out of the sky. She landed awkwardly on her left hip, but she wasn't high enough to break any bones. Nicholl turned and saw her. Eileen looked confused. What the hell was going on? Rek sat up. Nicholl turned and swung her sword, but stopped just in time.

'It's OK, Mand. It's me. I'm OK.'

Eileen walked over. 'So am I. I don't think I'm a...'

The sun rose over the tree-tops and Eileen held her face in its bright glow. She smiled and tears rolled down her face. It might have been the brightness of a sun she hadn't seen in a long time, but it probably wasn't.

Nicholl dropped her sword and jumped up on Rek, hugging him tightly and kissing him.

Rek smiled at her. 'You call that a plan?'

Nicholl laughed. 'It worked, didn't it?'

Rek left her down. They looked behind them and saw Kaaliz's body and head shrivel to a dried husk. Rek walked over and stamped Kaaliz's skull flat, just to be sure. Nicholl came over and took his hand. She led him away.

They joined Eileen walking across the battlefield in the morning light. There were a lot of bodies. Hybrids and humans. Twenty yards away they saw half a dozen members of Zero Squadron hacking up the last hybrid. Deirdre waved to them briefly, smiling, then got back to hacking.

Nicholl stopped and knelt down next to Claire's body. She felt for a pulse and didn't find one. Sarah and Tom had both lost their mothers in the space of a week. She hoped they would be able to comfort each other. Nicholl closed Claire's eyes.

They walked on and found Dave kneeling next to his namesake, crying. 'Come on, man. You have to get up now.'

Nicholl knelt down next to him. 'Dave?'

'No, no, he's all right. He's going to be all right, aren't you man?' He shook Dave's limp arm. Tears were running down Eileen and Rek's faces. Lynda walked over to them and dropped her torch. She knelt down on the other side of Dave. He turned to Lynda and hugged her, crying hard into her shoulder. Nicholl reached forward and closed Dave's eyes.

the beginning

Chloe managed to dress herself. Her fractured arm from the helicopter crash didn't hurt much and her hand was free of plaster. She looked in the mirror. There wasn't make-up in the world capable of covering up the cuts and scars she had received that night. She didn't care. Most of the others looked the same or worse.

She walked down the stairs of her mansion. The house she thought she had always wanted. Now sold for thirty percent more than she had paid for it to a man who sold pornography on the Internet. More money than she knew what to do with. She had come a long way from scraping by on benefits. And even though all the survivors of the Endtime War – that's what they were calling it – would be receiving a very generous cheque in the post tomorrow, she still had more money than she could ever spend.

The house echoed even more now with all the furniture gone. Most of it had been sold too. She was moving to a modest little bungalow close to Lynda's family. Lynda said she had the perfect guy for her. She'd heard that before, but she'd give him a try.

She walked around the empty living room. This was the last time she would be in this house. She found her scrap-book and opened it up. She looked again at the picture of her saving the baby that the vampire had pushed out into traffic. That's where this had all begun for her. The rest of the pages were blank, like the rest of her life. Not empty, just waiting to be filled.

She dropped the scrap-book in the bin as she left.

Chloe was early so she sat in the car and checked her make-up again in the rearview mirror. She turned on the radio.

Police say a group has claimed responsibility for the bombing... She twisted the dial.

Was found to have murdered his own parents and then used a hack-saw... She twisted the dial.

Kept the girl imprisoned since she was nine years old and sexually... She turned the dial.

Static hissed. She looked in the mirror for a long time. She turned the dial.

I would believe five people, maybe even ten, but in the UK and Ireland alone, eight-thousand missing persons show up in the same week? We're also hearing from America, Australia... basically everywhere! These people are just showing up in droves out of nowhere! And they're not only in perfect health, but none of them are willing to say where they've been or what they've been doing all this time.

Chloe laughed to herself.

Of course this story has brought every UFO nut in the country out of his parents' basement... She turned the radio off and got out of the car.

The funeral was huge. No newspaper or television station had carried the story of what Hal had done, but apparently word had spread. He had saved this town, this country, and probably the world, and it seemed everyone wanted to thank him for that.

Nicholl and Rek stood by the graveside holding each other. Both were badly cut and bruised and hiding behind sunglasses. They had posted Mr Takamura back The Fist of Merlin. Chloe smiled when she thought of him opening his post.

It would probably be even better than the phone call Kyle at Ministry HQ had made to Nicholl, apologizing. After all the vampires they had on level six suddenly turned human, he thought Nicholl might be onto something. Bureaucracy gets there... eventually. At least Nicholl had used her clout to secure pardons for all the zeros who survived the battle. They were really free now.

Eileen had called this morning. She had gone back home to her children and wouldn't be able to make the funeral. Chloe said she understood. She imagined it would be a long time before Eileen dared let her kids out of her sight again.

Chloe looked across as the reverend spoke. Tom and Sarah seemed to be holding each other up. They were both so young and had lost so much. Hopefully the money she was giving

240

them would help them start a new life together. Again the thought persisted in Chloe's head: why her and not me? Claire had a son. I have no-one. It should have been me instead of her. Claire gave birth to a boy who helped save the world. What had Chloe ever done? Wrote a few cheques. It didn't seem like enough.

The empty coffin was lowered into the grave and Sarah burst into tears. Tom held her tightly, trying his best to be the strong one.

Dave stood at a tree by himself, watching, looking uncharacteristically solemn. They'd all have to go through this again tomorrow at Dave's funeral. Dave had a wife too. Someone else left crying. If Chloe could've traded places with any of the dead she would have.

Chloe joined the queue of mourners. They moved slowly as each shook Hal's mother's hand and whispered a few comforting words. Hal's mother and Sarah had hugged. Chloe wondered how much she knew. Did she know the bad stuff? Did it matter? When it came down to it, he'd done the right thing. For love. Unrequited love, but love all the same.

The queue edged closer. Chloe never knew what to say at this sort of thing. 'Sorry for your trouble,' was a common phrase in these parts. She might just stick with that.

She looked forward to living near Lynda and Frank and the kids. She loved those children like they were her own. And now she could relax because they could finally grow up in a world without vampires. Of course there were all manner of other atrocities out there that mankind was capable of, but she wouldn't think about that now. This was a new start. A new dawn.

Hal's mother looked like wafer-thin white porcelain. Chloe feared if she shook the woman's hand she would break. She was staring straight ahead and when people spoke she didn't answer. Chloe shook her hand gently and said, 'I'm very sorry.'

Hal's mum held onto her hand. The woman's eyes refocused on Chloe. 'It's Chloe. Chloe Knight, isn't it?'

Chloe nodded. 'Yes.'

'I always wanted to thank you.'

'Thank me? What for?' Chloe asked.

Hal's mum actually smiled. 'You probably don't remember. About twenty years ago a vampire pushed my baby out into the street, into traffic, and you saved him.'

Tears started running down Chloe's face. 'Oh my god, that was…'

'Little Hal. Yes. Without you, I'd never have had the time I did with him. And without you…' She looked around at the thousands of mourners. 'Who knows what would have happened.' The woman broke into fresh tears and hugged Chloe.

Chloe walked away from the graveside crying, but also smiling.

Afterword

I'd like to thank everyone for their support and encouragement over the years. When I first started writing *Vampire Dawn* I had no idea it would become a trilogy, but I'm really glad it did as it gave me the chance to tell this epic tale.

Although I have taken liberties with history in this book, much of what I have written is true. The builders, architect and financer of Mussenden Temple are as I have stated, it's only their reasons for building it that I have embellished. The story of how Fairhead got its name is true, according to the legend, up to the point where Taisie falls to her death. Both Fairhead and Mussenden Temple are actual locations on the North Coast, and I urge you to see them whether you are a local or a visitor to these shores.

Thanks to all the readers who have followed me on this journey and spread the word about these books. I hope you'll follow me on whatever dark avenue my imagination takes me down next.

You keep reading, I'll keep writing.

P.H. 08/09/09